OFF THE BOOKS

OFF THE BOOKS

A Novel

SOMA MEI SHENG FRAZIER

Henry Holt and Company

New York

Henry Holt and Company
Publishers since 1866
120 Broadway
New York, New York 10271
www.henryholt.com

Henry Holt® and ⓗ® are registered trademarks of Macmillan Publishing Group, LLC.

Distributed in Canada by Raincoast Book Distribution Limited

Library of Congress Cataloging-in-Publication Data

Names: Frazier, Soma Mei Sheng, author.
Title: Off the books : a novel / Soma Mei Sheng Frazier.
Description: First edition. | New York : Henry Holt and Company, 2024.
Identifiers: LCCN 2023055947 | ISBN 9781250872715 (hardcover) |
    ISBN 9781250872722 (e-book)
Subjects: LCGFT: Novels.
Classification: LCC PS3606.R4294 O34 2024 | DDC 813/.6—dc23/eng/20231213
LC record available at https://lccn.loc.gov/2023055947

Our books may be purchased in bulk for promotional, educational, or business use. Please contact
your local bookseller or the Macmillan Corporate and Premium Sales Department at (800) 221-7945,
extension 5442, or by email at MacmillanSpecialMarkets@macmillan.com.

First Edition 2024

Designed by Gabriel Guma

Printed in the United States of America

10 9 8 7 6 5 4 3 2 1

To Adrian and Burgious—
the two sunlit stories of the structure I call home.

1

TAHOE TO TOOELE

Standing on the dusty shoulder, Měi squints down the length of the I-80 to track the gumball yellow cab of an eighteen-wheeler till it disappears around the highway's bend. Sugar pines tower above, massive trunks ruler-straight as though drawn by a steady hand. Nearby, she knows, the crumbling stone foundations of buildings are drawn, too: leftover traces in dirt of Sierra Nevada camps that once housed Chinese railroad workers.

In Chinese, the base component of the character for "road" is "foot," and Měi's caught wind of high school friends, now in their mid-twenties, finding the railroad camps on foot; spraying graffiti inside old train tunnels; scaling portions of the China Wall, a long stone embankment of excavated rock. Her own grandfather, eighty-six and active only online (where he posts rhetorical questions like "If raccoon is trash panda, is rat subway squirrel?" and "Why we don't say *salmon* like *almond*?" late at night) once told her stories of how two ancestors spilt sweat and blood here, laying transcontinental track, then returned to China with their earnings. "Two in fifteen, twenty thousand other Chinese worker," he added, leaving Měi unsure of whether that made it more or less significant. "Decades before I come here."

Closing her eyes in the towering trees' shade, she recalls the old man greeting her after school in his threadbare pink robe and ornate slippers, bending to her eye level. "That your textbook?" Lǎoyé pulled the heavy edition from her hands, a self-proclaimed history buff. "Got more boogers in here than facts."

Another eighteen-wheeler blows by, shaking her sternum. She opens her eyes but still sees her grandfather's face. She was six when her grandmother died and he retired from his part-time mechanic's job, relocating from the back bedroom of her childhood home in Oakland to the family's drafty, converted garage. There, he played video games and smoked weed with the ardor of a teenager, declining to go outside.

"Neighbors crazy," he'd cackle, dropping her textbooks on the rug as they settled into his ratty brown couch, grabbing game controllers in whatever sunlight made it through the murky window. "I got *Grand Larceny IV: Chinatown Wars*. What I gonna go out for? I need good conversation, I talk to myself"—smoke rings rising, spreading up over the bowed shelves of his leaning bookcase to pool between bare ceiling joists—"or you. Got no need for white folks."

"But I'm white."

"No, you just talk white. You a oriental cracker mix, like they sell at Trader Joe's. Baked in America, half Chinese ingredients." A crinkly grin. "You lucky you here at all." Coughing, he set his stinky joint in an ashtray. "I got interested in America from family stories. But your ancestors barely make it over to the Golden State, because Governor Leland Stanford call railroad men like them the 'degraded dregs of Asia.' Look it up online!"

"But he hired them anyway?"

"Not enough white guys show up for the job. He change his mind real quick." Lǎoyé snapped his fingers. "Poof! They upstanding citizens."

Lǎoyé, with his smack talk, is her favorite person. Her best childhood memories are of hiding out in his garage, which might as well have been a kids' fort with a Keep Out sign that her parents grudgingly respected. Even after moving into her own spot across the bay, she'd visited him regularly till the family fractured.

"Miss Brown?" The client's glinting Bulgari watch stretches from the rear passenger window of the idling, air-conditioned sedan as two bald eagles slice the sky.

She lingers another moment, reluctant to leave the densely clustered needles that shade her from a pitiless sun—cooling herself with the thought of shivering men trudging through shafts dug deep in the mountain snow, from tunnel rock faces to blizzard-battered living quarters. Men who'd journeyed to Měi Guó, the "beautiful country" for which she was named, only to live without daylight for months at a time.

But the sun is stronger than her imagining. The sun screams down at her to get back on the road; reminds her that this leg of the trip runs six hours, wheels turning.

Kicking debris over the vomit-soaked paper towels, burying them like roadkill where the woods meet the highway's shoulder, she strolls toward the car. "It still stinks back here," the client says as she nears. "The baking soda isn't working. Can't you spray an air freshener?"

"I'm sorry, Mr. Lee," she says through his open window before sliding into the driver's seat. "I only have citrus. The acid would exacerbate the odor." She gets in, slamming the door and adjusting the rearview mirror away from his eyes. Does not open the clear plastic partition that divides them.

Of course she has other air fresheners. Any driver who's handled a limo in prom season does. But this is no limo service, and the client's weak stomach is wasting her gas. *Let him bake in the stink*, she thinks. The blasting air conditioner keeps the front cool and fresh.

She readjusts the mirror after pulling back onto the interstate. Examines him surreptitiously. His *GQ* face is miserable as he loosens his tie, rolls the back windows up, and pops earbuds in, distracting himself with his phone. She softens. Cracks the divider open. "Leave the windows down if it's not too windy. It'll help with the smell."

He removes the earbuds. "Pardon?"

"Leave your windows down."

"No." A pained smile. "Don't want the car to get too hot for you."

"I'm fine up here," she says. "Trust me." But his earbuds are in again, shutting her out. She closes the partition.

Even as the Sierras flatten, hillside shrubs replacing colossal pines as they coast toward the flatlands of Reno, the client's windows remain closed. Normally, she'd make small talk: note the moment the I-80 becomes a viaduct, passing over the main floor of the Nugget Casino Resort. But she doesn't want to interrupt whatever he's watching on his phone. Nor does she want the intense puke smell in the front of the sedan.

She examines him again, this immaculate twentysomething, his tall form folded into the back seat with the large suitcase he's kept beside him, opting to fill the trunk with smaller things: his tablet and laptop, backpack, duffel, cooler bag. Miserable yet sincere. No way he snuck a flask by her. It would've marred the lines of his suit, the innocence of his smooth brow. Motion sickness, she decides. Or anxiety. He vibrates with barely controlled unease.

Watching his full lips curl as he forces himself to inhale, she softens. At the next stop, she'll spray the back with Big Sur Breeze.

Elko, Nevada, is home to the National Cowboy Poetry Gathering. And to Jarbidge Canyon, its name a clumsy anglicization of the Shoshone word describing a legendary, man-eating giant who carried locals off in a basket till native warriors managed to trap him in a cave. *Tsawhawbitts.* Exiting the car, Měi hands her client the Elko fact sheet she's printed for him: a personal touch, a new sheet for each planned stop along their way, designed to help clients remember the interesting trips they've taken. *It was in Jarbidge Canyon,* the printout explains, *that America's final, murderous stagecoach robbery took place.*

The client pauses a moment to glance the page over, looking confused, before hefting his enormous suitcase from the back seat. Despite his expensive clothes, Henry Lee's booked a dump: leaks have stained the inn's ceiling tiles, put ripples in the carpet, and the whole place reeks of mold. She chews a mealy apple from a bowl in the lobby as he checks them in.

"Gross," she murmurs as they walk to their first-floor rooms.

"The ceiling?"

She shakes her head. "The apple."

He grunts, rebalancing his suitcase on its wheels. Staring at the ugly, overpacked thing, she thinks perhaps she was wrong about him: perhaps he's not above carrying a flask. "You're still eating it," he says.

"That's my cheap Chinese side." She flashes a tight smile. "You know we can't pass up free food."

"I can," he says, "if it's bad." He watches her take another retching bite. "You could say something to the manager."

"Nah. I'll just keep complaining to you." She grins. "And that's my watered-down Texan side: all hat, no cattle." What she doesn't say is that, while her father had a two-semester teaching assignment in San Antonio the year she was born, they soon moved to temperate Oakland, where she grew up skateboarding around Lake Merritt in the yellow California sun; where cafés outnumber cowpokes and white-collar fields outnumber hayfields.

They pass a glass-walled swimming pool, tidy enough and empty aside from the elegant, brown-skinned woman who glances their way, startled, as though suddenly plucked from some luxury spa and deposited here in Elko by the hand of a pernicious god.

His room adjoins hers. He disappears through its dark doorway and she calls out to his broad back, "If you need me before breakfast, just pound on the wall."

"Or text, like a normal human being?" His door clicks softly shut.

She fumbles a bit with the key card, turning it every which way, before her own door opens. Inside, it stinks like an ashtray. She unlaces her high-tops; kicks them off. Closes the map on her phone and drops it with her overnight pack on the bed. Unlike the client, she's left her bulkier bag in the car: they will only be here till breakfast, after all—then back on the road. What could he possibly need so badly that he opted to lug his giant suitcase over the warped and sodden carpet? Or perhaps his belongings are simply too valuable to trust to an unattended parking lot. Peeling the covers back, slipping between cool, crisp sheets, she envisions him lifting the lid of the suitcase to examine neatly stacked gold bars packed in T-shirts and boxer shorts.

It's quiet in her smoke-saturated room, except for the thundering air conditioner. Nicotine, she thinks, smells like resentment and lingers just as long. She runs her tongue over unbrushed teeth. Forces herself out of bed, grabbing her toothbrush and flipping on the blazing bathroom lights. Squints, examining her tired face in the mirror. If the client were to guess her age right now, he might not say twenty-four. She bites her lower lip, bringing the blood back to pinken it. Tousles her lank black hair. And at last, in this bright, tiled room, she acknowledges the fact of her client's attractiveness. Prissy, yes. Pukey, sure. But the way he averts his eyes betrays his confidence: he's accustomed to politely dismissing women's stares.

Is he hapa, like her? American dad, Chinese American mom? He stands nearly as tall as her father—who was six foot two and had a comic book hero's jaw—his skin a warm, indeterminate gold. She spits toothpaste into the sink. Swishes water, spits again, wipes her mouth with the back of her hand. His last name is either Lee, like Confederate general Robert E. Lee, or Lee, the Chinese equivalent of Smith. And considering his quiet, clamped-down endurance of the pungent back seat, his parents were either uptight WASPs or zero-gen Chinese Americans who raised him to "swallow your bitterness," an idea Mao Zedong ingrained in his people, condemning psychology as a bourgeois pseudoscience.

Whatever. She shakes her head in the mirror. Strips to panties and bra, dropping her clothes on the cold tile floor. Turns side to side, examining her own slight form. "Welcome to the gun show." She flexes. Tiptoes gingerly back out to the empty, waiting bed.

In the morning, she stands in line for continental breakfast, watching drips fall into a bucket on the floor. Where does the water come from? Pipes? This is drought season, for Chrissake.

It's not just the Chinese, she observes, who can't pass up a free meal. Her own plate loaded up at last, she moves as far as she can from the line, the bucket—sits in a corner at the smallest table she's ever seen, wondering if its dimensions are meant to discourage lawless gluttony, and spreads concord grape jelly on four slices of toast. There is something festive about single-serving jellies, she thinks: the colorful array, the expectant unwrapping. When she's done, she gets more toast and begins again.

The client rounds the corner around eleven, as the inn's staff clears the breakfast bar. Dragging his luggage over buckling carpet, he looks rumpled today, as though camouflaged to match his surroundings. He's ditched the suit for jeans with a short-sleeved button-down, though his crocodile loafers still scream luxury, and yawns as he scans the room.

She stands, waving him over. "Got you this before they took it away," she says, handing him a banana.

"Thanks, but what I need is that." He points at the coffee dispenser, sticks the fruit in his back pocket, and goes to pour a cup, the female workers' eyes tracking his broad shoulders and tapered waist, his staunch forearm steering the ridiculous suitcase.

Sweet bananas are a mutant. This is a factoid she's learned from Lǎoyé, pulled, no doubt, from one of the quirky American history volumes in his leaning bookcase. She remembers how he offered her a piece of fruit; yanked it away before she could accept it. "You know where this come from?"

"Grocery Outlet."

"Before that?" She pouted. "Spanish missionary bring the plantain to America. You know: red and green cooking banana. But one day, Jamaican farmer find a yellow banana tree on his land, bright like the sun." Lǎoyé made a sun circle with his arms, like the normal Asian grandparents who stretched together in the park, near Fairyland. "He pull one down. Peel it, curious, and stick his tongue to the side. Whoa! Delicious, can be eaten raw. Xiāngtián kěkǒu." Bending forward, he waved the banana in front of her. "Late 1870s, white folks eat yellow banana with knife and fork, all proper, on a plate. Sell for ten cents each. You know how much ten 1870s pennies worth now?"

She shook her head slowly.

"Two hundred fifty buckaroos! That skateboard you asking for cost way less." And he relinquished the fruit to her waiting hands.

This, she thinks, has always been her grandfather's secret, superhero power: the ability to educate painlessly. Organically. Sneakily. To turn a kid's attention from the sweet treat in her hands to the American dollar's inflation rate. Presto! She glances at the banana in Henry Lee's back pocket—a treasure he doesn't even recognize.

When he returns, his wattage has increased. He smiles, and she smiles back. Of course, she will not ask what kept him up late.

She pulls the car keys from her bag. "Ready to hit the road?"

She has loved driving since she hit four feet tall and was permitted to race go-karts at the outdoor track where Lǎoyé worked. At first, he won every race. But eventually his arthritis ended their competition, and he gave up his secret strategy: "Very simple," he said. "Push gas pedal all the way down and keep you foot there. No matta what. And stick to inside lane." She nodded, eyeing the waiting kart. "Go on," he urged, giving her a little shove, a joint clamped between his teeth.

A pimply attendant buckled her in, shaking his head at Lǎoyé. The mechanics weren't permitted to smoke weed or anything else, but the old man was like the Olympic flame. He'd stay lit till the end. The sweet, earthy scent of weed drifted across the karts he repaired and through the chain-link fence that enclosed the twisting black track.

More than a decade later, after Měi withdrew from the Ivy League institution that had awarded her a generous scholarship—returning to the Bay Area to rent a room in the Lower Haight, where the neon blue cross of First Baptist Church blazed through her curtains every night—it was Lǎoyé who convinced her to quit her gig with Live Large Limo. It was Lǎoyé who bought her a nearly new sedan with the savings from his life as a mechanic, nostalgic, perhaps, for their racing days. And it was Lǎoyé who procured her first client: a mousy, pale woman named Ling Ling who called for rides at all hours.

Whether she was intensely private or had embarrassingly poor English was unclear, but beyond stating the destination, Ling Ling never spoke, and Měi grew accustomed to scooping her up near Grand Avenue and steering silently past the slower cars: West across the Bay Bridge. East into the Dirty Thirties. South to San Jose.

"Guess I'll apply to be a rideshare driver," she'd mused, blinking through the smoke that filled the converted garage, after a week of driving Ling Ling around. "Make it official. Score more than one client."

Lǎoyé scowled, revealing spotted gums. "What for? You like give half your money away?" He leaned closer on the couch and his hand grazed her forehead, sinewy and callused as if he handled railroad ties, like their ancestors, instead of Chocolate Thai. Pushing black strands behind her ear, he cleared his throat. "You need client, I get you client. Even Ling Ling get you client. She just waiting to see how it goes before she recommend you." He coughed. "Listen, you heard of karura?"

"Is it a new strain of weed?"

"Nah." He lifted his joint, examined it, and set it on a gold-gilded saucer that appeared to be from Mama's wedding set. "Going karura mean ride service off the books. Drivers in Nairobi do it. I hear about it on TV. And I tell you, smart driver everywhere do it." He released a smoke ring. "Customer call for ride, then cancel trip on they phone. Pay driver directly. No taxes neither."

"Wait—so, like, they're subverting the ride-hailing industry?"

"Subwhoing the huh? Yah. I think so. They riding dirty." He lifted the joint to his lips again. Protecting her health or his sense of propriety, or possibly just his stash, he never offered her a toke (though he'd informed her of exactly what he was smoking long, long ago). "You too young pay taxes. Besides, some customer really need go karura. So they pay more. Don't this country owe you that much? For so many decades we work longer, earn less. One of your great-great-great-great-granduncle lose his eye in a railroad blasting accident. What they give him for that?" He spoke around the dying joint. "A bandage."

"Is that really all?"

"Oh, no. I forget—he also get a nickname. Chi-clops." A wheezing laugh.

Soon after, Ling Ling began introducing Měi to family: cousins, sisters, aunts, all of whom kept similarly erratic schedules, till Měi finally understood that this was not a biological family but a family of sex workers.

If she'd been on speaking terms with her mother, Mama would've blown her top.

⤸

Halfway between Nevada and Wyoming, the client asks to stop for lunch. He pulls his earbuds out, tucks the phone into a pocket, follows her into a roadside café. "Where are we?" he asks once they're seated.

"Millie's Jam Jar."

"No. I meant, what state?"

Měi widens her eyes. "Didn't you notice the salt flats? We drove through them for, like, a long-ass time." He shrugs. "The Elect Jesus Christ SAVIOR signs?" He shrugs again; stares through the café's large, smudged window at her car, parked out front. "We're in Tooele, Utah," she says. "Home of the Mormons."

"Okay," he says. "So, Mormon food?"

She lifts her butter knife by its rounded tip, letting the handle swing like a pendulum; lays it neatly back on the scalloped white paper napkin. "What is it, exactly, you think Mormons eat?"

"More than one dish at once?" He grins a grin so quick she suspects she imagined it.

"Was that a polygamy joke? Like, they have their cake and eat it, too?"

"They have their wife and Edith, too."

"Yeah, but then Edith becomes a sister wife and everything's cool."

As an ancient waiter approaches, each step an obvious effort, Henry Lee fidgets. "Can I get the keys?" he asks when the man leaves.

"What? No," she says.

"C'mon."

She takes a mental inventory of everything in the front seat and glove box. Regional fact sheets to offer Henry at each stop. Gatorade. Overnight pack containing clothes, a dime-store toothbrush, and toiletries from the last inn. "Sure," she relents, dangling the keys above the table, "what the Hell."

The toiletries are a compulsion. Back home, in a bathroom cabinet, she keeps a stash from her travels: sample-size shampoos and conditioners and lotions. Bath bars, towels, robes. Even a hotel hair dryer in a cloth bag.

He grabs the keys from her hand, hops up, and heads out, a little bell jingling as the café's door swings open and shut. Hauling the enormous suitcase to the ground, he balances it on strained wheels, shuts the car door, and, glancing back, registers her stare. Gives a brisk grin. Rolling the case around the car, he pops the trunk. Slings the padded cooler bag over his shoulder. (Beer, maybe?) He slams the trunk shut again.

Starlings confer nearby, dipping their delicate heads toward one another, trading secrets, as she watches him drag the black monstrosity across the lot. And suddenly the birds take flight as one, becoming a tattered brown flag in the sky. She and the client look up in unison, the flag waving once before it shreds into bodies that wheel and dive. It is a moment that must be acknowledged.

Through the glass they share a quick, uncertain smile that makes him seem nearer than he is. *Objects in mirror,* she thinks suddenly, *are closer than they appear.* Glimpsing her faint reflection in the pane, she drags her fingers through the halo of sun caught in her hair. He lingers, watching. Then, offering her a crisp salute, he strides quickly out of sight around the corner of the building.

For a moment, she thinks of running out after him—"Mr. Lee!"—or at least wandering to the other side of the establishment to see if she can spot him through another window. But what he's about to do is none of her business. If he wants to shoot up or jack off or pull a pony costume from the suitcase, put it on, and dance around for a moment, that's on him. She grabs a red crayon from the bowl on the table; doodles cardinals across the paper place mat till the waiter returns with their food.

2

TOOELE TO YORK

Tooele is long gone from the rearview. Stopping in Rock Springs, Wyoming, for the night, she hands him a new fact sheet. This city at the base of White Mountain's sandstone cliffs is home to residents who represent nearly sixty nationalities. Most of these families immigrated for work in the coal mines that once supplied fuel for Union Pacific Railroad's steam engines. The city was once home, too, to Wild West icon Butch Cassidy, who earned his nickname working in the butcher shop. Now it offers Cowboy Donuts (popular with one local crowd), Iron Cowboy CrossFit (popular with a diametrically opposed crowd), and, of course, real cowboys.

This inn is exponentially nicer than the first. They wind their way through its well-appointed lobby, purple evening dimming to night beyond floor-to-ceiling windows, and she starts to suspect he didn't research any of the accommodations he booked after their initial call. Instead, he simply used the road trip map she sent to identify establishments nearest to the highway. Pragmatic. Hurried. Cost be damned. Stepping backward into the lobby's plush lounge area, she lurks between a sculptural wingback and a sleek leather sectional and observes him while he checks them in.

He's a chimera, Henry Lee, hapa or not. A single organism with two distinct genetic constitutions. From one angle, he's a swaggering, young, ethnically ambiguous hottie like the pop star Mama loves (and refers to as "Uyghur Bieber"). From another angle he's an aristocratic old man: manicured, pristine, stooped over the front desk. She amuses herself— blinking back and forth between his two halves—till he notices. "Chimera."

"What?"

"What?" she parrots back, cupping an ear. He scowls; turns again to the desk.

Closing the distance, she hovers nearby, watching the concierge now. JENNY, asserts the woman's name tag. She is a slender redhead in tasteful pearl earrings, silk scarf knotted at her neck. She half smiles at Henry Lee, pushing long bangs back with glossy pink nails.

"Just call," Jenny says, "if I can be of further service." Měi stares at her till her eager smile falters.

"I upgraded us," the client says as they walk to the elevators. He presses the button and they watch the little round lights till there's a ding and the doors yawn open. "I don't know about your room, last night, but mine was like this elevator car. Size, smudged walls and all. Only stinkier. And when I went to grab a tissue in the bathroom, a cockroach had already laid his claim. He, like, reared up on his tiny hindlegs."

She grimaces.

"Yup, he was all 'Get the fuck back, homes!' I thought I was going to have to fight him."

"Well, I mean, you probably would've won."

"I do have the height advantage."

Again, his room is next to hers. Before he can disappear inside, she darts a hand out, grasping his forearm. "Mr. Lee," she says—

"Henry. Mr. Lee is my father."

"—Henry, I probably shouldn't tell you this, but we could shave a full day off our trip." He tilts his head, dark lashes lowered to shade his eyes. "I mean, with all the breaks, we're only driving like six hours a day. If we did eight . . ."

"What, am I not paying enough?"

"More than I've ever been paid."

"So, then, you prefer being exhausted?"

"I mean, I just thought you should know—"

"Sitting for prolonged periods increases one's risk of death. Hit the spa or something. Okay? Put a massage on my tab. Or take a swim." He grins. "Catch up on the news? Watch a movie. Get room service. Browse the minibar. And I'll see you at noon, for checkout."

"But see, that's what I mean. We could leave right after breakfast instead."

He touches his key card to the sensor; yanks the ugly suitcase over the threshold. "Thanks, but no thanks. Goodnight, Miss Brown."

"Call me Měi. Miss Brown is my father."

A quick smile. The door clicks shut.

"Goodnight, Henry," she says to the empty hallway.

Měi's best dreams always sour to nightmares. It's been this way since she was young.

Arms wrapped tightly around Henry's neck, she lets him piggyback her up a steep road deep in the Oakland Hills. When the ground flattens, he lays her out on the front lawn of an expansive home; kneels over her.

The golden sheen of his skin reminds her of a cold, sparkling stream. Full lips lend a tender softness to his angular face. But someone is watching. Beyond his shoulder, a stoic woman appears. "Henry," Měi says, prodding his ribs, "I think they want you in the house."

"No." He tilts his head. "I don't think so."

The woman's narrowed eyes roll back in her head. Her mouth opens wider than it should.

"Seriously. Your maid is—"

"My what?" he says. The woman's teeth are black and broken. "I don't have a maid," he says. "That's Edith. My wife."

She wakes up sweating.

No matter how many times she drives through Wyoming, its emptiness still catches her by surprise. Henry raps twice on the partition and she opens the little window.

The faint tinge of vomit underneath the Big Sur Breeze makes her thankful for Lǎoyé's foresight in installing such a sturdy, airtight divider. If there's one thing her family knows, it's how things fit together, from railroad ties to Tetris tiles. But then, they also know how to break things apart.

"What are those weird fences?"

She takes in the slatted beams. "Snow fences," she says as though she possesses an innate understanding of Wyoming's mysteries. As though this were not something her fact sheet research turned up last month, when she'd driven a man she suspected of being a retired Triad cross-country to see his grandkids. "They really cut down on winter accidents."

"But, like, there are so many gaps. How do they catch the flakes?"

"They don't. They just slow the wind down till it lets go of them."

"Hunh."

"Otherwise, the gusts of snow make it impossible to see." She meets his eyes in the rearview. "The fences also cut down on plowing, sanding, and salting."

"Go figure," he says.

"Go figure."

With the partition window open, the sickly sweet Big Sur Breeze makes her gag. She cracks her own window. "Let's get it cleaned professionally," she'd suggested back in Elko, but he'd flat out refused.

"It's fine," he said. "Let's not waste the money"—tapping his exorbitant Bulgari—"or time." His erratic juxtaposing of frugality and finery reminded her of how, before her father left them last year, Mama had paired the mink coat he'd bought her with cheap department-store jeans. Spend, don't spend, hurry, don't hurry: he was a paradox.

In the back seat, Henry arranges and rearranges his long legs; still winds up looking cramped. "You're a fount of knowledge, Měi L. Brown."

"Ugh. Not my full name, please."

"Why not? It's on your highly informative handouts."

"It's the worst of cultural combos."

"What do you mean?"

She exhales sharply. "My mom wanted the character 'ài,' for love, somewhere in my name. She had all these pretty combinations of Chinese words picked out. But she didn't want it to just be 'ài,' and my dad thought a longer name would be hard for Americans, so they settled on Měi."

"What's wrong with Měi? I like it."

"I mean, sure, it's fine alone. But my mom was insistent about the love thing, so the *L* stands for—Love."

"Love?"

"Love."

"It's cute."

"Měi Love Brown? Like I'm stating my favorite color."

He clears his throat. "Wanna know my middle name?"

"Sure."

"Rocky."

"Rocky?"

"Yeah. Like, after China's sacred mountains."

"AAAADRRRIIIIAAAAAN!"

"See?" A snort. "I'm trying to empathize, and this is how you do me." In the rearview, a lazy half smile. "How long before we make it to Nevada?"

"Nebraska?"

"Yeah. That."

She glances at the clock. It's 4:00 P.M., meaning they've been on the road for three hours. "Three more hours," she says, "if we don't make too many stops."

But as always, he requests multiple stops—each time grabbing his cooler from the trunk, dragging his heavy suitcase from the back seat, and lugging it out of sight to do whatever it is he does.

At a gas station, she purchases an enormous ICEE, blue on the bottom, red on top. He only purchases ice, to refresh his cooler, and by the time he returns, she's down to purple sludge. And further down the road, at a truck stop, she grows so bored with spinning an enormous rack of plastic vanity plate key chains ("Martin," "Melissa," "Melvin," even "Myrna," but of course no "Měi") that she purchases one for Henry. When she hands it to him outside the car, his face does something so odd that she wonders how many women have given him gifts; whether perhaps he only associates with the kind who stay on the receiving end.

His car door's open, the heavy suitcase nestled inside, waiting. He fingers the trinket. "Thanks," he says slowly.

She wonders what his Chinese name is, if he has one.

His phone rings and he pulls it from his jeans pocket. Reading the caller's name, he stiffens. "I have to take this," he says tersely. She shrugs.

"Go on," she urges when he lingers.

He glances from the suitcase to Měi to his phone.

"Just—close the car door," he says. "Be right back."

And then he's off through the lot, sprinting toward the highway, as though to sprout wheels and make the rest of the drive on his own. She takes in his easy athleticism, his multicolored, limited-edition Dunks. He's ditched the suit entirely now, and the button-downs, too, reminding her of the way her favorite professor dressed and spoke formally at the start of each new term and, by the end, wore jeans, coffee stains, and smirks.

The threadbare gray T-shirt clings to the sculpted musculature of Henry's shoulders, his back. She has to force herself to look away by leaning into the sedan's open door, across the back seat, to press her palms against the black suitcase and shove it a bit further in.

And that's when the first thing happens.

Sidney, Nebraska, hasn't forgotten the intrepid equestrians who sped across nearly two thousand miles of wilderness, climbing mountains in the beat-you-down summer sun, fording icy rivers in the dead of winter, all to deliver the mail. And for anyone who has forgotten, Sidney offers a National Pony Express Monument: a galloping bronze mustang and its rider, flanked by the flags of every state the express traversed before the transcontinental telegraph replaced it.

"You know, Chinese also build telegraph," she recalls Lǎoyé murmuring, years ago, "when we make second transcontinental railroad."

"Second railroad?" They hadn't learned about a second railroad in school or studied the southern lines that the slaves built.

"Yah. I guess we couldn't get enough of those picks, shovels, wheelbarrows, horse carts, and supervisor who spit on us. We just gotta build one more railroad. And all along the tracks, stick telegraph pole and wire."

Waiting at a railroad crossing, blinking at the glove compartment that hides her next printout for Henry, her brain rumbles. *The suitcase—* But each time her mind starts to get somewhere, her train of thought derails, spilling its cargo, patrol cars with sirens on their way, so she's stuck at *The suitcase— The suitcase—*

The inn she parks in front of is part of a national chain, the staff comprised of cheerful and efficient young women in ponytails. Check-in is quick, and they head to the elevator.

This time, she's watching the protective way Henry manages the suitcase on its heavyweight spinner wheels. Even when they're standing still, he plants his feet wide to steady himself, shoulders squared, a soldier on duty—his long, able fingers gripping the rugged trolley handle.

"What?" he says.

"What?"

"Don't just echo me." He laughs. "Penny for your thoughts?"

"My thoughts," she says slowly, "are more expensive than that."

He purses his lips. "Okay?"

"I just—maybe it's not my business, but—" She thinks of Ling Ling: their silent rides, and the genuine sadness she'd felt the evening she pulled up to find the beaming woman perched on a hard-shell suitcase nearly the size of Henry Lee's.

"Airport," Ling Ling had said. "Oakland, not SF." And then, at Departures, when Měi opened her door, "I go back to my husband. He love me again, want me come home. I not see you no more, but I remember you. I make good money, thanks to you."

Should she have asked Ling Ling more questions?

Ding: floor four. The doors open, and they step out onto shiny tile. By the chemical scent of it, this is one of those establishments where someone's always cleaning something. She sniffs. Rubs at her nose.

On the wall in front of them, arrows point in opposite directions down the carpeted hall. "We're 409 and 410," Henry says. "To the right." But she can't move her feet. The elevator's doors close behind them, and they stand in silence as the car glides away. She watches the suitcase; feels him watching the watching, but can't take her eyes off it.

"Okay," he says decisively. And he's off down the hall.

"Wait," she says.

"See you tomorrow. Eleven A.M. checkout."

In her dreams, they are lost in a forest with the squirming suitcase, the glittering eyes of animals piercing holes in the inky dark.

Their next destination is under five hours away. Forgoing breakfast, she leaves him in the lobby, at the coffee bar, torn between dark and French roast.

Striding out into a hot breeze, she unlocks the sedan. Starts the car and blasts the air-conditioning. Fidgets in the driver's seat, feeling its gentle contours against her back, until he appears in the rearview. Still, she doesn't move. Watches him load his ugly suitcase into the back seat, shut the door, and walk around to the opposite side. She is accustomed to clients who refuse help with their luggage. This is the first time she's failed to offer anyhow.

She opens the little window in the divider as he pulls his long legs into the car. Fixes him squarely in her gaze. "Morning."

"Morning," he says, regarding her with a squint, calibrating something. Does he realize she nearly breached her own code yesterday? Asked him what he was transporting?

She closes the partition.

Nebraska, via the I-80, feels interminable: flatlands and more flatlands rolling by in a blur punctuated, here and there, by a brilliant sunflower field; a smoking, jackknifed semi; an overturned SUV. She would hate it, but she's saving her hate for the Three I's. Iowa, Illinois, Indiana. The interminable drive through those three states' rolling fields has nearly ruined her love for corn on the cob. She flips the music on; bumps her head to a '90s hip hop song till something large thwacks the windshield, then examines the stain it leaves. Grasshopper? Dragonfly?

When she glances in the rearview, he's looking at her. He's let stubble overtake his jaw; looks different, somehow, from when they met. Guarded, still, but not shellacked—his chimeric nature shed like a Halloween costume, the aristocratic elderly airs gone.

He is a client from Lǎoyé, who's never steered her wrong. "Good man," Lǎoyé assured her. And Lǎoyé is not one to dole out hollow assurances.

They pull into a rest stop full of fast-food joints and get in line for lunch. Ordering nachos, she's conscious of his eyes on her back.

It's almost a relief when he asks for the keys and heads outside to be with his ugly suitcase. She runs her fingers over the blue plastic tabletop; lets her mind drift from the rest stop back to Mama's home.

Aromas of hóngshāoròu—red braised pork, anise, rice wine—assailed Měi at the door. Another fall term of vegetarianism had obliterated her tolerance for meat, just as decades of barbarous honesty had obliterated her mother's tact. Her aunties, at least, feigned ignorance when she flew home from school for the holidays: "What? Vegetarianism mean even beef? Okay. You eat the meat this time and next time I get it right." But not Mama.

"Your friends don't eat meat, make sense. They got recipes to save their arteries, save the planet." Mama set the plate before her with finality. "But you can't cook to save your butt. So, for you, vegetarian is stupid."

Her father looked up from his plate. A faint smile, then back to his food. Ever a man of few words.

Eeny meeny miny mo. Catch a tiger by the toe. But Mama was not an Asian stereotype; didn't have claws. She'd never withheld physical affection or enforced stringent discipline. Despite her accent, her reluctance to deal with anyone lacking Chinese blood, she was imbued with American culture, and in twenty-four years Měi had never once doubted her mother's fierce love, which asserted itself in her very own name.

Mama was just very, very candid.

A little sauce dribbled down the D of her Dartmouth sweatshirt, and she swiped at it. "VOX CLAMANTIS IN DESERTO," a voice crying out in the wilderness, was printed in all-caps below the school's name—the motto bitten from the Bible in 1769 by Reverend Eleazar Wheelock, who founded the college in New Hampshire's woods "for the education of youth of the Indian tribes." Měi had come to appreciate the aptness of the Latin phrase; come to understand how her friends really did regard their undergraduate experience as a singular, four-year respite from the savagery of the American wasteland, despite all evidence to the contrary.

This went for Gabriel, who'd knocked his front teeth out trying to scale Bartlett Tower shitfaced; Una, still perky and smiling after being raped by four frat brothers who'd stalked her silently across the snow-hushed campus, chanting *slut-slut-slut* and laughing when she slipped on black ice; and Monica, who'd come home from a semester in India wearing saris and spelling her name Maanika, with a tricolor tattoo of a swastika on her wrist. Like the name, the tat was a symbol of her newly adopted Hindu faith ("reappropriated from the Nazis") and possibly also an icebreaker as her pallid face was disappointingly plain. "Its Sanskrit etymology is *su*, or 'good,' *asti*, meaning 'to be,' and *ka*, a simple suffix," she said loudly at parties.

But Mama was the opposite of her Ivy League friends. Mama spoke straightforwardly, neither clamoring to be heard nor shying away from the truth. Měi poked at the meat on her plate.

"You heard about Bo Xilai?" Mama asked, surprising her as she'd never seen her mother consume any form of reportage beyond Chinese celebrity news and cat rescue videos. ("Politics the most boring soap opera," Mama had said once. Then, waving a dismissive hand at Měi's observation that soap operas don't start wars, "Of course there will be war. Men going to fight over who got more like little boys battle on the playground with sticks.")

"Bo Xilai," Měi repeated. "The Chongqing Communist Party boss whose wife poisoned a British businessman? Years ago?" She lifted the pork above her plate with simple wooden kuài zi—no slippery, enameled chopsticks in this house.

"Yes. You heard?"

"Well, just the basics, really. I didn't delve into the more nuanced—"

"Who decide asylum?"

"What?"

"Chief of police help Bo Xilai cover up this bad crime, then he flee to U.S. consulate, confess, ask for asylum."

"Which was denied—"

"Who decide yes or no?"

Měi brought her kuài zi to her mouth. Delicious. In the vegan house at Dartmouth, they ate boiled kale and thirteen-bean soup: functional concoctions that Una prepared in a slow cooker at the start of each week. When Měi came home, though, she always gave in. What was a few days of guilt and gastrointestinal discomfort compared with Mama's cooking?

Mama waved a hand in front of her. "Asylum! Who decide yes or no?"

"Well, one applies for the right to asylum by proving"—she strained to recall a classroom lecture; an approximation would have to do—"a legitimate fear of persecution on account of a protected ground. There are five protected grounds." Wielding her kuài zi with her right hand, she raised her left, wiggling the fingers and thumb. Five. Her mother's utilitarian English had always been poor—Měi's Mandarin, far worse—so they augmented conversation with this homegrown sign language. "And the applicant must establish that the government is stomping on those grounds or allowing others to." More meat. So good! She chewed, swallowed. "Even then, once all that's proven, asylum can be denied."

Mama turned to Měi's father. "Persecution?"

"Unfair treatment." He wiped his mouth with a cloth napkin.

Her mother nodded patiently as Měi tried to elucidate. "Picture a psychopath waving a chain saw around on the busy street outside

Bellevue—which is like the U.S., right? The nurses at the asylum see the man on their smoke breaks. The doctors do, too, from third-story windows. But the maniac ends up walking home in the dark when the saw runs out of gas. Or, not having a home, wandering into a sleeping neighborhood. Because, sometimes, even the grandest loony bin gets too full to admit one more." She cocked her head at her own dramatic speech.

"Okay." Mama smiled. "So you don't know who decide." They ate the rest of the meal in silence.

∽

This leg of their trip is the shortest, yet it seems to drag. Her alignment is off: her thoughts—*the suitcase—the suitcase*—keep pulling her eyes toward the rearview.

She adjusts the mirror so she can no longer see its black bulk.

Steers her thoughts firmly back to Mama's cozy home.

After the hóngshāoròu, she'd tried to nap, closing the blinds in her childhood bedroom against the neighbor's obnoxiously bright Christmas lights. But she couldn't sleep and slouched back to the kitchen. Her father had wandered off to his study. At the little round table, her mother was reading his newspaper.

"What are you doing?" From the doorway, Měi gestured at the paper. "You hate the news."

Her mother didn't even lift her head. "Looking for used car for your auntie. But not so much classified ad nowadays—"

"Oh? Which one?"

"Toyota."

"No, Mama. Which auntie?"

"Auntie Amy: Ānmíng Āyí."

Měi wondered whether her white friends' parents did this: gave every loved one at least two names. Was Maanika's auntie Lizette also called something else, something more ethnic, the way Wonder Woman was Princess Diana of Themyscira as well as Diana Prince? Did Una's brother Robert have a secret identity revealed only when he removed his glasses? When she returned from holiday break, perhaps she'd ask. Still drowsy, she approached the little table. Took a seat. "Mama, why'd you ask that question earlier?"

Now, her mother glanced up. "What question?"

"About asylum."

"For your auntie."

"Oh." She rubbed at her eyes, wondering why one of her aunties— both ensconced in a gated San Jose development—wanted to know about asylum. "Which one?"

The house, an Oakland craftsman, was nestled in the curve of a free-way on-ramp, and the kitchen window was wide open. Evening sounds came in: neighbors and wind and cars. Fumes, too. Yet Mama's plants seemed to thrive on the pollution, honeysuckle sweetening the dirty air, morning glories spilling over and through the peeling wooden fence that enclosed the backyard and Lǎoyé's converted garage.

"You don't know her."

"What?" She stared at her mother across the table as an airplane rumbled overhead.

"What what?" Finally, Mama swatted at the air as though the issue were a housefly. "You don't know this auntie. Long ago, before Lǎolao finally come to America and we girls come with her, your grandma struggle in China. Lǎoyé send her what he can, but still, she make the tough decision to send two youngest girls to the South. I maybe fifteen, sixteen at the time."

Měi grasped the table's edge. "What?"

"What's on second," Mama said, making her voice like Abbott and Costello. But Měi didn't laugh. *How could you let that happen?* she wanted to say, but instead Měi asked why her faraway aunt needed asylum.

"She leave them with your great-grandma in Guangdong. Great-grandma die long time ago. Then we bring one girl over. But youngest āyí still stuck there, want to get away." Mama had shrugged.

"Wait, the older auntie is in the U.S.?"

"New York. With cat."

"Why haven't we visited her?"

"No good visit." Mama shook her head. "These two āyí speak Hakka. Very hard language. You not understand a single word. Plus"—she'd shrugged again—"she very different life from you. Live in small village."

Měi blinked her eyes. After the 1906 earthquake hit San Francisco, her Asian American History professor had told the class, San Franciscans rebuilt Chinatown as a tourist attraction: an exaggerated stereotype of the Orient. Its cluttered alleyways were so narrow they violated housing, health, and fire code—but the City turned a blind eye. Chinatown brought in money. Soon, other cities followed suit, building equally cartoonish Chinatowns. Měi guessed her vision of her family's birthplace was more Chinatown than China. "A village?"

"Plus, they old maids! Two youngest girls in they forties now. You got nothing talk about." Měi glared till her mother relented with a sigh. "United States auntie is Lán Āyí. Orchid. Though she always smell more like cheese. China auntie is Jú Āyí. Chrysanthemum." She put a veined hand over Měi's, to stop the drumming fingers. "You not gonna remember this."

"Of course I'll remember! They're my āyis, just like Ānmíng Āyí and Měilì Āyí." She swallowed rage while her mother shook her head. "Is Jú Āyí's life in danger?" Her mother shook her head again. "Then why does she need asylum?"

"I just thinking maybe easier than get the papers."

"The immigration application?"

"That take years." She shrugged. "Why you think we take so long to get here? Your grandpa just about to apply for citizenship when the man he work for convicted of a crime. He get so scared, he never finish papers. American history buff not even a full American when we finally come. So, your grandma and San Jose aunties get their papers illegal and Lán Āyí the same way. But that way not so good." Měi's mouth hung open. "At first, we think go smooth every time. But the supplier blackmail Lán Āyí. For him to leave her alone, she give things up, same as Ānmíng and Měilì before them."

"What does that mean?"

The corners of her mother's mouth turned down slightly. "Give more money, give other things. But that the decision they make."

"Did you have to—make hard choices, too?" Měi's head felt swaddled in cotton, and her stomach was doing something strange. Outside the open window, a motorcycle growled by in the dusk.

"Sure I did." Her mother turned back to the newspaper. "I marry your daddy."

They reach York, Nebraska, late and she forgets the fact sheet in her glove compartment.

This chain inn is so similar to yesterday's that the differences are slightly disorienting: Shouldn't the lobby be over on the east wall, instead of the west? Shouldn't the ponytailed girl checking them in be blond and not brunette?

Henry hands her a key card and they find their rooms in silence, then stand in the hallway, smiling politely across the carpeted yards between their adjacent doors.

What's in the fucking suitcase? I felt something moving inside.

But she says nothing. They enter their separate rooms.

Tossing her overnight pack on an armchair, she unlaces her high-tops, kicks them off, and paces. Picks up the remote. Clicks the TV on, flipping through channels. Continues pacing.

Měi has always had a hard time keeping still. Dropping out of Dartmouth the day after her father left them—just two more terms between her and an Ivy League degree—was the most obvious example. One Mama would never forgive her for. But hadn't the antsiness always been there?

Only Lǎoyé had understood. Lǎoyé, who'd never gone to college but crossed an ocean to work countless jobs in just as many cities, passing time with the homeless in libraries, sleeping in beds he didn't own, before buying the home his grown daughter now lived in. Hadn't he accomplished, without a degree, so much more than their ancestors ever could, given the 1875 Page Act (a forgotten piece of legislation passed before the infamous Chinese Exclusion Act, ostensibly to prohibit "coolies" and sex workers from entering the States, but more often wielded to keep railroad workers' wives out)?

Hadn't Lǎoyé laid down roots, regardless of his official status? Made them a real American family? Bought her the sedan. Introduced her to clients.

She forces herself to stop pacing and turn the television off. Grabbing a glass from the counter, she sets its rim firmly against the wall, pressing her ear to its cool bottom. And then, despite the urge to pace, move, fidget, she simply keeps still.

That's when the second thing happens.

Initially, she only hears the blaring TV and something like the sound of air whooshing through vents. She wants to slam the glass down and pound the wall; to charge out into the hallway and knock on his door.

But she stays motionless, silent, calm, till the surface noises peel back to reveal a hidden layer of sound. Though she can't make out the words, Měi can hear them talking. Henry and another person. Henry and the person from the suitcase.

3

YORK TO ROCK ISLAND

She skips breakfast and waits in the lot again, leaned up against the hood of the car. Around noon, he emerges, somehow managing the heavy suitcase without fumbling his paper coffee cup.

"Morning, sunshine." A grin.

"Mr. Lee," she says, sliding this formality between them like bulletproof glass, which the safety partition inside the car is certainly not. "Let me help with your bag."

Still a few feet away, he stops short.

"No. Thank you." His face goes serious.

She jingles the keys, thinking of the little plastic license plate key chain she gave him: *Henry*. A normal name. But he is not normal. None of this is normal. She jingles the keys again. Does not unlock the car.

"Look, Měi," he says, and shuts his mouth.

A cloud of mosquitoes forms suddenly above them, as though prelude to some larger insect storm. When it descends, she waves her hands about; flips her hair back and forth frantically till he closes the short distance between them, grabs her by the forearm, and pulls her out of the swarm into clear air.

The mosquitoes drift off—evaporate into the sunlit day.

Henry releases her arm. "Know what that's called?" The suitcase, a few feet away, stands unmanned.

"What what's called?" She gauges the distance.

"The little dance you just did. Swatting mosquitoes?" She tilts her head. "The Syracuse Shuffle!" He wears a determined smile.

"Great," she says slowly. "Our final destination's an insect-ridden swamp?"

"What can I say? I'm a nature lover. You will be, too, if you give the place a chance. I'll be happy to pay for whatever you do in New York. You should get out, while I'm in my meetings, and see the Green Lakes—"

"Henry."

"Two glacial lakes in this old-growth forest of sugar maples, white cedars, hemlocks, basswood, beech. You could add them to your Syracuse fact sheet. Because I know you've got one in that glove box . . ." He's backing toward the suitcase as he talks; grasps its handle. "The water at those lakes is like flat jade. In fact, the whole region's full of water. Lakes and rivers, bogs and ponds." He pulls the case to the sedan's back passenger door, where he stops and plants it firmly against him. "I mean, it'll help you understand climate deniers. Seriously. Because it's gotta be hard to believe the earth's drying up when water is, like, pooling in every dip and crack around you, pouring down for days on end. Did you know in Syracuse they refer to Manhattan dismissively as 'downstate'—"

"Henry!" She points to the case. "Stop yammering. I know what's in there."

He levels his gaze at her, serious again.

Narrows his eyes, biting his full bottom lip. "No. You don't."

"I do. I fucking felt something in there, like, moving."

"You got me," he says, throwing his hands up, tilting his head back in a barking laugh. "I'm smuggling puppies." An anime sun-flash glints off his perfectly white teeth.

Now a middle-aged blond couple, eschewing the veritable sea of empty parking spaces, pulls up right next to them. The man's balding head is sunburnt, while the woman has teased her curls to ludicrous proportions as though compensating for her husband's lack of hair. The couple kills the motor but remains in their car.

"I heard you," she hisses at Henry. "Conversing. In the room. Last night."

"You heard the television," he says, his face implacable though the proper word "television" somehow betrays his nervousness. "Just the TV," he corrects, reading her thoughts.

The couple climbs out of their car. Grinning. Nosy. "Great weather," the grinning man says to Měi, who shoots a tight smile back. Henry is pallid, looking at the grinning woman. He meets Měi's eyes.

She grimaces.

Returns to the driver's side. Unlocks the doors.

Whatever allegiance she has, it isn't to these people.

Henry hefts the case into the back seat's dark recess. They get in the car, and she drives.

This time, at the rest stop diner, he stays put after the gaunt teenage waiter leaves.

They haven't traded a word since York. Not in Lincoln. Not in Omaha. Not till now, in Des Moines, Idaho. "So who is it?" she asks, meaning *Who are you?* Meaning *Coyote? Kidnapper? Sex trafficker?*

He stares into his empty plate, and she thinks of riding silently with Ling Ling down 98th Avenue, toward Oakland International Airport, in the golden sun. Past the homeless encampments below the BART tracks. Past a businessman striding briskly out of a burrito spot, paper bag clutched in one hand. Past a smiling, dreadlocked father on a bicycle— two smiling, dreadlocked, bicycled children trailing behind like baby ducks. The only utterance she can recall Ling Ling making in transit, ever, is the "Oh!" she let loose that last day, near Departures, when they almost rear-ended a Prius as it darted into their lane.

She refocuses. *My motto,* she prepares to say, *is "My clients' business is none of my business." But I won't be complicit in bad shit.* She opens her mouth to speak.

"A kid," he says.

She gapes at him. "A kid?"

"It's not—whatever you're thinking," he says. "I'm helping her."

"Helping her sell a kidney?"

"No."

"Helping her blow men her father's age?"

He grimaces. "Měi."

"Or are you the father? Abducting your own kid from her mom?"

"Seriously?"

"Goddamn right this is mothafuckin' serious." She leans low over her place setting, directing the words at his chest. "You're a fucking kidnapper." Sitting up, she glances around. There is barely anyone to overhear her: just a hunched man in the far corner, drinking coffee.

"No," he says. "Please." His lower eyelid twitches. "Listen, you said you heard us, right?" She purses her lips. Decides not to explain the whooshing of air through the walls, the way it swept their words along in its rushing current so she couldn't quite catch what was said. "So you know she's Chinese. Speaks Mandarin. Refuses to travel outside the suitcase. But she's not scared of me. She's a"—the waiter appears behind the counter, walks around and veers away toward the hunched man's beckoning hand—"a Uyghur."

"What?"

"An ethnic minority in China's Xinjiang Province."

"Well, I know what a fucking Uyghur is. I mean 'What?' as in 'What the fuck?'"

A weak smile. "Do you always cuss this much when you're scared?"

"I'm not fucking scared. I'm angry."

"I'm pretty sure that's a product of fear. Like, a fight-or-flight thing."

"Great. First you explain China's ethnic minorities, and now a lecture on adrenaline production?" Her wobbly pitch and volume explode. "What the fuck, Henry? A fucking—"

Suddenly the rawboned, expressionless waiter is there with two sandwiches, close enough to spit in their ice water. "Wow," he says dryly. "Want me to leave and come back?" A high school senior, Měi figures, based on his careful nonchalance. The name tag reads ROBBY.

"Ignore her, please, sir." Henry tilts his gaze up at Robby, smiling in a teasing way that crinkles the corners of his eyes. "She's just hangry."

"Well"—setting their plates before them—"then I'm right on time."
The waiter seems to deliberate, hovering over Henry. "Hey," he says at
last, "maybe this is weird, but if my meemaw met you she'd just have
to comment on your eyelashes. She made me balance a matchstick on
mine." He bats his lashes.

"I've done that, too," Henry says, smiling brightly. "Balanced a
matchstick on them? At my own meemaw's insistence." Robby nods, face
and neck flushed, and the table goes silent. The diner is silent, too, except
for the clinking of the hunched man in the corner stirring milk into his
coffee.

"Let me know, okay," Robby says at last, "if I can get you anything
else." Then he's gone.

Instantly Henry's face goes slack, the banter having served its purpose. He regards Měi soberly.

"Your fucking 'meemaw'?"

"Wow. Now you're gonna disrespect Meemaw, too?"

"Chinese don't have meemaws! We've got a lǎolao and a nǎinai."

"Yeeeah—well. Not me. I don't have a lǎolao." He cups his chin,
fingers rubbing at his stubbly jaw, as she feels herself wince.

"Henry. I'm so sorry." Memories of her own lǎolao flood her: the
gentle way she'd held Měi's hand when they walked to school, so Měi
never felt dragged or even led; the sweetness of Lǎolao's desserts, of her
toothless grin. For one whole year, she'd insisted Lǎolao brush her hair.
Only Lǎolao, no other adult. And when her grandmother died, Měi cried
more than Mama. Cried more than anyone—though, days later, Lǎoyé
simply packed up his things and moved, without a word, out of the bedroom her grandparents had shared, into the freestanding garage.

"This California," he'd said, shrugging, when Mama complained.
"No hail, no snow. Climate change even take away the rain. You fine to
park in the driveway. Plus, now you got guest room." For months, he was
back and forth to the hardware store—making a racket out back, installing windows and heating, finishing the walls, tweaking the electrical system, tiling the floor. Tinkering was how he grieved.

"Oh, no, she's not dead." Across the table, Henry's perfect teeth flash. "I just don't call her Lǎolao. I call her Wàipó. And my dad's mom is Nǎinai."

She blinks. "So you're not hapa? Like me? Half white?"

"One hundred percent Asian blood. I'm just a tall drink of water." He picks his fork up; twirls it over the defeated lettuce next to his sandwich. "Now, are we gonna eat so I can get back to that kid out there, maybe let her stretch her legs, have one of the healthy lunches packed in my cooler, or are you gonna let her"—pointing, with the tines, at the sedan outside—"die of heatstroke?"

∽

Rock Island, Illinois, is not the original Rock Island.

Měi can't quite recall which mundane details about the city she's included on the handout in the glove compartment, but she does know one thing about the place: the original Rock Island, now renamed Arsenal Island, houses the United States Army's largest federal arsenal—and its products include small arms. This factoid sticks in her mind, thanks to a goofy memory that popped up as she researched the destination. "Dang," Lǎoyé whispered in her ear one afternoon as Auntie Amy emerged from her Toyota, arms laden with pink, string-wrapped boxes from her favorite San Jose bakery, "you know your lǎoyé think all his daughter beautiful. But you ever notice Ānmíng Āyí got teeny T-Rex arms? How she reach her head to put on that visor?"

Slowing, now, nearing their hotel, Měi's heart rumbles. She nearly threatens to turn the car around, like a scolding parent. Instead, inhaling deeply, she parks. Watches Henry sleep in the rearview mirror. She's read that twelve percent of us dream only in black and white; wishes she knew the colors of his dreams, that she could search them for clues to his character.

"You go back to your bedroom and dream." She recalls Lǎoyé's voice in her ear as he shook her gently awake on the saggy couch, drowsy himself in the flickering light of a Disney film's end credits.

"No." She must've been seven or eight.

"Your mama gonna worry. And couch not for sleeping."

"You nap here all the time." Her nose wrinkled with the injustice.

"Nap not sleep." He rose to his feet, stretching before her in his embroidered slippers and shabby robe. When his mouth gaped open, she yawned, too. "Got you," he said, triumphant, as she tried and failed to swallow the yawn. "You tired, like me." The shining white disc of the moon shone through the window like metal, like a headlight, like snow, and he clasped her hands, pulling her into a sitting position. "You know Americans used to sleep in two shifts?"

"Every night?" She rubbed her eyes.

"Yah. Go to sleep around nine or ten, wake up after midnight to putter for an hour or so, then sleep again till dawn."

"When you were young?"

"Psht." His smile showed yellow teeth. "I not that old. Americans begin sleep through the night in the 1800s, once we get gas and electric lights. Then we want stay up later and later! Like you. When we finally hit the hay, we too tired to get up and putter after midnight anymore."

"I could do it," she said. "I'm never sleepy."

And she stretched out and slept on the couch until she felt him shake her again.

Still, how Henry's nodded off now is beyond her.

The suitcase, too, is still. For all they know, the child could be dead inside. She wrenches around, opens the partition, and stares directly at the fans of his eyelashes, daring them to lift.

His lips twitch, but he doesn't wake. "Henry," she says. But with his earbuds in, he doesn't hear. And that's when the third thing happens, demolishing her trust in him.

His phone, gripped loosely in a hand, is playing a video of movement she can't quite make out.

She sticks an arm through the partition, but her wiggling fingers don't reach the device. There is a knot in her belly. As though in a dream, a film, as though in someone else's body, she slips quietly from the car. Opens Henry's door. Bends and, with a quick glance at the motionless suitcase, slips the phone from his fingertips. Rewinds the video. Plays it on mute.

On-screen: a child-sized, quick-eyed woman seated on a bed. The video, clearly shot surreptitiously by this woman on a cell phone hidden in her sleeve, pans unsteadily from her still, worn face to her drab clothing to her left arm, handcuffed to the bed frame. Then, slowly, around the bare walls and stained ceiling tiles.

A fly darts into the car, alighting on Henry's hand. He twitches and she stands quickly, dropping the phone on the seat as his eyes open. His fingers close around it. Instantly, she's back in Tilden Park as a child, watching a hawk snatch up a vole in the botanical garden. She fights the impulse to back away.

Disoriented, he glances at the suitcase. His mouth is hard, brow furrowed.

He blinks up at her.

A slow grin. "What's up, Měi Love Brown?"

∞

In line to check in, she fidgets.

Scanning the noisy lobby, she locates two police officers near an exit. Averts her gaze. Above the din, she asks: "Is this a casino?"

"Yeah," Henry says. "What gave it away? The slot machines, or the big sign that reads 'Casino and Hotel'?"

"What I mean is, is this the best place for a——" She rolls her eyes toward the suitcase.

He stares at her. "We're not planning on joining any poker games."

"But. The. Cameras"—she hears her voice rising—"are fucking everywhere!"

"Shh," he says simply, leaving her behind to approach the counter with a wide smile. "Henry Lee," he says to the concierge. "We have a reservation."

"Mr. Lee." The concierge (a luxury model of the standard ponytailed girls from the chain inns) pats at her elegant updo, managing to look Měi up and down without shifting her gaze. "Welcome back. We've got you in the penthouse suite this time."

His back straightens. "We booked two separate rooms. Not a suite."

"But we've renovated since your last visit, and we'd love your feedback. The new penthouse has two spacious bedrooms with en suites. Each room offers mood lighting, individual climate controls, heated bathroom floors, and, of course, automatic drape and sheer controls. I think you'll find it very comfortable." Her gracious enthusiasm is unwavering.

"We're on a budget."

She smiles patiently. "Upgrade's on the house," she says, wrinkling her nose in the direction of Měi's scuffed high-tops. "And the penthouse comes with VIP lounge access for you and your—friend. We hope you'll enjoy your stay with us."

Cutting his eyes at Měi, Henry flashes an indulgent grin. "Okay, sure. Thank you."

He is playing the role of the considerate paramour, she realizes, appearing to relent so his low-class lover can experience a penthouse suite. But his consideration is a lie extending back to Tahoe and the chivalrous decision to keep the back windows rolled up despite the stench, trapping the cool air—which, it's clear now, he didn't do for her at all, but for the child in the suitcase. The child who must not overheat. Who must stretch and eat. The child who must sleep in late, to recover.

She scratches at her neck, eyes roaming the surface of the mammoth black thing. Does he handcuff the child to a bed frame at night? She swallows, hard. Why not become that protective parent in her head? Why not actually turn the car around? But if Henry is a bad person, if he is trading women, girls, for money, and she just drops them off where they came from, who will protect the child? And if she calls the cops over, spills everything, admits she's been driving clients around without reporting one cent of income, who will protect her?

Once, for the client she'd pegged as a retired Triad, she drove a brown-paper-wrapped package to San Luis Obispo without one twinge of guilt. Keys of coke? A firearm and ammo? Or board books for his grandkid?

She shifts from foot to foot as the concierge beckons an aged bellhop.

"I'm Jacob. At your service. Take that off your hands?" He gestures from Henry's suitcase to his shiny gold luggage cart, bleary blue eyes locked firmly on Měi's small breasts.

Jacob looks insulted when Henry dismisses him, though less so once he sees the tip. Backing away, he gives her breasts a farewell stare. "Did you just tip that weirdo a hundred bucks? For nothing?" Měi hisses as they abscond. "What are you, a whale or something?"

They pass by the casino lights, his dark hair blinking neon red, orange, purple. "Callin' me fat?" He pouts. Hands her a key card. "I work out . . ."

Obviously. She rolls her eyes. "The other kind of whale."

"I'm no gambler," he says. "But I've been here on business with a betting man. A highly visible individual. 'Recognized,' as they say. Guess we're benefiting from his halo." A sharply dressed couple stumbles by and the man, even taller than Henry, clips his shoulder, knocking him gently into Měi. "Watch where you're going!" Henry shouts.

The couple spins around, the hulking man flushed and grinning. "WHAT IF EVERYONE YOU MASTURBATE ABOUT KNEW IT?" he yells, slurring, and the two disappear into the blazing, jangling slot machines, his date laughing giddily into his shoulder.

They press on through the crowd. "Casino randos." Henry shakes his head.

"When we get to the suite," Měi says without meeting Henry's eyes, "I need answers."

"I'd be fine with that."

Her posture softens, relief flooding her chest, as the case rolls smoothly along in his tight grip. If Lǎoyé trusts this man, surely she can, too. "Okay," she says. "Deal. So you'll tell me everything. And I mean everything. And then, I'll decide what happens."

"No," he says, flashing a sidelong grin. "I mean I'd be fine if all those women knew."

She stops short then. Grabs the handle of the suitcase so he must pivot to face her, and, placing her other hand on his cheek, draws upon a woman's innate ability to transform any man into a young boy.

He towers above her, his dark eyes turning contrite. "Měi Love Brown," he mumbles, "are you attempting to turn me into an honest man?"

"That is not on my to-do list. Just covering my own ass."

"Good." His eyes flash. "You have that concerned vibe that sets me ill at ease."

For a moment, before she drops her hand, they could be any couple in a classic film, the hero rebuked and entranced by the heroine in a crowd of poorly paid extras, the coffered ceiling and ornate chandeliers harkening to a bygone era.

But this is no star-crossed romance.

✦

The suite is smaller than she'd expected, but posh. Modern. Art Deco–inspired.

Henry scowls, dropping his key card on a brass side table. "It's no Bellagio," he says. "Be right back." He and the suitcase head into one of the bedrooms flanking the living room. The door closes.

For a few minutes she stands, expectant, in the center of the room. When he fails to reappear with the child, she slumps into a brilliant white Chesterfield sofa.

Lǎoyé would love this place. Despite his frat house decor, he's got a taste for old-school glamour—developed, no doubt, at his long-ago maintenance job in the luxe hotel owned and renovated by a Chinatown gang's dragonhead. He'd picked up his ornate slipper style, a twist on Hugh Heffner's iconic robe, from the gangster, she is certain. And perhaps also his weed habit—laughing and smoking with the individuals who would later comprise her client list. "I friends with Lobster Boy," he'd bragged when she was old enough for such stories. "He a good guy. Call me his right-hand man. And he never merk nobody. Not like them other ones. He deal drugs, not hits. Besides, he got a double chin and a lisp like the big boss in *Grand Larceny IV: Chinatown Wars*. Gotta feel bad for a guy like that. No?"

No, she thinks now. *No*.

What the Hell is she doing, trusting Henry Lee?

She chews her lip. She is considering whether to call Lǎoyé and cuss him out or run downstairs and grab the two police officers or bang on the bedroom door, when it opens. Henry crosses the room to her. As he sinks into the sofa, it shifts with his weight and she fights not to slide into him.

4

NEVERLAND (AN INTERLUDE)

"Anna's scared," he says. "To meet you. I gave her my tablet and stylus, hooked her up with Wi-Fi. She's in there doodling and scrolling."

She rearranges herself, cross-legged, in the corner of the Chesterfield while he drapes an ankle over his knee. Runs a hand through glossy hair. Somehow, even in his crappy T-shirt and jeans, he belongs in this opulence—a sleek, evocative silhouette.

Then she sees it, the trick to his composure: how he jokes and struts to keep himself from vomiting again, like smiling to fool yourself into happiness. Like faking it till you make it, something every skater who's fallen in a crowd and gotten shakily back on the board, fronting cool confidence, understands. She stares at the side of his face till he shifts, eyes meeting hers for just a moment. "How old is Anna?" she asks. "And what's her Chinese name?"

"Eleven." He taps at his knee with long fingers, catches her incredulous gaze before looking away again. "She's tiny, like her mom. And malnourished now. Don't comment on it." He chews at his lip. "You can call her Ānnuó, but the American version is fine, too. Her parents intended for her to have a name anyone in the world could pronounce. They never imagined she'd stay in China. When her father first came to the U.S. to interview for a professorship, the family accompanied him. He got the job and stayed. Anna and her mom returned to China, planning to come back soon. Then things got worse in Xinjiang—"

There's an energy vibrating under his skin, the seismic waves of some interior earthquake, and she recalls reading over and over, till she fully understood, a passage from her geophysics textbook on how the earth rings out with infrasonic sound for days, even months, after a high-magnitude event; how the study of each wave of energy illuminates more about what's under the surface. "Anna's original name," he murmurs, "was Medina." He clears his throat and the gravel of his voice liquefies. "Her parents changed it when she turned eight."

"To avoid Islamophobia?" Medina, if she recalls correctly, is where Muhammad campaigned to establish Islam.

"To avoid breaking the law. Can you imagine? Your parents sitting you down and assigning you a new name? But in Xinjiang, 'radical' names have been illegal for years now: Mecca, Medina, Imam, Hajj. She was named after her grandmother."

Fleetingly, she feels Lǎolao's fingers part her hair into strands to braid. "It wasn't illegal when she was born?" A shiver electrifies her back.

"No. But since the ban, kids under sixteen with the wrong names lose access to school. Healthcare. So they changed the family name, too, from a Uyghur name to Xīn. And her father, Ehmetjan, goes by Zǐmò or Jimmy." He leans forward over the gleaming, geometric coffee table to finger the petal of a white chrysanthemum in a maximalist black vase— "It's real." He releases the petal, looking mildly surprised. Meets her eyes again. "Even 'abnormal beards' are banned."

She thinks of her college friend, Gabriel, with his four-inch bristles and waxed handlebar mustache. "If the beard is weird and the 'stache is trash, they should probably be banned here, too."

He grins, shooting her a quick look. "Probably."

Inventorying her mind for what eleven years old looks like—how tall the child in the bedroom must be—she isolates a wobbly memory of her middle school friend Laura skateboarding toward her in the white light glinting off Lake Merritt. "I still don't get it," she says. "Stuffing your kid in a suitcase? This isn't China. Nobody's watching the Uyghurs here. She could've suffocated."

"It's specially designed with vents. Padding. Real wheels. And it's not like she came all the way over in it. She and the handler who accompanied her had fake passports with contactless smart chips. But once she was transferred to me, out of their hands, they felt they could take no chances."

"So the suitcase is a real vote of confidence?"

He smirks. "Hey, I'm not gonna trip. I want her to reach her dad, too. And put yourself in her parents' shoes. You know a Uyghur kid's corpse was left in a field, his organs cut out? Another was found frozen in a ditch. Desperate times . . ."

"But—there are other ways to disguise a kid. Bleach her hair blond. Get her gas station shades and a floppy hat!"

Palms to the ceiling, he shrugs. "Not my call."

"You can't talk sense into her parents?"

"Měi." Abruptly he sits up straight, his height dwarfing the slightness of her form folded in the corner. He drops a warm, heavy hand on her knee. "What do you think is going on over there?" Just as hastily, the hand is removed. He stares intently at the vase on the table.

"You tell me."

"Facial recognition. Armed checkpoints. Camps where people die of neglect—or worse. Communist Party spies moving into Uyghur homes. Forced abortions. Sterilization." A scowl blurs the perfect lines of his face. "Uyghur birth rates plummeted by nearly forty-five percent in a year. One year. That's genocide, defined by the U.N. 'Never again,' we said after the Holocaust. But it's happening now." The air conditioner switches on and she jumps. They listen through it to the silence from Anna's room. "Her parents are terrified." His voice lowers as his gaze rises to hold hers. "And I can't suggest anything at this point anyway, Měi"—he pronounces her name slowly, as though tasting it for the first time—"because nobody knows where they are."

"What?"

"Her mom disappeared first." His body falls back into the sofa, arms stretching along its leather spine. "To be clear, her mom *got* disappeared. Taken at night." Pulling his phone from a pocket, he unlocks it; balances it on Měi's bony knee. When she lifts it to look, she is face-to-face with the

petite woman handcuffed to the bed, the paused mouth in the little rectangle open as though choking. She presses Play and the woman clamps
her mouth tersely shut.

This time, with the volume up, the phone emits the scratchy sound
of words in the background. Some kind of broadcast in Mandarin, she
realizes, though it takes her a few moments to recognize the voice of Xí
Jìnpíng—his distinctive, presidential cadence. Then a woman's insistent
voice speaks in a language Měi can't understand.

Dizziness passes over her. She shakes her head. "What is this?"

"A vocational education center. Go in, and you may come out dead.
That's propaganda playing. Anna's mom bribed a guard to get her phone
back."

Wanting to be rid of the woman's unyielding eyes and handcuffed
wrist, she foists the phone at him. "And the dad?"

He shoves the phone into his pocket. "He's here."

She feels her eyebrows shoot up. "In the casino?"

A half smirk. "In the States. Syracuse. We think. He's a professor
there—a social anthropologist." Henry rubs at his stubbled jaw. "But the
thing is, he's got a readership in China, too, so he's on Beijing's radar. And
after our last conversation, he went on emergency leave. A worried colleague got the landlord to open his downtown apartment unit." The plane
of his brow shifts, deep faults forming. "Empty. Even the toilet paper gone."

"How do you know this?"

"He tagged Jimmy in social media. A rambling *WHERE ARE YOU*
post. Professors are babies that cry out loud about everything." He scowls,
ruminative. "Jimmy's still posting to social media. Only, the posts have
changed. Before, it was political stuff. Links to his articles. Ethnogra-
phies. Interviews about a phrase he coined, 'The Hollerith Age': a new
era of mass surveillance."

"Hollerith?"

"Every Holocaust death camp had an office where IBM punch-card
technology invented by Herman Hollerith stored data for identifying, iso-
lating, and exterminating Jews." The air-conditioning switches off again,
quick and efficient, and for a moment, they listen for any movement behind

Anna's closed door. "Now he posts pretty photos of downtown Syracuse instead. The civic center. The Palace Theatre. The Niagara Mohawk Building. No text, just images, except a response to his colleague. Telling him not to worry, everything's fine. But if everything's fine, why won't he pick up my calls? It's like he suspects someone is listening." The penthouse is quiet and slightly too cool now, a hint of citrus in the air-conditioned chill. Měi realizes she is shuddering. "The issue"—he stares out the wall of windows at Rock Island's flat, dimming landscape—"is that the Chinese also target Uyghurs living abroad, so we're not sure whether her dad's just laying low or—"

His lips remain pressed softly together.

"Or?"

"—or if he's disappeared, too. If they got to him. Threatened his wife. Lured him back to China and jailed him." She watches his jaw work back and forth. "Who knows—I mean, Xinjiang's an open-air prison, you know? CCTV everywhere. Everyone under surveillance." He sits up straight, leaning forward to finger the chrysanthemum again. "So, yeah. We're hoping to find him. That's the whole point of this trip. Because if he's got Anna over here to care for, to keep safe, keep free, there's less of a chance he'll try to go back." His fingers tap a restless rhythm on his knee again. "Anna fled a state-run boarding school with the help of concerned parties." His fingers quicken, tap-tapping across blue denim. "They call those places orphan camps, you know? The schools. As though the kids' parents are dead? So. Here we are. That suitcase may seem ridiculous to you, but . . ." His mouth snaps shut, trapping the words.

"Henry, it's—"

"I mean, it's not the approach I'd take, either. But it's not my call, right? I don't know the details. Whether it was the mother's idea or the person who contacted me, or both. I'm like you. Just doing a job. Except, of course"—a low chuckle—"I'm unpaid."

"Yeah?" The room is suddenly so cold she feels a headache coming on. "Then, why do this?"

His fingers drum lightly over his knee again. "The person who asked me to is important." Měi nods. *Important to China*, she thinks but doesn't say, *or important to you?* "Look," he says, standing, "I'ma order room service. Something to put a little meat back on Anna's bones. What do you want? And could you maybe give us a little privacy, just an hour or so, so she can eat, take her vitamins, brush her teeth, and acclimate to the idea of meeting you?"

∽

She stands in the stairwell, anxious, and dials Lǎoyé.

"Wéi?" The warm timbre of his voice steadies her instantly.

Someone has dropped an entire take-out carton of fried rice on this landing, an eggy scent rising from the mess, so she climbs a few steps; hovers there, remembering how she once saw her first boyfriend drop a spare rib on the ground, pick it up, blow on it, and eat it—and how, when her second boyfriend heard the story, he said "Oh, wow. The bar's set low."

"That you, kiddo?" She takes Lǎoyé off speaker. Presses the phone to her ear.

"Who else?" she answers as always, never daring to question whether he started asking to be cute or because his eyes are too poor to read the name on the screen. Now it's her turn to say, *That you, old man?*

"What's wrong?" he asks when she remains silent instead. "You get another speeding ticket?"

"No." She hears him shifting and can almost smell the stale weed, see his skinny legs stretched out on the fatigued brown couch. "I need to ask you a question. About China."

"China?"

"You know, our family's native land?"

"Oh, that China." Now, the sound of fabric dragged across fabric— the pink robe over his pajamas. "I think you talk about your mom's fancy wedding plates."

Despite herself, she smiles, recalling his pilfered ashtray. Climbing a few more steps, she leans against the wall, the handrail a dull irritation in her back. "Nope. Talking about the country."

"Okay. Shoot. But I may not know the answer. *American* history buff, remember?"

"This is more of a subjective question."

"Oh, okay. Then no way to fail. My favorite kinda exam."

"Do you think it's true"—she shifts from foot to foot, straddling two stairs: taller, shorter, taller, shorter—"about the Uyghurs?"

"What, that they got tails?"

"Jesus! Of course not."

"Good. That one not true." She hears the *ffft* of a lighter, and he inhales deeply. "Only white guys got tails."

She laughs, her free hand moving to graze her buttocks. "But I'm tailless."

"You a half-breed. Just got lucky."

"I'm wondering about, like, the detention camps."

"What about them?"

"For Uyghur reeducation."

"Yah?"

"Well, the Chinese government says they're one thing, and our government says they're another."

"Listen to Americans."

"Even though our president has a tail?"

"Look, I not saying America better. We do same thing."

"You mean the Japanese internment camps, after Pearl Harbor? The U.S.–Mexico border detention centers? Kids in cages?"

"No." A pause. He takes another hit, exhaling sharply. "I mean what we do to the Blacks. Even today."

She grinds her teeth. "Lǎoyé, please don't call them 'the Blacks.'"

"I call them whatever they ask be called. My friend Perlie say call her Black, not African American, 'cause the Africans sell her to the whites."

"You kinda missed my point. And I don't believe you for a minute."

"Shì zhēn de! That what she say!"

"No, I mean I don't believe there are still people named Perlie in this day and age."

"She old like me."

"She's not just an imaginary friend? Because you're always saying 'Friends are like vegan ham. Ew.'"

"I say that before Perlie. She real ham. Besides, what else I gonna do? My granddaughter stop coming around because she mad at her Mama. Force me to make a new friend. Anyway, back to point, I not saying no Black people do the crimes. Some do. Just like some Uyghur do crimes. But many arrested or killed for doing nothing."

"Now you sound paranoid, Lǎoyé. How much are you smoking these days?"

"Oh, I paranoid, huh? You know Xinjiang Province an obstruction to China's infrastructure project? Belt and Road Initiative?" She puts her hand on the cold metal rail; climbs to the next landing and kicks at the wall a few times, feeling the dull thuds vibrate in the stairwell.

"Oh, come on."

"No, you come on."

"You really think the Chinese government is sterilizing people for profit?"

A quick hiss. "You don't believe governments do that? You come home, borrow book off my bookcase. You never heard of eugenics?" She is silent. "Nah. You don't know," Lǎoyé concludes, taking another hit. "You don't even know what go on here in your own country." He exhales slowly. "Why you wanna know about the Uyghurs?"

"Look," she says, "if America's so evil, why are you advising me to trust our government's claims over Beijing's? What makes you think China isn't just protecting its people from terrorists?"

"Uyghur journalist is terrorist? Teacher is terrorist?"

"So you do have faith in America."

"Situation reverse, I believe Beijing."

"That's overly simplistic, Lǎoyé."

"Yah?" Now he is rustling around on the couch—reaching, perhaps, for cold green tea or a pillow or her mother's gold-gilded saucer to ash in. "You ask yourself: Who got the reason to lie?"

In the casino, distracting herself from the strong possibility that Henry and the suitcase will be gone when she returns, she plays Spot the John. This is something she learned from Ling Ling's associate, Cherry, who could talk a blue streak.

"In Vegas," she'd giggled, "they hold penny up to slot. Penny not work in machine. This a flag for us girls."

Měi has never caught this form of solicitation happening, but at every casino she visits, she watches the slot machines. Tries to calculate which men are on the prowl; which women, wobbling colt-like on four-inch heels, are at work.

"Are you for decriminalization?" she asked Cherry once, on the way back from a Vegas trip, expecting a blithe response. When she'd brought up the exotification of Asian women ever since the 1875 Page Act depicted them as prostitutes, Cherry had quipped, "Profitable business the *opposite* of exotification. Me and Ling Ling activists!" But regarding decriminalization, she just shrugged. Only later did it click that the issue might feel irrelevant. If Cherry had yet to gain citizenship, she was unprotected regardless.

It occurs to Měi that she will probably never know Cherry's real name.

She veers away from the slots, beelining for the bar. Striding between the machines' euphonic dings, she feels set in fast motion, the only sober soul in an altered crowd. And with so much alcohol flowing, it's no wonder these celebratory noises trick people into feeling like winners. They're designed to keep gamblers vying for that jackpot, no matter the puny size of the infrequent payouts they actually hit. The lights flash, too, every time someone wins—even if the prize is under a dollar.

"ROSÉ." It's not a question, but a statement. She pivots directly into the drunken giant who'd bumped into Henry. His date's long, bejeweled fingernails tap, one by one, at an enormous goblet that she shoves into Měi's hands.

"ATTAGIRL," the hulking man barks.

Měi shakes her head. "Really, it's not necessary—"

But the woman, all perfumed breasts and cascading hair, silences her with a finger. "Please accept a drink on behalf of this asshole. We're sorry about before. Besides, see him?" She points toward the bartender. "Honey, he ain't gonna pay you no mind when there's women dressed like me around." The tip of her chic stiletto taps the toe of Měi's worn high-top. "You belong on a playground." She clasps Měi's shoulders—leaning in to kiss her left cheek, her right—then reattaches herself to her gargantuan companion's arm and is gone.

Okay, Měi thinks, wondering whether the couple has a romantic or monetary arrangement. She sips delicately at the pink, then swigs it.

A barback swoops in, collecting her empty glass on a tray, as a nearby table's cheers draw her into its circle of spectators. "Poker switch," an older man in a cowboy hat says, leaning uncomfortably close, his dry lips an inch from her ear. "The bastard child of blackjack switch. No house edge." She sidesteps away; has no idea what this gibberish means.

Kitty-corner at the table are a slim white man in black and his doppelgänger, a slim Black man in white. The two eyeball each other over mountainous stacks of plastic chips. She stares at the round, colorful discs, wondering how much each is worth. Surely the black chips must be the most valuable: the players keep them closest to their bodies, like her grandmother hiding a four-of-a-kind mahjong hand.

One summer afternoon, Lǎoyé's garage getting battered by a sudden thunderstorm that slid a gray filter over Oakland's yellow sunlight, he'd shut the TV off. "Now I teach you play mahjong."

"But we'll miss the end of the show."

"This American sitcom! He gonna pull out last resort, overcome obstacle, then stand-alone joke, credits roll."

Her six-year-old body squirmed on the scratchy couch cushion. "But Lǎolao is the one who plays mahjong. You play RPGs and first-person shooters."

"You need learn how to bluff. Pivot. Make quick choices."

"But the tiles are all the way in the house. And it's raining. You hate getting wet."

They listened to the torrent's heavy, staccato beat. "You right," he said slowly. His veined hand tousled her hair. "I send you instead."

"No!" A distant boom and rumble. She'd snuggled in—clasped his narrow chest, fitting her head beneath his chin. "I want to stay here." Then, on impulse, she'd pulled out the three Chinese words she'd learned as a baby when Mama's face hovered like the moon over her long-ago crib. The words her mother still whispered when they hugged: "Wǒ ài nǐ."

The old man was silent. Rain threw itself at the little garage. They sat that way for a long time, till she wondered whether Lǎoyé had fallen asleep before he could say he loved her, too. But when she untangled from him to stare into his face, he was awake, dark eyes glowing softly like storm clouds backlit by the sun. "Oh, fine," he relented, waving a hand toward the frayed card deck on the bookshelf. "We play rummy instead. Almost the same."

She blinks at the poker players. Behind her, another jackpot, another jubilant whoop. For a while she tries to follow the game, till she remembers the single bills in her pocket: twelve dollars, all in ones, that Henry had fished from his wallet as he nudged her toward the door like a father urging his kid to play outside. Twelve chances to pin her specialness on a dollar slot machine. To invite the spinning reels to judge her in place of God. *Am I worthy of a win?* She sits, back stiff, at a machine.

Next to her is a woman Mama's age, in an electric wheelchair. They trade a nod and the woman pipes up. "Usually I play nickels online. You know. Start small. Prime the pump. But tonight my wireless went out. So here I am without my pugs, spending the big bucks."

Měi nods. Envisions multiple small dogs.

Feeding a dollar into the machine, she closes her hand around the lever. But when she glances to her side again, it's Mama there in the wheelchair. "What you doing," Mama asks, "with that Uyghur Bieber?"

She blinks. "What are you doing here, Mama?"

Her mother is unruffled. "I ask first. What *you* doing? Following you xiǎo mèi mei straight to trouble."

"Mama! That term is so problematic—"

"Only problem is you understand 'xiǎo mèi mei' mean 'little sister'" and 'vagina' but you can't order lunch at a Chinese restaurant. So you gonna take a gamble on this Henry? Go on, then. Pull." Her mother's warm hand closes over her own, yanking the lever down. Cherries, lemons, oranges, grapes tumble past her eyes, fruit salad stirred in a glass bowl, till the reels slow to a stop. Instead of fruit, there is a row of winking Henrys.

She gasps, turns to Mama, but Mama is gone. In her place, the older man with the cowboy hat who'd tried to explain poker switch. With a lascivious grin, he holds a penny up to the slot.

She comes to in the hallway outside the penthouse suite—spine cold against the glazed black door, phone gripped in her left hand.

In her right hand is a sweating water bottle, which she cracks open and gulps to wash the drugs from her system. She grimaces at the memory of the giggling woman, the hulking man. In college, she was dosed with MDMA by girls who thought they were doing her a favor—getting the party started—but whatever the couple slipped her tonight is something else. The high is jagged. Surreal. The patterned vines on the hallway carpet crawl.

Still, perhaps those college girls did her a solid because, downstairs, she'd recognized what was happening. That Henry's face in the slot machine was a hallucination. And as the hulking man's head bobbed above the crowd, the couple making their way back to her, she'd held her hand up and examined it. Her fingernails had lengthened into claws, and she'd understood she must escape while she could. Get back to the suite.

Gripping her penthouse key card like a talisman, she'd stumbled to the elevators; stuck her hand between closing doors. Boarded a crowded car. "No room," she'd called out to the couple as they caught up, the woman wobbling in her ridiculous shoes. "Nope."

"BABE," the man boomed.

"Catch the next one. I'm off to Neverland." She flipped them the bird—the gleaming doors pressing shut with a soft exhalation.

The first blackout had hit at the vending machine of a random floor, whatever floor the last passengers had deboarded on, lasting just a moment, throwing her off-balance. Carefully, she'd righted herself. Bent carefully to grasp the bottled water that thudded into the tray. Thank God for Henry and his dollars. Eyeing the elevator with suspicion, she'd made her way to the stairwell and—heaving the door open—come face-to-face with two women in enormous hats.

As she brushed past, stumbling up the stairs, they'd stared as though she were the one dressed for church in a casino.

On the next floor she'd left the stairwell. Found the elevator bank. Pressed the little metal buttons till one came and the doors opened, the car blessedly empty. Stepping in, she'd leaned her face against the cool, mirrored wall, making a smudgy ghost of herself to haunt the elevator. It was a moment before she realized she must use her key card to access the penthouse level.

Now, slumped against the door, she lets everything go dark.

I'm safe.

5

ROCK ISLAND TO ELKHART

She wakes again, head pounding, to the phone vibrating in her hand. Henry. She declines the call. Checks the time—10:59 P.M.

Surely the child is asleep by now, belly full of hearty food. But. Not yet. She can't go in just yet. She lets her head loll against the door.

When it opens behind her, her body tumbles backward into Henry's legs.

"The fuck?" His eyes are wide.

"I'm high," she squeaks, flat on her back, staring up from between his feet. "That couple you yelled at earlier put something in my drink."

"Shit," he hisses, glancing over his shoulder. He bends. Hooks his arms under her armpits and hauls her into the room and up to her feet, turning her body to face him as the door swings shut. "You okay?" His grip around her is firm. "Did they try to, like, seduce you?"

"Of course." A low laugh escapes her. "I'm irresistible." She glances at Anna's bedroom. "Is she . . . ?"

"Asleep," he says, dropping his hands to his sides. "I'm on the couch out here. She's still acclimating. It's"—a glance at his Bulgari—"eleven A.M. in China. You left hours ago. Your dinner's cold."

"Well, I didn't want to freak the kid out, dude. I'm tripping balls."

"Okay . . . dude." He rubs at the back of his neck, tense and tired. Still, he might've stepped out of a men's magazine, from behind overlay text reading *FALL FASHION GUIDE*. His golden skin emanates sex appeal. "How many fingers am I holding up?" he asks, not holding any up.

"Fourteen."

"Oh, yeah, I see. This is funny. This is something to make light of."

"I'm fine." She brushes past him. "Just need to sleep it off." Drops into the Chesterfield, where Henry's pillow and blanket wait. "This couch is, like, unbelievable. The leather? So smooth, like being cradled in a big, soft baseball mitt. The glove of sleep." She closes her eyes. Opens them again. "What do you use on your hair? It's. Shiny. But it holds its shape. Like the hair gel from *There's Something About Mary*."

"You're unbelievable." Looming over her, glowering, he shakes his head.

"Thank you. I really dug in the crates for that one—"

"That was not a compliment."

And yet, a half smile. Then his focus is elsewhere, somewhere beyond her, and she hears the slight sound of a door opening. Cranes her neck to see.

The girl. She is in cotton pajamas and does not look Chinese. Yet when she opens her mouth, fluent Mandarin pours forth: something about a dream, beasts pulling her hair out. Měi squints at her rapidly moving lips; the way she twists a light brown tendril around a finger, eyes glowing from a pixie face that could be Mediterranean, Spanish, Italian. She is tiny, more eight than eleven, with limbs like twigs. Speaking too quickly for Měi's altered consciousness to comprehend.

So she shuts her eyes and is back in her childhood home, seated at the little round kitchen table, straining to understand as her parents discuss secrets right in front of her. "Shēngrì lǐwù," she hears: birthday present. And that's all she can understand.

She rubs her eyelids; presses down gently, till she sees her father—blond, blue-eyed, erect in his military posture, towering over Mama. Yet it was Mama who'd powered their family, like a dam funneling water into the enormous blades of a turbine. Mama who sparked actions large and small. Mama who set the Dartmouth application on Měi's desk. Who told Daddy when and how to spend money. Who convinced him, once, to tell the new neighbors he was from Liqian, a village of blue-eyed Chinese rumored to be descendants of the Roman legion for which their village was named (a lie the neighbors believe to this day).

And years before, it was Mama who'd drawn Daddy down the aisle after a chance meeting in San Francisco; a day off from his teaching in Monterey, where he himself had once learned twelve dialects of eight languages in order to listen in on foreign military secrets. Měi hears gunfire. Then, behind her eyelids, fireworks are bursting over a field of families on blankets.

It's the Fourth of July, Měi home from college, working her summer gig at Live Large Limo, Lǎoyé dragged forcibly from his couch. Mama's on her knees, pulling pork buns from a picnic basket, Daddy standing in the grass like a staunch tree. "Hey," Lǎoyé shouts, "Paul Bunyan! This a public park. So park your ass! You blocking the view." Her father turns in silhouette, his chest an unyielding wall till Mama reaches up. Takes his hand. Turns him liquid, channels him down to the blanket.

Hours later, Mama is snoring on the pillow, looking annoyed as Měi shakes her awake. Annoyed that her oblivion has been interrupted. Annoyed because Měi has heard a bang like the fireworks neighbors are still shooting off, but louder, from inside the house.

When he evaporated in the night, disappearing himself, who else could Měi blame but her mother? Who else could she punish? She tries to return to where she was moments ago, happy in her childhood home, her parents discussing shēngrì lǐwù. Her birthday present. But those sweet thoughts have bubbled, boiled, crystallized into something else. An empty field. The smell of smoke and sulfur. The annoyance in her mother's eyes as Měi dragged her down the hall to her father's study, placing a hand on the cold, octagonal surface of the Victorian crystal knob, and opened the door.

She opens her eyes before she gets stuck in that place.

"Duìbùqǐ," she interjects, trying to will herself sober. She focuses intently on not slurring. "Wǒ de zhōngwén bù hǎo. Qǐng shuō yīngyǔ." These are two sentences she has practiced since youth.

"Don't ask her to speak English," Henry says. "She can't."

"Of course she can. Her dad's a Syracuse professor."

"She only knows Mandarin and Uyghur. In the camps, she was punished for speaking anything but standard Chinese." Měi shakes her head, disbelieving. The girl's eyes appear to follow everything, to know more than Henry believes. "I'll translate," he offers, gesturing to Anna to come closer, "lái lái lái." And then the girl is standing before Měi, even smaller up close, but authoritative. Like Mama.

"What was all that she said before?"

"Her name is Anna. She came from the orphan camp. She's grateful for your help with getting to central New York—" He pauses as Anna's slim finger reaches out. It lands on Měi's nose, the girl murmuring something in Chinese.

"What did she say?"

"'Like mine,'" he says. "Your nose is like hers."

"Boop," Anna says, tapping again before she removes her finger.

"What's that?"

Henry's mouth curls into a lopsided grin. "I believe that roughly translates to 'boop.'"

They stare at each other, Anna and Měi, silent. She wonders what Henry's said to the girl. Feels those glowing eyes scanning her, assessing her, making quick judgments.

When the girl spins and drops backward like a trust-fall, Měi startles. Her fingers fly up to catch something no longer in motion. But Anna is planted in her lap.

Does this mean Měi is trustworthy, or simply that the child craves female contact, a woman's touch, a woman's gentleness?

Grasping the small rib cage, she is overwhelmed by its mammalian heat. Holding this girl is like having a feral kitten in her arms, some stray, fragile life that's worked its way into her care. The girl twists around to hug her, impressing into Měi's chest how much Anna must miss her mother.

Fleetingly, in the past, she's toyed with the idea of motherhood—

When the girl stands suddenly, she lets go, startled again. Perhaps the hug was not acceptance but a politeness Anna's been taught. She blinks, unable to sort it all out in her altered state, shakes her hands as though to dry them. But of course, there is nothing to shake off.

At 3:00 A.M., she jolts awake. Someone is in the doorway.

Propping her head on an elbow, squinting, she can make out nothing beyond the diagonal line of her body across the bed. She props her head on an elbow and squints, then sits up, cross-legged, covering her breasts with a fat down pillow. "I thought you were on the couch."

He takes a step into the room. "I was."

"Is Anna—"

"Asleep." He shuts the door firmly against the living room's dim glow, so she can no longer make him out. The blackout drapes keep the moonlight at bay, and she remembers how, growing up, she'd thought "kept at bay" meant barred from docking. But in college she learned the term's origin: "abbay," from the Old French, meaning baying. To be held at bay, then, was to be in a standoff with a snarling dog.

"C'mere," she says.

"No"—closer in the room now—"you come here."

The flesh of her nape rises into bumps. She slides her fingernails lightly up and down her bare arms. "No."

When the mattress shifts under his weight, she holds still.

His hand is under the covers, strong and seeking, finding her knee. When it hesitates there, red heat in the black room, she reaches out. Cold metal pinches her wrist. She looks down. Sees the handcuffs, dark against bright white sheets. How did he—

It's not until the megaphone blares through the silence, broadcasting propaganda in Anna's insistent, unintelligible Mandarin, that she understands she is neither sober nor awake. She sits up in bed, blinking. Henry is beyond her closed door, sound asleep.

Měi waits in the car, head pounding, uneager to face Anna in daylight. How can Henry stand to feed her breakfast, remind her to take her vitamins, then pack her miniature body away in the ugly suitcase—even if it makes this traumatized, slight girl and her cowed parents feel safe?

Last night, sometime after the dream, she'd woken and tiptoed out of her room to find Henry snoring lightly on the couch, the door to the other bedroom ajar, the penthouse a silent jumble of clean shapes glinting in moonlight that poured through the sheers. Returning to her bathroom, she'd filled a glass at the sink and gulped deeply, hoping the swig might wash her high away. Stumbled back to bed. Soon after drifting off, she was woken again by her bladder. The chill of the bathroom tiles stiffened her feet—the toilet seat cold, too, and the frigid faucet-water rinsing over her hands. Still high and shivering, she'd refilled the glass, gulped, woken shortly after, returned to the bathroom, and repeated the cycle.

She shakes her head. A few dark strands graze her cheek and she tucks them behind her ear, then fumbles for a hair tie in the console between the front seats; pulls the jet-black mess up into a sloppy bun. Nearly 10:00 A.M. now. The sun cuts through the windshield, slicing her eyes.

She pulls the sun visor into place. Squints down at her phone, skimming articles by Jimmy Xīn, Anna's father, about arbitrary detention. How Xinjiang's Communist Party Secretary called on officials to round up Uyghurs in a "profligate effort to eradicate Islamist extremism." How isolated incidents of Uyghur-led violence were not entirely unprovoked. She reads about a riot sparked by the lynching of Uyghur factory workers baselessly accused of rape; how the province is now split into a grid, each closely monitored square housing a police station and approximately five hundred citizens tracked with regularly scanned ID cards, cell phone searches, and an annual government program called Physicals for All that provides free medical exams while storing participants' biometric data.

It's like a dystopian novel. Her skimming slows at a photo: a girl with Anna's malnourished form, her honey hair. She zooms in. The girl is not Anna, but the daughter of a Uyghur activist whose real name

Jimmy withholds. "When she came home from the state boarding school," the interviewee recalls, "she'd been hit with rulers. Forced to sit against the wall, no chair, for long periods. Locked in a dark basement. But worse, she'd been scrubbed. Erased. Her mother ran to hug her, and she didn't even lift her arms. She was so small. Skinny. Both younger and older than when she left. We asked what she wanted to eat in our language, and she answered in Mandarin. She will not speak our language anymore."

Is it possible Anna understands English, as well as her native Uyghur tongue, but does not dare speak either anymore?

She squints at the author photo, then pulls up social media and finds Jimmy Xīn quickly on an app she generally ignores—Dr. James Xīn, Associate Professor of Social Anthropology at Syracuse University— despite the fact that his avatar is a photo of a dessert sandwich: two doughnuts with a vanilla ice cream center, drizzled in syrup and what appears to be bacon bits. Social media is just like riding a bike, she thinks. Finding her old, familiar rhythm on the app, she cruises through his page.

The only posts he's left up are innocuous shots of downtown Syracuse, a blue-collar wasteland repositioning itself as an attractive reshoring option: its shuttered industrial buildings ripe for renovation, an affordable alternative to outsourcing, its proximity to Lake Ontario an attractive option for tech manufacturers that use up to twenty million gallons of water a day.

Each photo is easily identifiable with a quick image search. Jimmy Xīn's shared a historic hotel constructed during the Roaring Twenties; a Mexican restaurant converted from a church that was once a stop on the Underground Railroad; a Queen Anne Romanesque Revival mansion; a cathedral whose sanctuary and bell tower were built in the space that La Concha Turkish Bath House occupied till the early 1870s, when the parish purchased and demolished it; a STEAM school built in 1900, morphed to meet the city's evolving needs.

It's just as Henry described. She's certain that he and Anna have scrutinized the page ad infinitum, yet she tries to find a pattern in the posts. A clue to Jimmy's whereabouts. Nothing emerges. She closes the app. Yes, she thinks, social media is just like riding a bike: a stationary bike that only makes you feel as though you're getting somewhere.

Měi maps directions to Elyria, Ohio, their final stop before Syracuse—then sets the phone in its mounted holder and runs a finger across the dusty, warming dashboard. Heat drips down her skull, coating the back of her neck. Despite her night of sipping, peeing, refilling, her throat prickles dryly and she coughs. Watches idle shadows of the day's growing heat drift over the dash, the air warming, expanding to bend the light.

And there they are in the rearview—Henry and his suitcase. She straightens her back. Adjusts the mirror. Turns on the car, gets the air-conditioning going, and steps out to greet him. "Need a hand with that, sir?"

He grins. "Get away, druggie." Today he's in a T-back tank, jeans, and a frayed blue baseball cap, golden shoulders gleaming in the sun. She takes him in slowly as he opens the back door on the driver's side, her proximity no longer an issue. Should she pull him away from the car to talk? "Gotta do some laundry at the next overnight stop," he says, lifting the case into the back seat with a soft grunt.

The grunt travels through the narrow passageway of her ear canal to vibrate on her eardrum and travel up her auditory nerve as an electrical signal. She draws a sharp breath.

"Elyria," she says. "Nicknamed *the Rustbelt* in the seventies and eight-ies, when industrial restructuring killed its car manuf—" but his finger lights on her lips, just long enough for her to feel her own softness pressed into her teeth.

"Don't spoil the fact sheet," he says, lifting the finger away.

She snorts, sliding back into the driver's seat.

Atkinson. Annawan. Mineral. Lasalle. Joliet. Tinley Park. Valparaiso.

Cutting through or zipping alongside, she imagines each city's resi-dents: small-town girls dreaming of basketball scholarships, hoping their growth spurts will take them all the way to the position of WNBA center. Boys sneaking out shirtless to ride four-wheelers over undeveloped land or hunched in darkened bedrooms, headphoned, organizing playlists.

By Elkhart, Indiana, hungry for a late lunch, she's drifted back to her own teenage years. Mama's voice spikes from her parents' bedroom, Daddy silent, or silent enough not to be heard. "So do it, then. Don't just talking, talking, talking." In retrospect this could've referred to anything, a purchase, a household chore, a car repair, but she can't help replaying the comment—

Suddenly a white van is on them, enormous in the rearview. She stretches up toward the mirror, annoyed, the tailgating driver's expression inscrutable behind his mirrored shades and full blond beard. Flipping her blinker on, she pulls into the slow lane.

Immediately the van is beside her car, the driver leaning forward to stare across his passenger, a smaller man with identical glasses and beard. His intensity brings her back to the elementary school playground where Chris Pringle sat on her chest, eyes narrowed, and spat *Chink*. She recalls the novel feeling of gravel ground into shoulder blades, the other kids circling around, time slowing enough for her to marvel at how close this bully's name was to "Kris Kringle." The van keeps pace, the men staring, until she lifts a hand off the wheel to wave.

That's when the van swerves toward her and—jerking the wheel to avoid a collision—she experiences time moving strangely, simultaneously speeding up and slowing down. For an instant she presses her eyes shut. A millisecond or an eon later, she opens them as the bumpy right-hand shoulder of the highway rattles her teeth. Road signs and scrubby trees fly by close, brownsilvergreen. And then the sedan shudders to a stop on the side of the road, the van whooshing past, a stream of words spilling from her mouth.

"Oh Hell no. Shit! What the muthafuckin' fuck? Fuck."

"Calm down," Henry shouts, the suitcase shaking as though about to hatch. He unzips it and the girl unfolds in the back seat, eyes round and darting.

Měi lowers her voice. "Fuck. Shit. I'm so sorry. You guys, that was—"

"Just a careless driver. That's all. We're fine." Henry smiles a big smile at Anna. "Méi shì! Dōu méi shì. Yǐhòu yào gèng xiǎoxīn!" But Anna's face is slowly crumpling: balling into an ugly wail that she hurls at the driver's seat. And though Měi has slept through the cries of children on planes, eaten through them, oblivious, in restaurants, her heart crumples like the girl's face till it's a dense, desperately beating thing.

"Xiǎo Bǎo," she says instinctually, in her mother's most soothing bedtime voice, "bié dānxīn," but the girl is climbing over Henry, scrabbling out of the car, so Měi follows.

In crumbled dirt, surrounded by flowering weeds with brilliant snow-white petals, they sink down, her body wrapping the girl's in a soft, warm shell.

They rock on the side of the road, entwined like that, till Anna's heaving sobs dwindle to sniffles. When the girl looks up, dry-eyed, they stand. And when she interlaces her hand with Měi's, her small fingers fit like the teeth of a key—raising invisible pins inside Měi's chest to open some previously locked room.

Henry has exited the car. He is asking if they're okay, and the girl is nodding.

Wordlessly, Měi pops the trunk, pulls the monstrous black suitcase from the back seat, and stashes it inside, closing the lid. They get in the car in unison, she and Anna, the girl belting herself into the back seat before Henry can help. From now on, she will watch the road, too.

6

ELKHART TO ELYRIA

Elkhart, Indiana, the RV Capital of the World, is also home to the best Amish creamery in the state. As Henry pulls the door open, they inhale deeply: Blazingstars are in season, and the fragrance of fresh-picked peaches mingles with scents of spiced ice cream and homemade waffle cones.

Inside the quaint facility, under high tin ceilings, four ruddy women bake fresh oatmeal raisin cookies and pecan pie bars, whip up pans of caramel cashew crunch and bowls of peanut butter marshmallow fluff, then mix each treat into a small batch of vanilla—delivering flights of four flavors on wooden cutting boards.

Anna glows, watching them work, clearly glad to be out of the car for an unexpected treat. "Qiǎokèlì!" Her small finger points at the tub of chocolate. Henry nods. Hands her a sandwich and banana from his cooler, with two gummy vitamins. The price of dessert. The near accident forgotten, she skips to a booth and slides in, tucking into her lunch.

"Měi?"

"I'm mostly vegan—"

His nose crinkles. "Mostly?" She shrugs, lingering at his side before the gleaming maple counter, hands still quaking with adrenaline, while he selects a flight to share. Bananas Foster, salted caramel, birthday cake, elk tracks. The order placed, they watch the tallest woman bend into the freezer, her scoop disappearing into ice cream bins. "So"—biting her lower lip, eyebrow raised—"who were they?"

"Who?"

"Who? Seriously? Who do you think? The guys in the van."

"Assholes?" he says.

She blinks slowly. "Okay. Assholes. But why'd they swerve at us?"

He shuffles from foot to foot, loosening his long legs. "That's kinda the thing about assholes. They don't really need a reason." Edison lights gleam from vintage metal bulb cages—a weak supplement to the sunlight shining in from South Main Street. In the tidy wooden booth, Anna gazes out the window at a pub across the street, drinkers toasting one another on the balcony.

"Do you think they're"—lowering her volume—"Chinese spies?"

He nods his thanks as the woman ferries their laden cutting board down the counter to the cashier. "They're freakin' white dudes."

"Or Chinese dudes with bleached hair. Think about it: the shades hide their eyes."

The foot-shuffling stops and he stands stock-still. "When I was a kid," he says, "I thought the *Danger Man* theme song was 'Secret Asian Man.' Not 'Secret Agent Man.'" He grins.

"I'm serious."

"So am I. The lyrics are actually pretty sinister, if you swap out that one word." He glances up at a framed feature on the creamery's wall, printed by *The Elkhart Truth* (an ambitious name, Měi thinks, for a small-town newspaper). A celebrity grins in black and white, sampling flavors. "Like, living a life of danger? To everyone he meets, he stays a stranger? Odds are he won't live to see tomorrow? I thought being Asian was pretty risky . . ." She rolls her eyes.

"I like your nails," the cashier says as Měi cuts in front of Henry, forking over a few crumpled bills.

"Thanks." She takes in the teen's bedhead, his sleepy smile. "They're kind of a mess. We're on the road." She holds her hands up, studying the chipped black paint.

"That's what I like about them." A coy grin. He hands back her change. "They make it look like you've been digging in dirt."

They join Anna at the booth, Měi sliding in next to the girl, passing plastic spoons around. "That was weird," Henry says. He sets the bowl of chocolate ice cream before Anna; the flight in the middle of the table.

"What? Nobody's allowed to compliment my nails?"

"No. I mean, you've never treated before."

"Oh," she says. She'd had an impulse to spoil the girl. "Yeah, well, you know." She hands out napkins. "I'm rolling in dough now. My dumb client overpays."

"Shit," he says, laughing. "Don't I know it."

"Language," she growls.

"She only speaks Chinese. Remember?" They dig in.

Měi scans her memory for the words of praise her mother's friends would heap on Mama's dinners. "Zhēn hǎochī," she says, Anna nodding vigorously. "Honestly," she says to Henry, "I think it's the best ice cream I've ever tasted. Possibly the best food."

"You know," he says, shooting the tousled cashier a slightly territorial glance, "Chinese doesn't have to be a last resort all the time. You can speak it with me, Secret Asian Man, to practice."

"I can't."

"Sure you can."

"My Chinese sucks." She scoops sweet coldness into her mouth, conscious of the cashier keeping furtive tabs on her, smiling whenever she glances in his direction, while Henry keeps furtive tabs on him.

"No, it doesn't."

"It does." She swipes at her mouth with a napkin. "My mom reminds me all the time."

"Chinese moms." They share a smile. "They don't pull punches, huh? So, what's your dad like? I believe you called him 'the original Miss Brown' back in Rock Springs?"

"Um." Another bite buys her time to think. "Absent, I guess. He left us, a year ago."

"Really? I'm sorry!"

She shrugs. "What's yours like?"

There's commotion outside: an enormous sheepdog dragging a leash, loping across the street diagonally. Anna's eyes widen as traffic stops, the middle-aged owner running after his escapee.

"Uh . . . Hui," Henry says.

"Gesundheit."

"He's a Chinese Hui Muslim. My dad. He used to be in commercial real estate. Now he and my mom are semi-retired. They teach English online." Henry scowls. "She never converted, so it's a scandalous inter-faith marriage."

"No shit?"

"Language!" He grins. They glance at Anna, who's still following the drama outside. "But yeah, no shit." He dips his fork in the salted caramel. "I'm not Muslim," he says quickly, as though she'd asked, "though my dad raised me in the faith. I got shipped to California when I was nine. For boarding school. Lost my religion and my virginity by sophomore year. Didn't tell them I planned to stay in the U.S. till I'd earned a full ride to Pomona College. You know: the Chinese parent's abandonment nightmare."

"Wait—doesn't boarding school start with freshman year?"

"Not mine. It went third through twelfth. Formal dinners four nights a week. A mandatory horsemanship program."

She envisions him in a tiny, crested uniform, riding a pony across the grounds of Hogwarts. "I don't know anything about the Hui."

"Well, my parents live in Ningxia. It's an autonomous region, like Xinjiang. But less scary to Beijing." Měi raises her eyebrows as he dips his spoon into a new flavor. "Most Hui are visually indistinct from Han Chinese nowadays." The spoon disappears into his mouth, reappearing clean. "They speak Mandarin instead of a Turkic language. In fact, they're so widely acclimated across China that extremist Uyghurs urged their followers to *Kill the Han, kill the Hui* during the Xinjiang riots." He licks salted caramel from his lips.

Under the table, she pinches her wrist in an effort to stop watching his mouth. Lifting a corner of her napkin, she rubs its paper layers between her thumb and forefinger till they separate, then pulls them apart. "You say 'they.' Aren't you Hui, too, since your dad is?"

"Nah. 'Hui' isn't just an ethnicity. Basically, it means 'Muslim, but not Uyghur.'"

"Wait—the Uyghurs teamed up with Britain or Russia to establish their own East Turkic state, yes?"

"Yup. Got their name from Russian expansionists. And helped Japan in the Second World War."

"But not the Hui?"

"The Hui consider themselves Chinese. Still, my mom's afraid Beijing will come for them next. Look what Islamophobia's done to non-extremist Uyghurs—and the government's already shuttered, demolished, or renovated most of the gold-domed mosques that made Ningxia special. Shut down Hui schools. Started reeducating Imams. Detaining Hui travelers." He sets his spoon on a napkin, drums his long fingers over the wooden tabletop. "Officials in Ningxia also offer rewards for reporting 'suspicious behavior' like advocating for Islam or teaching the Quran."

"So, is your dad—" Suddenly, Anna's tugging at the phone in Měi's pocket, eyes frantic.

"Bāng wǒ," she says. "Qǐng bāng wǒ."

Měi frees the phone. Hands it to the slight girl, who searches through the apps.

"You're worried about spies," Henry observes, "and your phone isn't password protected?" She rolls her eyes; tries a new flavor.

"Dizzy dough," Anna murmurs. Then she is on her father's social media page, scrolling, squinting at every picture, pausing to enlarge a few. "Ice. Cream. Sandwich," she says, placing the phone in the center of the table. Měi and Henry exchange a look. "Dizzy. Dough. Ice. Cream. Sandwich. Wǒ bàba hěn xǐhuān! Zài tā xiāoshī zhīqián, tā shuō tā xiǎng gěi wǒ chī." She points at a photograph.

It's an image Měi researched when she e-stalked Jimmy Xīn: an immense stone cathedral with stained glass windows and cornices. Parked nearby is a blue food truck. Anna points, points, points insistently at the vehicle. "Nǐ kàn."

They lean in. *Some Like It ~~Hot~~ Cold* is airbrushed across the side of the truck, above a cartoon ice cream cone. Henry lifts the phone and scrutinizes it till the girl's fingers snatch it away again. Scrolling to the next shared photo, she zooms in. Placing the phone in the center of the table, she points. Parked in front of the Niagara Mohawk Building, an Art Deco classic with blindingly bright stainless steel details, is something that could be the same food truck—only its blue top showing, the rest of the vehicle cropped out.

In the next photo, there is just a tiny corner of a blue vehicle. But the girl nods, furiously pointing.

Now she taps at the phone, opening the website for *Some Like It ~~Hot~~ Cold*, navigating to the menu page. "Dizzy Dough," she says, pointing at a photograph of the same treat in Jimmy Xīn's avatar. Crossing her arms, she leans back in the booth.

Henry leans over the phone. Taps at the screen to open a new page. *Upcoming Locations*, the header reads, and below are dates and addresses. "Jīntiān shì jǐ hào?"

"Jīntiān shì liù yuè èrshísān hào," Anna says.

"Today's June twenty-third." Henry scrolls to the date on the phone. "Bīngqílín chē zài Clinton Square."

"Duì ah! Suǒyǐ, jīntiān, wǒ bàba zài Clinton Square."

The bell above the door rings as two women in flowy dresses enter, holding hands, to peer up at the chalkboard menu. "OMG," one says, "they've got strawberry brownie cheesecake."

Sliding the phone out of Henry's fingertips, Anna hands it back to Měi, beaming.

Měi shifts in the booth to stuff it back in her pocket, her brain putting the rudimentary Chinese words together. And slowly, she beams, too. Jimmy Xīn has been tracking the ice cream truck. Making it possible for them to track him. They sit that way for a moment, the three of them, grinning in silence.

But when they walk outside, the white van is parked across the street next to her car. The two men, with their identical beards and glasses, are on the pub's balcony.

∽

It wasn't till her freshman year of high school that it occurred to Mĕi to treat all men with skepticism. Before that, her world had been neatly divided: there were the Chris Pringles and the non–Chris Pringles.

"There are no known side effects." "This war is unavoidable." "We value diversity." "I did not sleep with that woman." History is riddled with untruths. Oftentimes, only those suffering by the lie hunger to expose the truth. Well, here it is, the truth about two boys we go to class with. Shutting her laptop, she'd sat quietly on the colorful bedspread Lǎolao had stitched together by hand a decade ago, the fabrics lugged from China. Her bedroom in the little craftsman faced the freeway, and the warped window casing admitted tiny beetles and moths along with the susurrant sounds of Oakland's Sunday-night traffic.

The start of her lede was too heavy-handed, even for an op-ed piece. She chewed at her ragged fingernail. "Student journalists shape monthly issues of *Just the Facts* in concert with a faculty advisor," the journalism club's web page proclaimed, but Mr. Murphy barely skimmed the headlines his student staff wrote. He fancied himself a free speech activist, though his own infrequent stories only ever appeared in a local indie rag. Perhaps she should text her classmates, the Nguyen twins, again, she thought. But the twins wanted to keep the peace.

"Can I write something controversial?" she asked on Monday, an illicit wad of mint gum burning under her tongue. Her idea had to do with "The Blade," a long boulevard cutting through the Nguyen twins' neighborhood, where cars crept along beside hairdressers who just wanted to buy cigarettes down the street and fresh-faced schoolgirls walking home from the bus stop—forcing them to ignore the men beckoning in low, expectant tones, as though every Asian, Latina, Black, or poor girl were in "the life."

"Absolutely." Murphy smiled. "You know I champion journalistic freedom." He straightened one of the knit ties he wore every day with corduroy slacks and a tweed blazer. He'd turned himself into a sitcom-worthy journalist stereotype—made all the more ridiculous by the fact that his own writing had never made it further than Oakland. (He, him-self, had taken just one semester of journalism, decades ago, and still heavily referenced Iran-Contra. In encouraging Měi's writing, he'd touted the rise of Connie Chung.)

She shifted the gum subtly into her cheek. "It's about people who don't want me bringing attention to them. Like, anonymous subjects."

Murphy stuck his chin out, lips pressed into a squiggly line. "Is this about the faculty's push to unionize?"

"No."

"It's fine if it is." He looked hopeful.

"It's about a party. Saturday night? In Tilden Park?"

His face went slack as he rolled his desk chair backward. "Just let the facts lead you, Miss Brown, and you'll be fine." He stretched his arms toward the buzzing fluorescent lights, then laid his palms flat on the desktop—poised, she thought, to whip out his latest piece in *The Oakland Independent Star*. Instead, he hefted himself up and relocated to his arm-chair to doze while the paper's coeditors, Mindy and Matt Johnson (no relation), took turns managing the staff.

The men from the van do not see her. They're drinking beer on the bal-cony; having a good old time. Měi keeps her head lowered as she crosses hot pavement to the car.

From the driver's seat, Anna and Henry safe in back, she locks the doors. Turns to open the divider window and point the men out. But it's Anna's bright eyes, and not Henry's, that meet hers first. She leaves the partition shut. Flashes a cheery smile. Starts the car.

Excited feet kick at her seatback, the girl's body ringing so loudly with anticipation that she's got Henry grinning, too. Měi adjusts the rearview as Henry runs his tongue over his top teeth, savoring the day's lingering sweetness. The Amish creamery is as charming from the outside as from within. Large, shimmering windows in its canary-yellow storefront mimic the sheen of a small pond just down the street, in a park where children chase after fat geese.

Pulling out into Main Street's traffic, she glances up at the balcony: just normal men, she assures herself, drinking normal beers from normal pint glasses. As she steers toward the freeway, squashing her nerves, they pass the giant runaway sheepdog. Docile on its leash once more, the dog ambles down the sidewalk, pausing calmly as a woman leaps up from outdoor café seating to greet its owner with a quick kiss.

The perfect Americana picture.

Nobody else is thinking crazy thoughts about spies.

Not Henry, who looks sleepy. Not Anna, who never saw the van in the first place; only experienced its aftermath. She switches the radio on. Steers carefully up the on-ramp.

Swanton, Indiana. In the back seat, her passengers snooze.

The radio station's been eaten by static. She shuts it off, rubbing furiously at her eyes.

Back in the journalism club's computer lab, she'd stared at the dramatic opening sentences of her lede. She needed some kind of introduction to the who, what, where, why, when, and how of this, didn't she? She shifted in the uncomfortable plastic chair. Mindy—a strong writer whom she would remain friends with after graduation—flitted about. "JER, WAIT UP!" a boy shouted in the hallway as Murphy continued snoring in the pleather armchair he'd shamelessly abducted from the faculty lounge. Měi redirected her focus, struggling again with her paragraph.

The Nguyen twins were absent. Skinny, big-eyed girls who spoke with lilting accents and handled ad solicitation for *Just the Facts*, they'd joined multiple after-school clubs because their mother, who worked late, would not allow them to ride the bus home and wait unsupervised in their apartment. Ms. Nguyen had left Vietnam to marry an American, but it hadn't worked out and now she was waiting to learn whether her employer would sponsor her to remain in the States—or at least, that's what everyone said.

The twins were shy. They ate lunch with the Asian American crew that Měi floated into and out of, but everyone knew they weren't Asian American. Not like Jason Kuo, the water polo goalie who posted videos of his pit bull carrying the family cat around gently by the nape of her neck. Not like Grace Truong, who held the high score on every old school video game at Alameda '80s Arcade and had earned her private pilot's license at seventeen to impress her girlfriend, Langley Zou. No, the twins were not legally American, if the stories were correct, and not culturally, either. They were just Asians living in America. She'd been surprised to see them on Saturday night up in Tilden Park—where the silence, crisp air, and deep, true tones of sky were deliciously unnerving for city kids like Měi—even though Mindy, a senior and managing editor of *Just the Facts*, had thrown this party and instructed the entire staff to attend.

"You like?" A sylvan catering duo, the twins were circulating with Jell-O shots lined up on a pilfered cafeteria tray. Měi marveled at their ability to glide smoothly over roots and fallen trees despite their obvious drunkenness.

"Thanks, Mademoiselles. Don't mind if I do." Lifting a cocktail napkin and miniature paper cup from the tray, she'd tapped her jiggling orange cube against Mindy's in a toast and downed it. The Nguyen twins spun away with a small bow, leaving some shameful part of her angry with them for playing server.

As Mindy dug in an enormous cooler for low-calorie beer, Měi glanced around.

The kids at this party, Mindy's middle-class friends and minions, would end up at good colleges. Caste might separate them socially from the rich kids, who dumpster-dove, used street drugs, and shopped at the Salvation Army on Webster—playing poor kid, just for fun—but they'd have the opportunity to make real money someday. Even Jay "Sully" Sullivan and Todd Hanscom, who'd joined the journalism club and fencing team despite being semi-popular and lacking any interest in writing or swordplay (to help score scholarships to Stanford and Cal) were here, honoring this bond.

By dawn, she was on her fourth Natty Light. Only seven kids were left. The Nguyen twins were off in the woods someplace, puking together, while the rest—silent, ecstatic—clustered around a dying bonfire. With a jolt, Měi realized she didn't want the party to end. Rising exhausted to her tiptoes, she proclaimed, "Cheers to all y'all fellow nerds."

"All of us? Even Sully's dumb ass?" Mindy ventured, ever the fact-checking editor.

"That's right," she answered solemnly. "Even Sully's dumb ass." They raised their cans and red plastic cups, sharing a quiet moment of journalistic fellowship.

"Well, on that note," said Sully, disengaging from the circle, "this dumbass is going to see a man about a horse."

"Our best accommodations await you," Kumani DeCato sang out, throwing an arm toward the dark wall of trees, and everyone laughed again.

"Me too." Todd Hanscom nodded at the group, following Sully into the woods.

Me three, Měi thought, but she held it, shifting foot to foot. She didn't want to catch the boys with their pants down.

When they didn't return, she gave in: striding into the eucalyptus, she squatted near a splintery shed where the park probably stored maintenance equipment and (cursing herself for forgetting the communal toilet paper roll) used her soggy cocktail napkin to wrap up the paperwork.

Wobbling to her feet, refastening her jeans, she exhaled warm breath into the pure, cool air. From the shed there came a slight buzz, and she approached it cautiously to spot a wasps' nest under the eaves. She'd read that wasps did not attack at night but that they didn't sleep, either. Instead, they lingered at home, tending to their nests and offspring. Now that the party had died down, the woods were coming alive in a new way, white sun sifting through leaves and needles to light the stirring undergrowth—the wasps venturing out again.

At first, hearing the wail, she thought it was a cat. Sometimes cats made sounds like this, dying sounds or mating sounds or fighting sounds. But when she peered around the little shed's corner, she saw Sully and Todd. The boys' backs were toward her, so she couldn't see their faces as they hunched atop one of the twins—Todd at her waist, Sully at her neck. But the bare body beneath them lay perfectly limp, and she could see the other Nguyen twin's face clearly. The girl crouched a few yards away, stricken. It was her shaking body that produced the wail.

"Stop—" Měi shouted, blind with fear. "I called the cops!" And as the boys jolted backward, zipping up, she stumbled back to the bonfire.

The sun was powering up fast now, its heat falling heavily through the overgrowth. Despite what she'd said, there was no cell service this deep in the park, so she hovered beside Mindy and Kumani, who flirted heavily, turning her phone over and over in her hands, till the boys emerged from the woods, both twins dressed again and following behind with the plastic cafeteria tray.

Then Mindy drove Měi and Kumani and the twins slowly back down the hillside, into the waking world, while Todd and Sully stayed behind, burning hot dogs.

She'd closed her eyes in the back seat, jammed up against the door. Tried to focus on Kumani's banter and forget the smirk Todd had shot Sully when the Nguyens were put in charge of soliciting ads and Murphy, oblivious, said, "You two will be naturals at solicitation."

She'd texted the twins immediately from her bedroom, and immediately they'd texted back: Please do not tell anyone.

As the club dispersed on Monday (Mindy gently shaking Murphy awake), Měi painstakingly completed, then deleted, her lede. What exactly was she getting at, anyway? Race-based objectification? Some subconscious assumption that every Asian girl is a child prostitute? She clicked Don't Save. Watched the screen go dark.

On Tuesday, the twins showed up as usual and she sat staring again at a blank screen, her eyes darting occasionally from the Nguyens to Sully and Todd, waiting for something to happen. Nothing did.

On Wednesday, nothing happened, either. She mustered her strength to write the article Murphy clearly wanted, on the faculty's push to unionize.

Nothing happened on Thursday. Or Friday. Or the next week. Nothing ever would.

But the memory of that sound, the sound emanating from the shaking girl crouched in the woods, never left her.

Perhaps it's that sound, and not the driver of the white van or his passenger, that still frightens her. That feeds her reservations about Henry. About half of the world's citizens.

Up ahead in the slow lane, a dump truck fishtails, snapping her back to attention.

Měi's entire body tenses as its rear tire detaches and rolls across her lane, straight up onto the concrete divider, where it continues rolling and bouncing. Behind her, it drops into opposing traffic and a black cloud explodes into the air. There is the squeal of brakes, the sound of crunching metal. Her right hand flies to cover her mouth, her eyes moving to Anna in the rearview, but the girl does not even twitch.

Nerves jangling, she gives in to her compulsion to check the mirror, every few minutes, for the van. Fucking gotdamn muthafucking asshole muthafuckas. But they're nowhere to be seen. They are back in Elkhart, she assures herself, daytime drinking on a balcony.

I am not a helpless child, she thinks. *These men cannot chase me down and push me backward into gravel, spitting* Chink! *in my face. Cannot straddle me on the forest floor.*

Sometimes she hears the Nguyen twins' lilting voices; wonders whether they ever said a thing about the party to their mother. Their exhausted, abandoned mother who already had enough worries to chew on. Or were they afraid that involving the law might send them back across the ocean? Back to a land they thought they'd lost, their homecoming as unsettling as the reattachment of a phantom limb? Once, she'd asked them to teach her some Vietnamese words and they'd refused.

Měi is privileged, she knows, to be the child of a protective family that she is not, herself, compelled to protect; to be a protected citizen in the larger sense, too, comfortable with speaking any language she likes. Cruising across the Ohio state line, she remembers how hard Mama tried to teach her Mandarin, from attempts at Saturday school to books borrowed from the library's Chinatown branch. Perhaps she could've paid more attention—prioritized her own family, her own heritage, over fitting in and getting by. Perhaps, at the next stop, she'll phone Mama.

Glancing in the rearview at Anna's smooth cheek and fluttering eyelids, she floats back to a later Mindy Johnson extravaganza. For this party—thrown the month after Daddy's funeral, after she and Mama had stopped speaking—it was Měi and not the twins Mindy recruited to help out, a welcome distraction. She'd found herself in a bright Potrero Hill sublet, blowing up blue balloons as round as her friend's enormous belly and dumbfounded by the fact that Mindy, only three years older, was already on baby number two.

"You know Kumani married one of our classmates?" She shook her head. "Josh Katz. The chess guy. They swore they're coming today! With their son."

"What's their son's name?"

"Festus."

"No."

"It means 'joyful'—"

"It means lifelong virginity."

"Ooh, that's facts." Mindy grinned. "McCarthy Dolan's coming, too—you had the biggest girl boner for her."

"Bringing her own little Festus?"

"Odessa Dolan-Karp."

"You're shitting me."

"What? Odessa's a strong name."

"Odessa's an old dog dying slowly on the porch. And Karp? Why take that on? Does nobody love their kids anymore?"

Mindy paused, a blue crepe streamer dangling from her hand. "Not for nothing, Měi—but you don't know jack about love till you're a parent. I know that's rude, but it's true." Picking at the fraying sleeve of her sweatshirt, she'd climbed off her footstool to swipe a few Cheerios from the counter into the sink. "It's like, all love is imbued with yearning. But this type of yearning answers itself. And all love is selfish, but this kind of love is more selfish than the lover. It'll crack you before you can crack it, and even then, you'll thank it on your knees. You know?"

Měi hadn't known; couldn't fathom knowing, though she was impressed, as always, by Mindy's knack for stringing words together.

Before she'd had Austin, her first, unplanned, Mindy was set on becoming a poet and journalist. Instead, she'd remained a housewife. "Be right back," she said. "I need to change into my dress."

She checks the rearview. No van. Of course, no van. The men's presence in Elkhart was coincidental.

In the back, Anna's head lolls gently against the seat. Měi can almost see the girl's pulse beneath the delicate skin of her neck. If her tenderness toward this child she barely knows is even half of what parents feel—

She tries to put herself in Mama's place: the child grown now, gone now, the father gone, too. But she cannot quite conceive of her mother's feelings as some vast, unfathomable sea. Her mother's sensibilities are clear, crisp, and directed. Sweeping everyone straight into the turbine's blades.

She's been so, so mad at Mama, ever since Daddy left.

Even now, the bile rises to burn her throat as she recalls Mama's face that night. The Fourth of July. Fireworks popping off outside, in the dark.

7

AN IMPASSE

Elyria, Ohio, described on travel sites as a diamond in the rough, adds its sparkle to the lusterless decay of the rust belt—its majestic, unexpected waterfalls shining up the dirty air of Cleveland's metropolitan area. Even the city's name is a gem, a hybrid of its provincial founder's surname, Ely, and Illyria, the eponymous Balkan region that lends its four soft syllables to Shakespeare's magical kingdom in *Twelfth Night*.

She leans forward against the seat belt, squinting, as they enter the city limits. Examines Elyria's evening sky beyond the windshield (deep blue at its center, bleached bright along the horizon) as, from the back seat, Anna and Henry, awake now, call out words describing what they see in the cirrus clouds above.

Some, Měi recognizes: èyú, a crocodile like the ones her mother had shown her at the Oakland zoo. Huā, a flower like the ones in her aunties' dueling San Jose gardens, captured in photos they post online. Jiǎo, foot, a word Měi has always known but occasionally confuses with tuǐ, leg. Other words, she must repeat to Henry.

"Lèigǔ?" she asks through the open partition.

"Rib."

"Biān?"

"Whip."

Treetops and rooftops peek over the freeway's noise barrier. Passing a water tower, a cell tower, a line of latticed steel transmission towers, she imagines the sleepy town they serve: Elyria. A flickering candle in the window of a larger bedroom community, boasting a few small businesses of its own.

"Kàn qǐlái xiàng yì zhī húlí," she says to Anna, pointing at a steel tower. She hopes she's gotten the words right. "Looks like a fox with pointy ears?"

"Shì de," Anna says, glancing at the transmission tower's geometric face. Měi's heart lifts.

"Look at you," Henry says, meeting her eyes in the rearview, "gettin' your Mandarin on."

"Damn straight," she says. "Mǎ mà māmā ma?"

"Do you even know what that means?"

"It means, 'Does Mom scold the horse?'"

He snorts. "Close enough."

"We are, actually," she says. "This is our exit. And I looked the inn up this morning. It's got a laundry room guests can use, and a swimming pool—in case she wants to, you know, yóuyǒng."

"Now you're just showing off," he says as she noses the car off the interstate.

"That's why they call me the Mack Daddy Polyglot."

"Nobody has ever called you that. You know you got the horse sentence wrong—"

"Psht. You don't know me, son." *My father spoke eight languages.* But she doesn't add this tidbit.

"Yeah, well, everyplace we've stopped has had a pool. It was Miss Anna's only request." His words hurl her back to Elko, Nevada, and the glass-walled swimming pool they passed on their way to the ashtray-scented rooms. "And we've swum in all of them, too. So maybe *you* don't know *us*. Son."

"Hunh." A twinge of envy. Turning into the parking lot off Lorain Boulevard, she chastises herself—reminding herself she is only the driver. Not the child's parent, for Chrissake. And why would anyone introduce a human life into this teeming mess? She thinks of her father's arm flung out across his mahogany desk.

Fiery sunlight pierces the windshield as, blinker on, she pulls into a space near the entrance. Puts the car in park, recalling the day Cherry slid into the back seat with a ridiculous tan. "Did you—just get back from the beach?" she'd asked.

"Nah." Cherry waved a hand in front of her face, obscuring herself in the rearview. "Just trying out *Jersey Shore* look."

It had taken a good five minutes of furtive glancing to discern that the spray-on camouflaged a shiner. Some client's ugly purple legacy, a reminder that Ling Ling and Cherry were "outlaw" workers with no pimp for protection. Of course, pimps are known for leaving legacies, too.

Shutting off the ignition, she stares through glass doors at the gaily lit lobby. *Maybe someday I'll adopt*, she thinks. *Take in a life, rather than pushing one out. After all, when I want a bookcase it's not like I go out and collect acorns, plant them, water the roots, raise the tree, chop it down, saw and sand and assemble the shelves, then paint the thing and put it in my house. No. I buy one online.*

"Hullo?"

Already outside the car, Anna's small fingers wrapped in his, Henry raps at the driver's-side window with the knuckles of his free hand.

"That was wild, right? Those two beardos in the van?"

"Are we back on that?" As their elevator rises to the third floor, Henry hands her a key card.

"They were at the bar across from the ice cream parlor. Back in Elkhart."

"What? Why didn't you point them out?"

"I only saw them as we were leaving. Then we hit the freeway, and you two were out like a light." She snaps her fingers unsuccessfully, producing only a soft, grazing sound as the elevator stops and the doors glide open.

Anna hops lightly over the threshold onto the third floor, taking in the elevator lobby's console table and mirror before turning to look at them expectantly. It is hard to believe this miniature child will be a teenager in two short years.

"You think they followed us? But they were ahead of us on the road. And Elkhart was an unplanned stop."

"They passed us initially, yeah, but that doesn't mean they stayed up ahead."

"Were they watching us or anything? Taking pictures?" He puts his hand on her back, guiding her gently out of the elevator to the expectant girl.

"No, but—" Anna leads them down the long hallway. Not knowing where she's going, she plays some game with herself, leaping from yellow flower to yellow flower. (The carpet's design, Měi knows, is intentionally busy: nearly all hotel carpets are, their loud patterns and high contrast meant to obscure dirt and stains.)

The girl is far ahead now, her knobby knees and narrow, sneakered feet spiriting her on till she pauses at the end of the hall, unsure.

"Yòu zhuǎn," Henry calls out when they are near enough to read the posted sign, and Anna turns right, disappearing.

Měi's throat is dry. She wishes she had eyes on the girl—wishes they'd share a suite again, not split up into separate rooms. "I don't know." She fights an odd, growing panic. "It was weird to see them again. Don't you think that's a big coincidence?"

"Not really. I've bumped into other travelers multiple times. On lots of trips."

"This is different. They tried to run us off the road."

"Did they? Or were they shitty, distracted drivers? Were they, like, texting?"

"Henry." She stops, grasping his bicep to halt him mid-stride. "They weren't texting. They were staring into our car." With a half smile, he is studying her fingers on his skin. She releases his arm, heat rising in her cheeks. "Why won't you take this seriously?"

"I am. But, look, we get targeted all the time. People punch Chinese grannies in the streets, right? Trash Asian bodegas, spray-paint slurs on the walls. And a cop shot an Asian grandma in her own home when she opened the door holding a vegetable peeler. Does any of it make sense? No. I mean, it's not like the cop was Mr. Potato Head."

She frowns. "They're gender-neutral now."

"Who? Cops?"

"No. Potato H—never mind. Your point is?"

"My point is that it's not unusual to get targeted by race, if that's even what happened. Not in America. Not anywhere in the world. It doesn't mean they're spies." They're in front of her room now. "I've gotta catch up to Speed Racer, okay? You take advantage of the alone time. Eat dinner. Watch TV. And don't worry: we're not being tailed."

"You can't be sure of that."

"Yes. I can." The light in the corridor flickers. The inn is neat: updated, even, but inexpensive. She turns the key card over and over in her hand. When his lips twitch into a genuine smile, she can't help but smile back.

∞

The closest Měi's come to the horrors Anna endured at the state school, she supposes, is the closet.

When she was little, and acted out, her father would lock her in the hallway closet. It was tiny—a narrow, upright box—yet there was certainly enough room for a tall man, maybe a zombie, to stand directly behind her, staring down at the top of her head. Closing her eyes tightly as she heard the lock catch, she'd sing songs under her breath. *This old man, he played two; he played knick-knack on my shoe.* And as she sang, the four walls seemed to expand, sound ricocheting for miles. She wouldn't open her eyes till Daddy returned to let her out.

Years later, after his incense-blanketed funeral (where the Chinese guests bowed three times before the closed casket as the Americans watched awkwardly), she would visit the cemetery alone. There was an oak tree over her father's grave, and she'd climb up to sit in the gentle curves of its broad branches, wondering why he'd left them for this place. Was it the quiet?

Inhaling the scent of freshly turned dirt, she'd picture her father below in his final resting place, face disfigured by the bullet, arms folded across his chest, six feet underground. Her daddy. Hidden inside the polished wood with its ornate golden hinges, grass growing overhead as he lay stiff in his own narrow box. There would be no light where he was, ever again, and nobody to let him out. Was he scared, too? Did he regret what he'd done, too? Sense a silent presence behind him in the dark?

Yet those awful moments locked away alone are so much more forgivable than her mother's blunt, inscrutable answer to the question of what hard choices she'd made to become an American. "I marry your daddy."

Surfing from channel to channel, studying the room service menu, she thinks of the night she dropped Ling Ling off outside a hotel and found her waiting there, one hour later, with a cat carrier. Inside was a calico kitten. Days passed and she asked Cherry about it. "Oh, yah," Cherry giggled. "Client give her that little guy. He imagine Ling Ling in love with him. She name the kitty 'Trick' in Chinese. Say she gonna starve it. Kick it. But I see cat toys in her bedroom today. So maybe they *are* in love."

And what is love if not transactional, Mĕi thinks. *You say it first, I say it back. You give me a bit of you, I give you a bit of me.* Yet coming from Oakland, where people order people like food, where adults with options creatively express their sexuality for a profit alongside the poor and desperate, the turned-out teenagers who spill from dark doorways into the gleam of sun or streetlight to make their quotas—she cannot stomach Mama's comment. Her parents' marriage was more than mercenary. It had to be.

When it's dark out, she clicks the TV off. Moves her room service tray to the floor. The hotel's bleached sheets are cool. Impersonal. She tosses a bit, trying to evade her own body heat (as discomfiting as a warm spot in a swimming pool). Going to the mini-fridge, she brings tiny bottles back to the bed with her, then kills the lamp, drinking in the dark.

"American independence a sham," Mama had commented once at the kitchen table, baiting Daddy, who was a true patriot. "People need people." When he snorted softly, she'd pointed to Mĕi's glass. "You know how to make a reusable, nontoxic water glass? Make water drinkable so you don't get sick?" Begrudgingly, he shook his head. "Yah, I don't think so. Without other people, your life gonna be like that TV show, *Naked and Afraid*. But with other people help, you get to drink soda pop and stick your glass in the dishwasher."

"And yet you're here," her father answered, "in hypocritical America."

Tossing blankets off, Měi lets the air-conditioning prick at her skin. Lǎolao, she recalls, never used the dishwasher. Once, wiping it down, she'd accidentally turned it on. "AIYA!" Měi grins at the memory.

Under the hotel's nondescript ceiling, she feels Lǎolao's soft, dry hand in hers and the Californian sun on her back. Fluffy white dandelions lean out over the sidewalk, inviting Měi's free hand to pluck them up—tempting her lips to blow wind into wishes.

Thrashing in the chilled air, she shifts the pillow beneath her head. Through the sheers, the parking lot glows reassuringly as she makes out dim, nearby shapes: armchair, lamp, small oval table. Across the room, the desk looms large and indistinct as a pirate ship across a misty cove. It draws her thoughts through time's murky waters to another desk: the desk in her father's study, his body slumped over the glinting mahogany as she burst into the room.

One of his arms was flung across its surface. His heavy pen holder overturned, fountain pens spilling to the floor. And in a folder in the drawer of that desk, a neatly typed goodbye note.

When the police were through with their questions, she'd sunk into Lǎoyé's ratty couch. The dark garage reeking of weed, her grandfather puffing quietly in a far corner, producing perfect O's like *O, it'll be okay. O, I've lost someone, too. O, don't cry, don't cry*, each reassurance dissipating between the bare ceiling joists.

"Why'd they ask me all those things?" Měi sobbed.

"It's they job."

"But there's a note. It says he loves us."

"It still a unnatural death. How they know you not a murderer?" From the dismal distance he materialized, thin robe like some pink second skin, ornate slippers shimmering in the moonlight from the cloudy window. Perching on the arm of the couch, he rubbed at her back awkwardly with hands unused to this sort of physical contact. "You know," he said, "your great-great-great-great-granduncle find a dead body, too."

"Yeah?" She stared up. Who else but Lǎoyé would've thought to share this morbid family story now? Would've understood how sometimes it took a blow to counteract a blow.

"Yeah. In the early spring. He take a nice walk, wanna see what kind of wildflowers near the railroad camp. Instead, he find another Chinese guy's frozen body. From a avalanche. Still got the shovel in its hands."

"Now that's dedication to your job." Eyes red-rimmed, she felt herself smiling.

"You telling me! Nobody gonna find me holding a spark plug in rigor mortis."

"Can you imagine? I wonder if any fluffers have ever died on the job."

"What this? 'Fluffer'?"

"They assist porn stars in getting—ready to shoot."

"What you mean?"

"Like, get them hard?"

"How you know this?"

She rolled her eyes. "The internet, Lǎoyé."

"Okay. You don't need no fluffy side hustle supplement your summer limo job." He puffed his joint contemplatively, rubbing her back in precise circles. "Besides, you paid so bad you already getting fucked. We gonna find you new job, okay?"

Grinning up at him, Měi shook her head.

Then, rolling onto her stomach, she'd buried her face in a dusty couch cushion and laughed and cried.

Her mother did not understand her nonsensical reactions. Her mother did not rub her back. Nor did Mama cry. At the funeral, when the preacher spoke of loss, Měi watched her mother's impassive face and wondered whether she even felt Daddy's absence.

On July fifth, she contacted Dartmouth and withdrew from school. Certainly, Mama would feel that.

∽

The pool area is empty in the wee hours, of course, the other troubled insomniacs tucked away in their rooms to read or drink or watch TV.

She's walked past this door twice, earlier, heading to and from the laundry room. A sign reads OPEN DAILY, 6:00 A.M.–10:00 P.M., and she figures the key card won't work, but when she swipes it the light flashes green. She pushes the glass door open, inhaling the warm scent of chloramines and cleansers.

Everything is neat and tidy: stacks of neatly folded towels in an open-faced cabinet, pool noodles stashed in a large box. The cleaning crew has come and gone. Still, she worries that someone may spot her through the glass door if she risks a swim. Glancing into the room's far corner, she sees a hot tub half-hidden from passersby. Yanking her high-tops off, she balls her socks up inside them and pads toward it, barefoot.

By the tub, she pulls her tank top over her head and shimmies out of her jeans, aware that her white bra and panties will turn transparent in the water. If she's caught by the portly, hirsute night manager, whose eyes ate her up as they checked in, it'll help her talk her way out of trouble. A dial on the wall brings the dormant tub roaring to life, its surface an eruption of bubbles, and she steps in. "People stew," Mama always says when invited into a hot tub, "no thanks." Submerging herself to her chin, she shakes this irritating thought from her head. Carefully, she removes her earrings (tiny diamonds Daddy gave her when she graduated high school) and sets them atop the fresh white towel with her phone and key card.

After the funeral, the house was quiet for days. The police had taken Daddy's laptop, then returned it without explanation, so she opened it and tried to guess his password. She typed in her own name, Mama's name, and the name of Daddy's beloved childhood pet, Muldoon, a basset hound who'd howled along when the family sang. She even tried the name of the river flowing beneath a truss bridge Daddy had once scaled.

This was one of a handful of stories he'd shared about his youth. His friends had jumped already, he said (one girl executing a breathtaking dive, thumbs interlocked, legs taut, chin tucked) and were waiting on him. But standing on the top chord, staring down past the triangular beams at the tracks that ran below—the strident gray current even farther down, rushing under the railroad span—he'd chickened out. Inched haltingly back toward the end post to shimmy to safety, his friends booing. He was still in the center of the bridge when his feet began vibrating. Glancing down, he saw his buddy pointing off into the distance. "TRAIN," the boy shouted, and when his gaze followed the bend of the tracks, he saw the glowing eye of its headlight. The vibrations grew stronger. More insistent. He jumped.

It was one of his most vivid memories, he said—falling through the air to plunge into brown water; opening his eyes under the surface as the current tugged; using all his remaining energy to thrash back to the riverbank in a daze. Later, the girl who'd dived headfirst learned of a sunken railroad car hidden beneath the water's surface, near enough to where they'd plummeted in that any one of their bodies, their skulls, might've struck it. "I guess that's what they call a near miss," Daddy chuckled. "But my cowardice was gone after that. I enlisted the very same summer."

On the Fourth, he'd been cowardly.

And this time he hadn't missed.

She tried everything she could think of but failed to guess his password. The laptop that had proffered his parting words would remain a closed mouth, never to spit out another utterance. The house, too, was silent, beyond the apologetic creaking of floors and doors.

Throughout a week of long, late-summer afternoons, Měi ignored the limo company's calls. She lay across her father's faded Persian rug or draped her body over his leather armchair, letting the silence saturate her. Waiting for Mama to call her out of his study. Waiting for Mama to say anything at all.

During this interminable wait, she barely thought about the cluttered Lower Haight room she'd rented, her new roommates, Shayla and Tim, waiting with concerned faces. She offered to help Mama with the housework, but Mama said she had her own system. She asked to help handle Daddy's affairs, but Mama said things were taken care of. So they paced around one another toward separate destinations—the study, the kitchen, the powder room—till evening, when they sat at the little table together and ate the foil-covered dishes people had dropped off, the hum of the refrigerator audible.

In the end, Mama won their game of chicken, her silence only broken by unavoidably mundane things: zǎo, good morning; lái chī, come eat; wǎn ān, good night. Měi waited for a hug, a conversation, a night-time sob or wail. Watching her mother sort through Daddy's things, she waited on a gift: something meaningful he'd had given Mama, perhaps, or something Mama chose to pluck from his belongings for Měi. But none came, so she went back to the Lower Haight, to her roommates' hugs, talks, tears of sympathy; these virtual strangers' gift of acknowledgment that her world had changed. Back to the welcoming neon blue blaze of the cross of First Baptist Church illuminating her bedroom at night.

And she hadn't returned home since. When she occasionally tried Mama on the phone, her mother stuck to cheery banter. "You hear the latest about Florida man?" Mama would say, or "They got a good sale going on at Ranch 88 today. Kumquats!" And because Mama had been the go-between connecting Měi with her aunties, uncles, and sincere, nerdy cousin Warren, those relationships faded, too. In this way, just as Mama's gravity had once held their family's little galaxy together, her dreadful levity now flung it apart, sending everyone out of orbit into the vast solitude beyond.

She lifts her hands out of the hot tub and stares at the pruney pads of her fingers. Dabbing them dry on the towel, she snatches up her phone, dials Mama's number, and is shocked when her mother picks up. "Wéi?" It's the middle of the night in Elyria and past midnight now in Oakland. "Wéi?"

She hangs up. Drops the phone back on the towel. Shuts her eyes.

When the door to the pool area opens, she startles, braced to explain herself to the night manager. But it's Henry striding toward the hot tub, black flip-flops slapping against his heels, photoshoot-ready in a matching black T-shirt and trunks, water bottle gripped in his hand. With a glance at her small pile of clothing, he grabs the hem of his shirt and pulls it quickly off—all muscle cuts and luscious skin. She shuts her eyes tight again.

"Knew it." His voice is low and close. She opens one eye as he discards the flip-flops and water bottle, sinking into the frothy water.

"What?"

"You aren't just conked out in your hotel room every night."

"This is the first night I've left my room at all—"

"Besides Rock Island, when you were almost in a throuple?"

"Because of you! You kicked me out to tell Anna the jig was up."

"Did I tell you to accept drinks from strangers?"

"But she wasn't a stranger. As I recall, you and her gentleman friend had an intimate dialogue about the women you . . . enjoy contemplating."

"I never discussed Angela Merkel or Rebecca Solnit with anyone in Rock Island."

"You know what I mean. Yeesh." She twists her head left and right, rolling her shoulders back. "Though I am impressed that you know Solnit's name."

"You never asked what I do for a day job."

"What do you do?"

"I'm a writer."

"A writer."

He shrugs. Splashes water up over his shoulders, runs wet fingers through dark, glossy hair. "Met Solnit at a book release."

"I've never seen your name on a book."

"And you never will."

"Why not—are you, like, an ekphrastic poet? A misunderstood genius?"

"I'm a sneakerhead, and poetry doesn't buy limited-edition Dunks."

"Oh?" She splashes water on her cheeks. Dabs at her temples. Lifts her hair from the nape of her neck and lets it fall again, eyeing his sweating water bottle.

He's nodding. "I'm a ghostwriter. We make bank. And we never have to do an interview."

"Wait, really? So the high-visibility client who got us an upgrade back in Illinois—"

"Steph Curry."

"You're shitting me!"

"I am." A slow grin. "But I do work with high-visibility individuals." Without thinking, she slaps his muscled shoulder. Instantly regrets the contact. "Can't tell you who, but more than one of my subjects' projects have been adapted for the screen. And guess who gets to write the scripts?"

So he's a screenwriter, too. She narrows her eyes. No way is she sharing her off-and-on journalistic ambitions with this guy. Running her smooth palms up and down her thighs, she wishes she'd booked that massage and gone straight to sleep afterward. Then she realizes this isn't the sort of inn that offers spa services. No matter. She tries a relaxation trick she's learned from Ling Ling's associate, Cherry—releasing the small muscles in her forehead, her jaw, her neck, her tension dissipating, floating away in the warm water.

"Hmm," she manages. Somewhere nearby, a metallic sound starts up. Loose debris inside a vent? A nail, perhaps, rolling around in there, rattling.

"How about you?" he asks after a minute. "You must've driven some A-listers around?"

"Well, nooo. But once, on Divis, I stopped at an intersection and Weird Al Yankovic was in the crosswalk. Does that count?"

"Did you shout at him through the window?"

"No."

"Not even a friendly 'Hello'?"

"Nope."

"Did he give you a little wave?"

"No."

"Smile?"

"No."

"Then, yes, it definitely counts."

"Mmmhm, that's what I'm sayin'. This one here knows how to hobnob."

She opens her eyes, peeking at his biceps as he shifts to rest his arms on the tub's rim.

He smirks. "So, give me some top secret private chauffeur stories."

"Nope." She licks dry lips, wishing she'd brought water, too. "And it's *driver*, not chauffeur. I'm paid to operate a vehicle; not take care of the client's every need." He chortles, throwing his head back. Regards her through dark lashes that hide his eyes. "You, of all people, Henry, should value my discretion. That said, I guess I might have a few tales from my limo-driving days . . ."

"Your limo days? Like what? Teenagers getting wasted on the way to prom?"

"How about two strippers and four cops—one of whom took a dump in the center console?"

"Did you report them?"

"To whom?" She shifts slightly, positioning a bubble jet between her shoulder blades. "The cops?" He raises his eyebrows, conceding. "Even worse, one of the officers called the next day to say they'd left something in the limo. Uh, yeah. Yeah, buddy, you did." She glances pointedly at the water bottle.

"What?" He lifts it. Takes a long swig, keeping his eyes on her. "Thirsty?"

He tilts his head. Holds the water away from her reaching hand. "Maybe I am," she says, her breasts grazing his chest as she stretches toward the bottle—

A buzz startles them. The wall timer. The bubble jets die, the nearby vent still rattling.

"Um," he says, lifting his dripping frame from the tub, "gotta make a call."

When he doesn't return, she towels off quickly. Resolves to get some to sleep. But she passes on by her room instead. Knocks softly on his adjacent door.

In the unflattering light from the hallway, flawless Henry Lee appears a bit haggard.

"Remember how I told you I was doing this for someone important?" he asks, not meeting her eyes, staring down the corridor as though to count the light sconces. She nods. Waits for him to disclose what she probably should've guessed: he's got a young, beautiful fiancée in China. "Well"—he beckons her into his dark room—"that person's my mother. She knows the Xīn family. Went to graduate school with Jimmy. Recruited me into this." She stifles a relieved grin. "I think they've taken her," he says. "My mom."

They move through the room quietly; sit side by side on the small sofa, no lights.

On the farthest bed, the girl is a cocoon of cotton blankets in the bracing air-conditioning. "We don't need to whisper," he whispers anyway. "She could sleep through anything. Told me she even fell asleep in the suitcase."

"I burn with envy." She is grateful for his quick grin in the dim light filtering through the sheers. "Wait, but your parents aren't Uyghur, right? Why would they take your mom?"

"True." His voice is strained. "And it's not like they're activists. They teach English online. They have a framed photo of Xí Jìnpíng."

She sits for a time without speaking. "So, then. Are you thinking they might've taken her because she's connected to the Xīns on social media, or something? Or because of us?"

"I mean—"

"Because we're helping Anna? They found out somehow?" She thinks of the men in the van.

He glances past the sheers, into the magical kingdom of Elyria beyond panels of pleated white polyester that diffuse the light. The air conditioner is loud, seeming to never turn off, to never deem the room cold enough. His worry vibrates between them. "I mean, how would they know? There's no public link between us. And I'm barely visible. Clients find me through word of mouth. Like you." They lock eyes. "That's why I chose you," he says, barely audible, "after I met your lǎoyé." She slides imperceptibly closer, wanting to press into his side. "I would've driven Anna cross-country myself, except for the possibility she'd, like, die or something while I was up front at the wheel. That fucking suitcase . . ."

"Look, I get the suitcase thing now. I really do. I read Jimmy Xīn's articles." She thinks of the white van, the bearded men. "It's gotta mess with your head, getting screwed by your own government"— Lǎoyé's words ring in her ear—"just ask any Black civil rights leader. That hasn't been assassinated . . ."

He scratches at his jaw, skin reeking of chlorine, and she fights an impulse to press her lips to his forehead. "You haven't told anyone?" he asks.

"Of course not."

He tilts his head, staring down at her. "Yeah. That's what I thought. Like, besides your lǎoyé, anyone who knows what you do is too shady to talk anyway." She feels her eyes narrow. "No offense. I don't mean your clients are bad people. Just not the sort to run to the cops."

She thinks about Ling Ling, missing her with a pang. "Wait, how'd your mom even get involved?"

"Jimmy Xīn's an old friend, as I said. And my mom tutored Anna online. Said she was an excellent student, though she clearly hasn't retained much English. Mostly, she's into digital art. Could animate characters by age eight. And she's a gifted gymnast."

"Well, that explains her stamina. Balled up in that ugly case."

He nods. "She wants to be an acrobat. Or an animator for Disney. Her parents are well traveled and big on expanding her options. So they signed her up for digital art classes with a university professor. And English sessions with my mom. When she missed one with no follow-up, Mom got nervous. It was the middle of the night in America, so she called Mrs. Xīn. No answer. But the next day, Jimmy phoned from the U.S., upset. Said neighbors watched some men visit Mrs. Xīn late at night. They took her; sent Anna to the state-run school." In the near-dark, Henry's eyes narrow. "The schools prevent Uyghur kids from practicing Islam. Change their language, enforcing standard Mandarin. Make them eat pork. It's Basic Genocide 101. And Mom's fearless, with friends everywhere, so . . ."

"So here we are."

Henry nods. "At an impasse." Unscrewing the cap of his water bottle, he gulps. Tightens the cap again. "When Mom didn't pick up earlier, I called my uncle. But he didn't answer, either, which is why I couldn't sleep. I wasn't exactly worried, but I was happy to find you in the hot tub. I was just planning on giving you a heads-up that we might need to call things off. Then we got—"

"—distracted."

His smile sets her at ease so she leans into him briefly, warmed by the momentary contact before pulling back. "Yeah. So, uh, after I cleared my head I got hold of my uncle. Finally. He says nobody's seen her. My mom."

"Wait. Rewind. Did you say 'call things off'?" she inquires softly.

His face is pained. "I did this to help my mom. Not put her at risk."

A cold front is forming in her stomach, working its way up into her throat, her mouth, to freeze her tongue.

"Look," he says, "I didn't fill you all the way in. They took Anna's mom to get to Professor Xīn, who's outspoken and respected—to intimidate him, maybe lure him home. Make him stop writing about the Uyghurs. He's got some dirt that hasn't come out. And he can back it up."

"Yes," she manages. "Yes, I get that."

"But also, a week before Anna's mom disappeared, a Han Chinese 'uncle' moved into her house."

"A what?"

"A Communist spy, Měi. A fucking informant, reporting to Beijing. If he found Jimmy's contacts list . . ."

"Wait, he moved into her house?"

"Into her bed, too, maybe—who knows. I mean, I can't have my parents go through shit like that." The shame of helplessness presses his head down. He stares into his lap. "The 'uncle' denounced Jimmy's unpublished manuscript, *The Hollerith Age*, which he found in Mrs. Xīn's email. And who knows what supposed offense Mrs. Xīn committed: praying, maybe, or reading the Quran. Refusing to eat pig's flesh. Or—refusing other things." He looks up again, meeting her eyes. "I mean, they were lucky to even have a house. Many Uyghur homes were razed by the government, the families relocated into boxy high-rise units that replaced them . . ."

"But your parents aren't in the same boat. They aren't Uyghur."

"Yeah, but"—he's shaking his head now, tapping his foot on the carpet—"I told you, the Hui may be next. Look, we've got this neighbor, Mr. Xu. His family's owned the store on the corner since before I was born. And for years I've asked after him because he was always so kind. Gave out penny candies to us kids. So, a few years back Mom tells me a police officer visited his shop, wanting liquor and cigarettes. Being Hui, Mr. Xu didn't stock those things. So they called him in to the station. Over cigarettes. Mom was incredulous." He pauses, his jaw working back and forth. "Mr. Xu said the interrogation chamber was like a cell, with an iron chair and floor shackles; that a dried, faded river of blood ran under his feet. They took handwriting, voice, and biological samples. Scanned his face. He agreed to do what they said, and was released but never complied. Never bought the booze and smokes."

"And then?"

"A few weeks later, he was gone. Nobody knew where. Not even his son, who took over at the store. But tonight, my uncle said he stopped in to buy oranges. And there he was, back behind the counter: Mr. Xu. While he was ringing everything up, he rattled off the names of other neighbors he'd seen in the camp. 'Tell their families not to worry,' he said. 'I was treated like a king. They must *not* protest against this wonderful program. I went off to school,' he said, 'and came back a wiser man!' He smiled so widely, my uncle saw the holes where his back teeth were missing. And his eyes—they held a warning. A warning to heed the stories leaking out of Xinjiang, of women in the camps getting raped systemically by masked men in 'black rooms' without surveillance. Losing babies after being dragged and beaten. Of men abused till they're paralyzed. Sick and untreated. Dead. My uncle was terrified by what he saw in Mr. Xu's eyes. So, like, my family"—he pauses, anguish steaming off his body in the dark; Měi can almost hear it hissing—"they can't go through that. You know? Not because of me."

"But what about—" She gestures toward the girl's still form.

"I mean, she's not family. And who knows if her ice cream truck theory's correct? Jimmy Xīn was supposed to call me. Never did. We may never find the man." He gulps cold water from the bottle, brow furrowed. "And it's not like boarding school will kill her."

His body stiffens and Měi straightens, too.

Lifting her bare feet up onto the couch, knees hugged to her chest, she grips the cushion's edge with her toes. "Before, you called it an 'orphan camp.'" He looks away. "If we don't succeed, at least we tried to help her, right? So the risk your mom took wasn't wasted." She leans close again. "Henry—"

"I've gotta think," he says, his jaw clenching and unclenching. She moves to cup his face but, clasping her hand, he sets it in her lap. Then he stands. Pulls a clean shirt from his overflowing bag as fear rises slowly in her throat. There is something about the careful aversion of his eyes that reminds her of Daddy in those final days.

"Henry." Her voice is calm, but inside her two imperiled galaxies swirl, destined to collide like Andromeda and the Milky Way. The first galaxy is her family—one star inert, one hidden in smoky stellar fire, the others threatening to explode like supernovas. The second galaxy is this new, evolving system: Henry. Anna. Měi.

"Henry," she repeats, almost under her breath, "don't leave."

8

ELYRIA TO CORFU

Later, she wakes on the couch, shivering, from a dream of his return, the muscles under his golden skin shifting like tectonic plates, pulling her body close. But he is still gone, the clock glowing 3:30 A.M.

She stands in the center of the room and spins slowly, taking stock. His open packet of overpriced trail mix. Clothes spilling over the edge of his unzipped luggage. On the little writing desk, next to a complimentary notepad and pens, his watch and the small envelope containing his second key card. She snatches the envelope up. Tiptoes to the girl's bedside.

The delicacy of what she feels is alarming: a deep and tender fear. A longing to run, and the certain knowledge that she'll stay. The girl is still as a stone.

Chlorine pricks at Měi's skin. Scratching at her forearms, she backs slowly away. Returns to her own room for a quick shower and change of clothes. When she enters Henry's room again, he's still AWOL. The cotton cocoon on the bed does not stir. She approaches, fearing the worst, but the girl's face is angelic, half-smiling in sleep, and when she puts out a hand she feels warm breath.

She grabs at her own earlobe to turn the earring there. A nervous tic. But her jewelry is missing. Daddy's gift—

This time, striding down the hallway toward the pool, she feels centered and clearheaded. There's a jolt of nerves as she tries her key card, but the light flashes green again, no problem, and she pushes the glass door open. Passing the glowing white towels in their open-faced cabinet, she glues her eyes to the deck. Near the hot tub, she finds one of the diamond studs. She stares into the water, hoping the other isn't in there at the bottom of the tub. Did she scatter them when she snatched the towel up? She has never misplaced the earrings her father gave her.

"You get her diamond?" Mama had marveled when Měi opened the red leather box with its neat ribbon bow. "For high school graduation?" Daddy nodded. Mama shook her head. "Well, now you in trouble. What you gonna get for her wedding? Rolls-Royce?"

And later, as she'd packed for college, Daddy's military presence had shifted the air in her bedroom. He rarely entered her room, she'd realized then, respecting her privacy. But now he stood there, eyes shining a bit too brightly, and opened his arms for a hug.

Měi circles the tub, breathing measured breaths, when the second earring's brilliant wink catches her eye. She wipes the posts and slides the studs, one by one, back in—making her way back to the glass door—when two figures pass by in the hall. It takes her brain a moment to accept what she's just seen.

It can't be? But it is. She would recognize those beards, those glasses, anyplace.

She freezes like a deer, but the men are gone.

For a moment, time skips. She's back on the highway outside Elkhart, Indiana, the white van barreling toward her. She squeezes her eyes closed, opens them, exits the pool area, and runs toward the room.

Inside, in the white light filtered by the sheers, there is only silence around the girl's unstirring form.

"Anna," she says. Nothing. Crossing to her, she grabs the child's slight shoulders. Shakes gently.

Big, lustrous eyes open. "Shénme?"

"Wǒmen xiàn zài bìxū zǒu le." This is something Mama would say throughout her childhood when they had to go, though never in such dire circumstances—just when they were running late for a party, say, or a movie or appointment.

The girl stares. Sits straight up in bed, rubbing at a ragged dent in her hairline that Měi hadn't noticed till now. Has she dreamed about beasts yanking her hair out again? For a moment, Měi thinks Anna will scream and does not know what she'll do if that happens. They blink at each other. Without thinking, she wraps her arms around the girl. Smooths her warm brow with a cool palm. Leans back to meet Anna's eyes again, tucking soft strands of hair behind the girl's ears.

This child has lost her given name. Been assigned a new name. Lost her language. Been assigned a new language. Lost her home for an austere campus, a plane, a suitcase, a hotel room—

She cannot lose her parents, too.

This is not the first time Anna's been shaken awake in the night. Kicking the covers off, she stands barefoot on the carpet, rubbing her eyes, and peers at Měi. Performs calculations Měi could never understand. Begins, mutely, to pack.

Always, we worry about the wrong things. We fear we're developing arthritis while the CEO pinpoints the perfect day to fire us. We shriek at spiders as the tornado's spindly finger draws a line toward us on the map, or check the sex offender registry for a dodgy neighbor's face while the kids are with eccentric Uncle Ervin.

Since graduating middle school herself, Měi has religiously avoided middle schoolers with their incessantly rolling eyes, made-up slang, and snappy comebacks; their finely attuned sense of others' insecurities. Now, driving at daybreak with an eleven-year-old, she sees through the hubris to the vulnerability and can't believe how wrong she got it.

No white van in the rearview.

No white van in the rearview.

No white van.

Traffic is light under a pink-bellied sky as they pass the Cleveland Metroparks Zoo billboard. Měi would like to visit the zoo with Anna and pretend, for a few hours, they are only on vacation. She imagines the girl tiptoeing up to the giraffe, proffering food and giggling as the animal's long tongue curls around the acacia branch in her hand. They could walk slowly through the darkened bat enclosure, buy rainbow snow cones, gawk at the sun bears rolling on their backs. "They're called sun bears," she'd tell the girl, recalling her own trips to the Oakland Zoo with Lǎolao and Lǎoyé, "because of the golden fur on their chests. Don't those patches look like the rising sun?" Her hands twitch the steering wheel toward the exit, but she rights the course. Holds herself steady. Anyway, it isn't yet 6:00 A.M. Surely the zoo is still closed.

In the rearview, she sees that the girl is awake. Opening the little partition, she catches strains of a vaguely familiar melody. Whatever Anna's humming in the back seat is something Mama's played in the kitchen, dancing around with a pot and a dishrag in her hands.

"Uyghur Bieber?" she asks Anna, wondering whether the girl has heard of Justin Bieber, and Anna nods energetically, cracking up. Everyone, Měi realizes, has heard of Justin Bieber.

"Wǒ shì yī gè Belieber. Nǐ ne?"

"Enh. I wouldn't call myself a Belieber." Shaking her head.

The girl smirks at this lukewarm response, and they ride on in silence—Měi suddenly able to envision Anna as a teen.

When Měi turned sixteen, her parents threw a party. But it wasn't the sweet sixteen she'd wanted. In the living room, she and her friends clustered beside the picture window, surrounded by adults chattering in Chinese. "Can we go out on the porch?" Mindy said.

"My mom doesn't trust it. It's rotted."

"Can we just *go*?" someone else said, and her friends laughed, and she laughed the loudest.

There on the couch where they ought to be sitting, giggling, four elderly Chinese women from Mama's YMCA swim class sat and giggled. And on the coffee table where she'd imagined liters of soda, maybe even a few wine coolers, there were sesame candies and birthday noodles and thousand-year-old eggs. Her mother had begun preparing the eggs last week, dragging her to Chinatown, where swarms of noisy grannies crossed the street wherever they pleased; tried to bargain down every price.

"Not those!" she'd yelled when Měi returned to their cart with plain white cartons. "Those chicken eggs!"

"Okay?"

"We need duck eggs. Don't you know nothing?" Her mother had slapped her playfully on the bottom, which would've embarrassed her anyplace but here.

"No, Mom. I don't know *nothing*. I can't even talk right." Her sarcasm was lost on this crowd.

"Yeah," Mama agreed. "You and me talking is like chicken talking to duck."

Later that night, up on a footstool, all four feet and ten inches of Mama strained to pull an enormous ceramic Crockpot down from a high cabinet. Squinting in concentration, she'd coated the eggs with paste, rolled them in rice chaff, and set them beside the pot. "Hey," she'd said, glancing up once, "you wanna learn?"

In the doorway, Měi had squirmed. "Don't those go in the pot? Not next to it?"

"First they gotta dry. I gotta coat the pot, too."

"What's—what's in that brown stuff?"

Mama had smiled. Mud. It was lime, ashes, and mud.

Her friends shifted their feet uncomfortably as Měi stared at the eggs—avoiding their confused eyes, their fixed smiles—till McCarthy, the pierced, outspoken senior she wanted desperately to impress (who had come to her party because she went to every party) followed her gaze. "Ew! What are those?" The group regarded the neatly arrayed, gelatinous eggs. "Why are the whites black and the yolks green?"

The girls laughed, Měi the loudest. Fiddling with her chain (actual chain, heavy and cold, purchased at Ace Hardware and closed around her neck with a small padlock, to impress her friends), she concluded, "Some kind of Dr. Seuss thing. Green eggs and ham, or something. They treat me like I'm turning six, not sixteen."

And that's when Mama put on Uyghur Bieber. "Pop music," she

hollered across the crowd, over the incomprehensible foreign lyrics. "You girls dance!"

McCarthy put a hand over her mouth.

Měi glared an S.O.S. at her father, but he was stuck in a corner with old Mr. Wing, her parents' travel agent. Leave it to them to find the only remaining in-person travel agency in Oakland. In the world.

"OMG," McCarthy breathed through her slender fingers, "boomers."

She inhaled; relaxed her grimace. "Neutral face," Lǎoyé had instructed, over and over, till the day she finally beat him at rummy. "Cards close to your vest. Otherwise, I see everything. And—this important— pay special attention to what people discard. Then you gonna understand how they play the game."

"Hey, McCarthy," she said quickly, before anyone else could speak, "I bet that guy wears sock garters." She pointed at Mr. Wing. "And them?" She gestured at three elegant servers from the noodle shop her mother frequented, still in their black restaurant uniforms. "They're a coven."

Slowly, McCarthy turned to her, face stony. Then, the purest giggle. Real laughter, with a little bit of snorting. After that, Měi was invited to all the parties, too, which made her happy though she rarely went. She preferred to meet her friends at cafés or in the mall. She had not forgotten Tilden Park.

Buffalo, New York, was once the final port of the Erie Canal. Then, for a time, America's second-largest railway hub. *This place has been industrialized and deindustrialized time and again*, she thinks, *the cityscape shifting around our nation's first-ever urban parks system.* Heavy clouds formed from the vapors of Niagara Falls drift low over the buildings—so unlike the West Coast's untouchable cirrus streaks. Měi often thinks of California's high-up clouds as cotton fluff stapled to heaven's ceiling by a team of DIY angels.

Albeit surrounded by urban blight, by boarded-up businesses and derelict houses with their windows busted out, Elmwood Village is lovely as a travel brochure. Packed with restaurants pioneered by ex-Manhattanites seeking to revitalize this historic Buffalo neighborhood, it's as good a place as any to stop for lunch, she figures. She pulls into a parking space.

The calls from Henry began around 7:00 A.M. Now, mounted on the dashboard, her phone lights again. She ignores it.

"Buffalo wings," Anna says when she asks, in halting Mandarin, what the girl is hungry for. "Wǒ bàba ài chī Buffalo wings. Wǒ cóng méi xiǎngdào wǒ huì qù Buffalo."

Not really a breakfast food, she thinks, but whatever.

"Wingspot"—the girl's lips twist around the English words—"is halal."

"Wingspot? Noooo." Měi grins. "I'll do a quick search for what's good." The girl frowns.

They choose Edna's Burger Venture based upon its five-star reviews and halal wing selection and sit outdoors where the hipster waiter delivers the hottest wings Měi's ever seen. Not spicy hot. Hot as in sizzling, as though the plate is a porcelain burner. "Xiǎoxīn!" she warns as Anna pokes at the bounty with a fork, the word transporting her to her own childhood. *Xiǎoxīn!* Mama would yell when she slid across the living room in her socks. *Xiǎoxīn!* as she and Laura wobbled past Lake Merritt Boating Center on their first skateboards, her parents half jogging to keep up.

"Don't mall grab," she'd chide. "It makes you look like a poser."

"Hey, you're the one in *Thrasher* gear."

She wonders now whether Anna had good friends in Xinjiang—whether they, too, were assigned new names. But even if she were bold enough to ask such a prying question, she still wouldn't have the words.

Anna's wings are flanked by a pickle and a tiny stub of carrot. The girl eyeballs this odd assortment, then tests her meal with a finger, wincing back before poking at the food again.

Měi wonders what she ate at home with her parents, before the state school stole her hunger. Would her mother approve of this sticky orange meal? Would she simply be happy the girl was eating? Her thoughts turn to her own mother.

In her mind, Mama's staticky voice says *Wéi?* again.

Had she intuited who it was last night? Recognized the caller ID on the landline? Does she know her daughter hung up on her without a word? *Wéi?* She'd sounded so old.

Across the table, Anna tucks into the cooling wings.

"Hǎo chī ma?" This is a phrase she knows because Mama's asked it all her life.

The girl looks up, grinning with sauce-smeared teeth. "Tài hǎo chī la!" Delicious. And Měi feels her own face break into a wide smile of pleasure—relief, even—that the girl is satisfied.

For the first time, she considers the possibility that her mother's many efforts to teach her Mandarin might've been about more than academic success, more than job opportunities. Perhaps Mama, dissatisfied with her own English, had only wanted to be able to speak with her daughter in a language they both fully understood.

"Wǒ kěyǐ jiè nǐ de shǒujī ma?" the girl ventures. "Shǒujī?" The girl lifts her hand to the side of her face, pantomiming *phone.*

"Kěyǐ," Měi says. "Of course." Digging the device from her pocket, she slides it over.

Anna bends in concentration. When she returns the phone, she's tapped out a text message:

------(--------<@

"Huā," Anna says, and elation blossoms in Měi's chest.

"Flower?"

The girl nods.

Měi types in her own number and sends the text to herself, grinning at the girl when the phone dings—received—and taking her time on the reply:

Satisfied, she sends herself this text as well, to preserve it. "Elephant," she says.

```
                    /  ‾  \ ~~ /  ‾  \
            ,-----(        oo       )
            /       \___      ___/
           /\            (\   |(
          ^  \    /_\_\  / \..|
          |_| |  |_| |
```

The girl grabs Měi's phone, stares at the screen. Smiles up at her, Buffalo sauce smeared across her lower lip. "Dà xiàng." Her impossibly slim fingers type away and when she turns the screen forward, Měi sees:

><(((*>

"Yú," the girl says, and Měi smiles.

"Fish?"

Anna nods. Types again.

/_/\
/>^ ^<\
\ _ y _/

"Māo." The girl holds one finger in the air, like a teacher.

"Cat!" This is a word she recalls from childhood.

The girl turns the phone inward again, bending over it to study what she's created. She looks up as the waiter passes by with an enormous bowl of ice cream for another table. "Bīngqílín," she says, pointing across the patio.

"Yup," Měi says. "Ice cream." Another word she's always known.

For a moment, Anna stares down at the remaining wings on her plate. Looking up again, the girl pushes her light-brown hair back, her expression someplace between sad and hopeful. "Bīngqílín shì wǒ bàba zuì xǐhuān de tiándiǎn." Then she lifts another wing to her mouth.

"It was my daddy's favorite dessert, too." Měi smiles.

Bàba, father. Her own father would've known, could've explained, why the word sounds the same in so many languages. She recalls the last time she ate ice cream with Daddy, quizzing him about the aunties she'd only recently become aware of. Yes, Daddy admitted, he'd accompanied Mama on a visit to the women's village once. No, he couldn't really describe them, other than physically: one petite like Mama, the other big-boned and tall. "It was hard to communicate," he said.

"But you speak, like, a zillion dialects," she'd persisted as Mama joined them at the small, round kitchen table.

"Well," he said slowly, dragging his spoon around the bottom of the bowl where the fudge sauce had pooled, "Hakka isn't one. We only stayed in the village for a week. And everyone was so excited to catch up with your mother, she was barely available to translate." Reaching across the table, he'd squeezed Mama's hand.

"But you were fine on your own?"

"Sure, I was fine. But let's just say people misinterpret those studies about nonverbal communication. Spoken language is important." Her father smiled. "In fact, that's why I'm employed!" Unfurling to six foot two, he bent into the bottom freezer to extricate the carton and scoop another mound of vanilla into his bowl. "More?"

She shook her head, imagining the vegan house's scorn and amazed by this fit, trim man's ability to ingest vast quantities of sweets. "So how'd you handle the situation?"

"I can draw a bit." Her parents exchanged a quick smile over their dessert.

"So?"

"So your mother bought me a notepad."

"Yah," Mama chimed in at last. "Little red one. He carry it everywhere. I not there, he draw. Like they point to his belly, *What you want eat*, he draw pig. Then they know: cook pork."

Now, under their giant patio umbrella, the girl flicks away a bee drawn by the food. Pulling her knees up onto the seat of her stool, she leans over the tabletop to show Měi what she's pulled up on the phone. "Xiǎoxīn," Měi says as the stool wobbles.

"Xiànzài shì liù yuè èrshísì hào." Anna blinks rapidly at her. "Nǐ tīng de dǒng ma? Today? June twenty-four?" Gently, Měi nods, taking the phone from her hands to set it on the table between them. Anna has opened the upcoming locations for *Some Like It ~~Hot~~ Cold*.

She zooms in, locating June twenty-fourth on the schedule.

From 11:00 A.M. to 2:00 P.M. today and tomorrow, the food truck will be parked at a place called Farmstead Acres, in a town Měi's never heard of. She tries to imagine it: an apple orchard outside the urban center? A dairy barn or vineyard on some picture-perfect Syracuse region hill?

Her mind drifts westward again—out of the East Coast humidity and history to Oakland's drier air and infectious, freewheeling spirit. Even Daddy, at times, could disregard the rules. She recalls waking, five years old, from a nightmare—padding down the hall for a swig of milk. In the dark kitchen, she stalled before the refrigerator. Anything could be behind that door. Tarantula? Tentacled beast? Her small hand hesitated, then reached to grasp the stainless-steel handle of the bottom freezer instead. *Ice cream.* Cold. Sweet. Better than milk. She heaved the freezer open, then shrieked as Daddy's voice came from behind. "Why are you out of bed?"

"Milk?" she stammered, spinning to find him in the doorway. He drew near, hovering behind her. And bravery seized her heart the way it sometimes did in school, when she talked back to the teacher despite herself, and she heard herself say, "Why are *you* out of bed?"

His mouth was still, but his eyes smiled. The clock read 3:00 A.M.

"Not for milk," he said at last, softly. "How about some ice cream?"

The girl is restless now, rubbing a napkin fiercely across her lips and chin. "Gǎnkuài zǒu," she says urgently, tossing crumpled paper onto her plate.

What will happen if Mr. Xīn doesn't show? Shelving her pessimism in the farthest reaches of her mind, where it's wedged between other awful hypothetical situations, she summons the waiter. Pays the bill. Glances down at her phone's clock.

9:30 A.M. Two and a half hours, wheels turning, and they'll be in downtown Syracuse.

The sign for Corfu, New York, means they are still in Genesee County. Beyond that, she knows nothing about this little village, its travel plaza modeled after a rustic lodge replete with a river-washed stone facade and cedar shingles. Even before they enter, she can envision the exposed beams.

No white van in the parking lot. The girl rushes ahead to find the restroom—probably shouldn't have fed her buffalo wings for breakfast.

Inside, she stretches her arms, fingertips reaching upward toward a tiered wagon wheel chandelier. They've only covered a half hour of highway, yet her neck is stiff. She turns her head this way and that, perusing a small gift shop. The cashier, name tag clipped beneath her hijab, sipping a milkshake, nods hello. "Help you find anything?"

"Do you have notebooks?"

"Just small ones, with a mini-pen attached."

"Where?"

"Back wall."

She nods her thanks. Browsing the shelves, she dials Lǎoyé.

The phone rings so long, she nearly hangs up. When he answers, his voice startles her. "Wéi? That you, kiddo?"

"Who else? That you, old man? Did I wake you?"

"Nah. I been up since five A.M."

"Why?"

"Got to start early. The older you get, the earlier it get late."

She grins, bending to examine an intricate coloring book intended for grown-ups. "So—" She lifts the book; flips through its pages.

"Yah?"

"How you doing?"

"Old. We establish that already. Why you call?"

"Can I ask . . . about Henry Lee?"

"You want my approval marry him?"

"Jesus! No."

"Why you gotta invoke Jesus? Don't you know I Budapest?"

She sets the coloring book back on the shelf. "Budapest?"

"I Buddhist, but go Baptist church now."

"You do not!"

"I do. Perlie try and save my soul."

"Good luck with that . . ."

"That's what I say, but she a glutton for punishment." She hears him shuffling around in his slippers. "What you wanna know about Henry Lee?"

"Do you think he's, like, dangerous?"

A hoarse laugh. "Henry Lee a writer."

"So?"

"All writers are wimp! He pull a muscle lifting his pen."

"Lǎoyé—"

"He call Santa's elves 'subordinate clauses.' Henry Lee not dangerous. He such a pansy you can plant him in the garden!"

"Lǎoyé, that's homophobic."

"What? I not say he gay. I say he a delicate flower!"

Locating the notebooks, she selects a blue one. "So. You don't think he's, like, shifty?"

"No," he says. "Not Henry Lee."

"You sure?"

"Sure."

"Okay . . ."

"Why you ask this now?"

"No reason. All good."

"All good?" More shuffling; muffled sounds. "Okay. Now that we settle this matter, I got me some breakfast to smoke."

At the register, waiting for her receipt to print, she scans the rest stop's sprawling interior. There is something ubiquitous about these places, no matter how picturesque their design, that makes her feel she's deep, deep underground in some janky, sprawling subway stop. Sniffing fried food and Windex, her eyes skip over shelves of packaged baked goods. A rack of cheap sunglasses.

A few yards away, above a line for fountain drinks, a TV broadcasts local news. When she tries to read the ticker, the words are too small.

Her gaze drops to a nearby fast-food poster on an enormous stand: WINGSPOT.

"Get the lemon pepper wings," the cashier says. "They're, like, dreamy." She shifts her hijab, slurps her milkshake.

"Wait—Wingspot *is* halal?" She squints at the poster as two bearded men in glasses pass by, obscuring it from view. Her breath catches. They're older, more portly, than the men from the van. Still, she yanks the bag and receipt from the nodding cashier's hand. Rushes to the women's room, bursting in. "Anna?"

A stall door opens, the girl emerging with an inquisitive expression.

She swallows her anxiety. Holds out the little paper bag, which Anna peers into. "Draw? To communicate?" She thinks of Daddy drawing pigs for a left-behind auntie. "Bǐjiào róngyì," she says, pointing to the notepad. Easier than texting images, perhaps, or typing into an online translator. Certainly more fun.

"Ah," Anna says. "Búcuò!" She opens the notebook, gets the ink flowing, draws a thumbs-up.

"C'mon. Let's hit the road." Měi watches her stuff the notebook in a pocket.

They exit against a stream of incoming families: parents and grandparents stretching their legs, kids exploding with cooped-up energy. She wonders whether the locals eat here, too.

In the parking lot, scanning for the white van, she silently curses her paranoia. Of course, the only van here is a plumber's van—an enormous woman in her stained uniform inside, eating a folded slice of pizza.

Měi pulls her hair up on top of her head and releases it to spill across her shoulders, the sun soothing her forearms, her neck. Glancing up at the taxonomic collection of clouds, she sees a lumbering èyú, crocodile, slowly crossing the sky on the heels of a tùzǐ, rabbit.

As a kid, weaving through a fish market in Oakland's Chinatown— rock cod and red tilapia swimming in tanks and metal buckets, LIVE CRAB advertised on sun-bleached canvas awnings that also shaded pomelos and tangerines, melons and squash, ginger and fresh cilantro—she'd heard a visored granny spit "Tùzi!" at two men who cut her in line.

"Mama," she'd whispered, "is 'rabbit' a bad word in Chinese?"

Mama burst into cackles, barely audible over the crowd's transactional barking in Mandarin or the makeshift, abbreviated English that non-Chinese customers were prone to misinterpreting as intentional rudeness. "She not mean bunny rabbit! She say they gay together. Like call two man 'duànbèi,' from that movie. If a person say it nasty like she do, yah, that make it a bad word."

Floating in this noisy memory, she slides into the heat of the driver's seat, clicks her seat belt closed, and starts the car, slowly registering its silent disobedience.

The engine won't turn over.

Shit, she thinks. *Fuck. FUCK. MOTHAFUCKIN FUCKETY FUCK!* She wishes she had a Chinese expletive, but the only bad word she knows is "tùzi."

9

CORFU TO SYRACUSE

"Could be the battery, could be the alternator. The starter or connection cables," the squat man says as she fills out the paperwork. RAMON is stitched into his old-school mechanic's shirt. "I can diagnose it this morning, if you want to wait."

She nods. "Yes, please. That'd be great."

"There are a few cars ahead of you, but I'll be quick. I'm off at noon. Shouldn't really even be here today."

She hands him the clipboard. "Is there someplace I can bring her while you take a look? Other than in there?" Eyeing the small waiting room with its coffee machine, generic creamers, and Styrofoam cups, she nods at Anna. She's unsure of exactly where they are, of exactly where the tow truck dragged them after their long wait in the travel lodge's parking lot.

"Been on the road awhile?"

"Yup."

"There's a nice trail out back, running along the forest's edge. Short but scenic. Got a restaurant at the end, if you go south. I can call you when I figure out what's wrong. I know road trips are tough on kids"—he lowers his voice—"and tough *with* kids."

"Thanks," she says. She glances at Anna, who's studying an out-of-place flyer posted on the wall among ads for discount car services. YOU DON'T HAVE TO BE A DOCTOR TO SAVE LIVES, it says. BE A HERO. SUPPORT

YOUR LOCAL BLOOD DRIVE. If she didn't know better, she'd swear the girl was reading the words.

"You're very welcome."

If only this kind man knew half of what the girl's endured, that hours in the back seat of a car, left alone to her daydreams, are lovely in comparison. But few people are aware of the Uyghurs' predicament. She, herself, had barely skimmed the news stories till it became personally relevant.

"First they came for the socialists, and I did not speak out . . ." She remembers Martin Niemöller's eerie poem. Would the United States have stepped in and helped stop the Holocaust if the Nazis hadn't posed a threat to our European allies? During World War II, liberating camps was a secondary mission. Yet we've adopted that heroic task as integral to our national identity. So, what is our real responsibility toward children who suffer, parents without protection, populations being squashed under a boot? How bad does it have to get, she thinks, before we do more than impose sanctions? Before we apply real pressure to the United Nations? Increase U.S.–Uyghur ties? Become a true safe haven for refugees whose freedom does not constitute a political advantage? How long before we plant ourselves firmly on the right side of history? Or at least, closer to right?

The trail behind the repair shop, half-hidden behind scrappy hedges, is an oasis for mosquitoes and retired, strolling couples. Sunlight filters through the hedgerow to gild the dark forest's edge. "Měilì de fēngjǐng," the girl says, and because her own name, Měi, means "beautiful," she supposes this must be a comment on the scenery.

The girl skips ahead, making room for a white-haired couple to pass, and they continue on single file, Anna skimming the shrubbery with her fingertips, Měi peering into the dense tree line. The East Coast's unkempt forests are a marvel. In Oakland, even the wilderness of Tilden Park has been tamed, cultivated, leaving only the savagery of humans. Veering off a hiking trail there, one finds restrooms and hippie shrines and homeless encampments; gum wrappers and condoms and cola cans. Evidence, everywhere, of human trespass. Here, the undergrowth is so thick she can't imagine people walking through the woods. Only foxes, coyotes, and bears.

Checking the time on her phone—10:54—she finds more missed calls from Henry. If she ever wants to turn the ringer back on, she'll need to address them. **WHERE ARE YOU TWO** reads his latest text. She squints at the letters, trying to discern whether they transmit worry or anger.

Near Buffalo, Corfu.

His response is instantaneous. **Rest stop? Café?**

Woods.

???

Taking a break from the road. Hiking. And now the guilt seeps in: yes, he is wealthy enough to find his own ride, but she left him all alone.

Worried sick

Sorry. You scared me, too.

Y???

Thought you might give Anna up.

To??

Don't know. But she's a bargaining chip. The three dots blink: he is typing. She types faster to cut off his response. **Weird night, right?**

The dots stop. Start again. She has set him on a tightrope, she realizes. Forced him to balance his responses lest she abscond with the girl. He sends a smile emoji, a cringe emoji, another smile emoji. Then,

Behind u by 30 min

Where?

Buffalo. Stopped 4 wings

She thinks of the sizzling plate she and Anna shared. **Ew, how cliché . . .**

Guilty as charged. Meet up @ Corfu?

She chews at her lip. Up ahead, Anna has paused where the path intersects a narrow road. On the other side, the restaurant. Glancing back, the girl waves.

Her calves seem no bigger than Měi's biceps. She bends to pluck a dandelion, lips pursed to blow the fluff, and Měi suddenly feels small, too. She thinks of Lǎolao's soft, dry hand in hers. A girl needs someone to trust.

I don't know

?!?

You won't send her back to China?

Hell no

And you're going through with the trip?

Of course! That's y I hired u—the three dots blink, stop blinking, start up again. Sorry. She waits, watching the dots. Know ur own dad left and that sucks. But I promise I'm all in. Not leaving again

She hadn't meant to lie to Henry about her father, she thinks, closing the distance to Anna as the girl plucks weeds, exhaling wish after wish into the air. Is she even wishing? Do Chinese girls know about this magic?

She should've told him, but she just can't bear to watch people's faces when they learn Daddy took his own life.

Even saying he's deceased is problematic. Conversation screeches to a halt as the other person must readjust everything: facial expression, tone of voice, assessment of who Měi is and how she's damaged. "It's okay," she ends up reassuring them afterward.

Besides, *he left us* is exactly what happened. And once she says it that way, people shy away from questions, assuming it's another woman— someone prettier, or less Chinese, than Mama. Maybe even a man. Měi has no real explanation to give, anyway.

She's racked her brain, since that Fourth of July, for some indication of depression. Yes, he was vague and evasive in the days leading up to his death. But beyond that, he was always just himself: the calm, kind, nerdy Daddy he'd always been. A quiet, contented man.

Once, he'd brought her to campus for a party celebrating his tenure, and she recalls how his colleagues had joked. "His life is dedicated to language," one said, lifting his glass in a toast, "but he doesn't like to talk."

"It's true," he'd replied. "I love language. It's been an honor to make it my career. But I also know too much about it"—a wry smile— "to trust it!"

And it was true: conversations in the Brown family had a way of shifting, their meaning morphing into something else entirely, as though the words were trying on new roles. For instance, when she finally confronted Mama about slut-shaming her the day she'd set out for Dartmouth, her mother had looked bewildered.

"What you mean, I make you feel like a whore?"

"Are you denying this conversation occurred? In the airport?"

"I never call you whore. Give me potato." This was during Thanksgiving break. She'd flown home to relax and eat her mother's cooking. Instead, she found herself sweating in the overheated kitchen, helping Mama prepare a meal for Old Mr. Wing. She handed the potato over. Watched Mama peel it quickly. "Mr. Wing will be very grateful. First, he lose his travel agency. Then his wife, five years ago. You remember. Then he lose his giant mansion. Live alone now, in drafty old run-down duplex." Měi glared. It was just like her mother to distract, to deflect. "He fall in love with white lady's ginormous breasts. The next thing you know, she got his money." Mama quartered the potato, dropping the pieces in a pot of salted water. "You wanna talk about whore? Reba a whore!" With a few clicks, the gas stovetop flared to life.

"You're right," Měi spat through clenched teeth. "Technically, you never called me a whore. You called me a tramp."

"Well"—wiping her hands on a dish towel, her mother turned to attend to the turkey—"you dress like one, get on the plane with strangers like that."

"What I do with my body, my femininity, is my business."

"What that got to do with it?"

"I'm allowed to dress as I like. And have sex!"

Her mother barked a laugh. "Why you talk about sex?"

Měi inhaled deeply, pursing her lips. "You called me a tramp because of my sheer black blouse?"

"No. For your pants. Why you wear jeans with rips everywhere?"

"How. I. Choose. To. Dress. Does. Not. Make. Me. A. Slut."

Mama's face fell. "What that mean? Slut?"

"A slut. A whore. A tramp. And even if I were, that's my prerogative."

"No," Mama said slowly, brushing the turkey with rosemary-infused olive oil. "Tramp is a hobo. Wear ripped clothes because they got no money." She sprinkled the bird with dry herbs she'd mixed in a rice bowl, began rubbing the seasoning in. "We got money! Look at my mink coat."

In the end, they clarified that her mother had not slut-shamed Měi.

Yes, her father had devoted his life to the study of language: its meaning, sound, and function. How it evolved over time. Yet the note he'd left said very little—only basic logistics like what to do with his body, and that he'd loved the time he'd spent with her and Mama.

Měi bites her lip, the pinch bringing her back.

Reaching out, she takes Anna's hand gently.

Something rustles the underbrush, and they glance. But the twitching leaves obscure whatever's inside. Looking both ways, they start across the road.

The restaurant's filling up with an early lunch crowd. They follow the balding host to a rear booth, Anna staring at his ink-black spray-on hair. "Nà shì jiǎfǎ ma?" the girl murmurs up at her, but she has no idea what this might mean.

At the table, they order from an extraordinarily tall waiter—roast chicken for Anna, a salad to split, and root beer floats. Měi wonders if Anna is lactose intolerant. If so, she wishes she could joke with the girl, it may be a long car ride.

Digging in a pocket, Anna pulls the notepad out. She presses down lightly, then heavily, with the pen, intent on her work. When she's finished, she holds up a picture of a cake. "Dàngāo."

"Cake," says Měi.

"Cake." Anna nods, pushing the pad across the table so Měi can appreciate how skilled the sketch is: its composition elegant, its shading intuitive. She lifts the plastic mini-pen, which is cool and smooth between her fingers. Holds it over the notepad, thinking. Then, slowly, she attempts to draw Henry.

"Nánrén," the girl says, pointing excitedly.

"Henry," she answers. The girl stares at the sketch—so much clumsier than her own—then pulls the notepad toward herself. Adds a little shading to the drawing. "Henry will be here soon," Měi adds. "Henry kuài láile." The girl nods, intent, and when she lifts the notepad to show her work, Měi's shocked to see her own sketch transformed: the man in the picture now is actually Henry.

The waiter's back. Bending, he sets their plates and mugs heavily before them, root beer foaming up around scoops of vanilla to overflow the frosty glasses around long-handled, stainless steel spoons. Měi stifles her vegan guilt. Sips greedily.

"Henry kuài láile?" Anna repeats when the waiter is gone.

"Right. Duì."

The girl's lips part in a smile. Is it the language barrier, Měi wonders, that's precluded questions about his absence? Or is the girl simply accustomed to changing hands? "Sháozi liángle," Anna says, sipping her float, then "Děng yīxià: wǒ mǎshàng huílái." Scooting out of the booth, she skips to the doughnut case near the register and peers in. The only thing capable of distracting an eleven-year-old from sugar, Měi thinks, is more sugar.

Fried dough is something nearly every culture has in common. When Měi was young, Mama would prepare it on special occasions, handing her a wooden spoon, letting her mix the ingredients in an enormous bowl. They'd shut the dough in the refrigerator, the yeasty scent of anticipation lingering in the kitchen till early the next day, when Měi rushed in to extricate the heavy plastic bag. Dumping the dough on the counter, she shaped it carefully into a log, which Mama sliced into strips. Then it was her turn again. Wetting the tip of a chopstick and dusting it with flour, she'd layer two strips, pressing the stick into their center to create the yóutiáo's distinctive shape before Mama fried it up and drizzled it with syrup and powdered sugar. She'd savored the stirring, the waiting, the shaping, perhaps even more than the eating.

"Chinese also like eat yóutiáo with soy sauce," Mama said one day. "Salty."

Měi wrinkled her nose. "Weird."

But Mama was used to being called weird by her daughter. She laughed. "We put sugar on french fries, too!"

The girl returns from the doughnut case, slipping into the booth to munch her chicken, stir her float, and slurp it fastidiously. Měi watches, the sight more refreshing than her own drink—just as the anticipation of yóutiáo had been sweeter than the fried dough itself.

Anticipation. She glances at the door.

The girl draws new pictures between sips, naming each in Mandarin, thrilling Měi with her artistic talent.

Hǎilí, beaver.

Màozi, hat (which she already knew).

Mótiān dàlóu, skyscraper. *Perhaps this is a literal translation*, she thinks, recognizing the word for "sky." And now she envisions the girl in a sun-baked high-rise full of classrooms where a Han Chinese teacher points to pictures of animals, objects, plants. Asks the children to repeat their Mandarin names.

With each addition, Měi thinks, a subtraction—each word written on the whiteboard, spoken in perfect tones by the instructor, erasing a Uyghur word. Each lesson learned at school replacing one learned at home. How to think, feel, speak, identify, what god could be believed in, if any.

No laptops, but a full-coverage surveillance system. No athletic fields, but perimeter alarms. No reprimanding notes about truancy, but the shock of a 10,000-volt electrical fence.

When he enters, doubled in the reflection of the glass door he holds wide open, he looks unfathomably taller. Shoulders broader. Skin a smoother, shinier gold. She's taken aback.

It's just absence, she tells herself. *Absence makes the hot grow hotter.* She stares till his eyes find her. And as he looks her up and down, she feels herself dividing in two: actor and audience. One smiles at him. And the other assesses the smile, wondering how it must look to Henry. One waves. And the other coaches herself to wave less energetically. She wants to run across the room and press against him, but he takes his time, still patiently holding the door as two men pass through. They're familiar. She stiffens.

It's only when the three of them—Henry and the men from the van—draw near that she understands he is with them. Without the beards, their clean-shaven faces are young and soft. They are younger, she sees now, than she is. Her toes clench in her high-tops.

"Remember this asshole?" Henry claps the taller man on his back. "Almost ran us off the road?" He slides in beside Anna, who beams at him, as one man pulls a chair up from a nearby table.

"My bad." He grins, dropping into the chair.

Měi is dumbstruck.

"We're so sorry," the smaller man says. He hovers, sheepish, over the booth. Extends a smooth, uncalloused hand, which she shakes limply. "We were sort of zoned out."

"Not to say we'd spent the month camping, on shrooms, or anything." His friend bleats a laugh. "Not to say we're still not quite right. I'm Hog. That excuse for a man is Jake. We didn't mean to scare you or your niece. We thought we heard reggae. We were trying to listen to your radio."

"Like, through the window," Jake adds with a breathy, skittish giggle. "We were really high."

Hog clears his throat with a porcine grunt. "We're headed to Syracuse, too. We're business majors. Met your man here in the bar. Cold feet's a bitch. Oh! Excuse me." He winces in Anna's direction, but she only smiles blandly back, stirring her float.

"She doesn't know English," Henry says.

"Oh. Good." Hog grunts again. Stares at Měi. "You weren't lying. She's even prettier than you said. Hurry up and put a ring on it, huh, if she'll still have you?" A quick, conspiratorial wink at Měi.

She glances at Henry, who shrugs mildly. "That's what she keeps telling me," he says, reaching across the table to take her hand. "And you're right, Honey Bunches. I've been a fool." Her lips twist tight. Is he enjoying this charade? "I got cold feet last night, with the stress of wedding planning and our families flying in. Can you forgive me?"

The little bell on the door dings as a family enters, the restaurant's volume rising around them, the balding host scurrying now. Hog stands. "You two have lots to talk about. We'll snag our own spot before there's none left. Right, Jake? And hopefully there's wireless here. This dumbass still hasn't registered for fall classes."

"Guilty as charged."

"Yeah, they're *gonna* charge the shit out of your ass, in late fees." Hog smacks his buddy's arm; turns back to Měi. "Cut him a break, miss—okay? Guys are stupid. But he really loves you. I can tell." Backing away, he drags the chair back to its original table. "You got our numbers, Henry. Hit us up! We expect an invitation to the wedding."

Henry raises a hand. "You got it." A languid smile.

"It was nice to meet you," the smaller man says. He follows his friend.

Henry slides Měi's mug toward him, bending to sip.

"First you puke in my car," she says softly, Hog and Jake out of earshot. "Then you leave in the middle of the night. Then you make up some whopper to talk innocent strangers into giving you a free ride. And now you drink my float?"

He stares up through his impossible lashes. "You were letting it melt."

"So, when is our wedding again?"

"Next Sunday. We're on our way to Syracuse now, to prepare. You know—make sure they string the lights up in the barn."

"It's a barn wedding?"

He lifts his hands, palms up, in a shrug. "I thought that was what you wanted . . ."

"What I want is to get to Farmstead Acres in Syracuse by two P.M. tomorrow, before Jimmy Xīn turns into a pumpkin again."

His eyes go serious. "That's where the ice cream truck will be parked?"

"Alternator," Ramon says. Subtly, he eyeballs Henry.

"So, what's that"—she asks—"four hundred bucks or so for parts and labor? An hour to change it out?"

He returns his gaze to hers. "Took the words out of my mouth."

"My granddad's a mechanic. Knows his way around cars, go-karts, you name it."

"Hunh." He hands her a clipboard and pen. "I'll have the part in by tomorrow. But as I said, I'm overdue at home already. Sign here, if that's okay." She scrawls her name, hands the clipboard back. "Your vehicle's got the cleanest undercarriage I've seen. Not a spot of rust."

"California," she says, and he nods.

"If I was you, I'd be itching to get back. We'll have you on the road by eleven. Probably earlier, but let's say eleven to be safe." A shaggy blond mechanic appears behind him, gives a wave, hand covered in grease— taking in Henry, Měi, and Anna, who's counting the gumballs in a machine by the door—and disappears again.

"Need a ride someplace nearby?" Ramon smiles a wide smile, his durable coveralls sparking a memory of Lǎoyé at the go-kart track, work uniform zipped over his street clothes.

It's hard for her to envision Lǎoyé in anything but coveralls or paja- mas with a robe. He'd looked so unnatural in the black suit he wore to Lǎolao's funeral that she had a hard time envisioning him as the ladies' man he swore he was before he met her. He wore the same suit when Daddy died.

Henry pipes up, "Know a nice place to stay?" Anna's tugging at his pocket. He shoves his hand in, producing a few quarters, and she skips back to the gumball machine.

For a moment the mechanic is quiet, as though trying to gauge what Henry means by "nice." They listen to the sounds of Anna turning the metal crank and the gumball rolling down the chute to clank against the little metal door, which she lifts quickly, claiming her prize. *In a world of rampant inflation,* Měi thinks, *at least fifty cents still buys this.*

"Nice little bed-and-breakfast down the road," Ramon says, watch- ing as the girl studies her red gumball in delight. He chews at the inside of his cheek. "C'mon. Let's get your luggage into my truck. It's on my way."

❧

The dirt road cuts straight uphill, through dense trees. *Nope,* she thinks, *this cannot be on anyone's way.*

But then the pickup turns onto a meandering paved drive. CORFU HILLS MANOR B&B reads a quilt hung from a white gazebo. "So the wilderness isn't that much wilder here," Měi says, thinking of California.

"What?" Henry says from the back seat.

They hop out at a stone path that bisects a manicured lawn dotted with Adirondack chairs. While Henry deposits their bags on the flagstone, Ramon unrolls the driver's-side window, addressing Měi. "My guy can pick you up here tomorrow, okay? We'll call first." With that, he's off.

"Zhè shì shéi de fángzi?" The girl eyes the enormous, shingled Victorian with its cross-gambrel roof and windowed turret.

"Zhè shì yījiā lǚguǎn," Henry says, "just a hotel." The girl's eyes widen. She skips toward the door.

"We are staying in one room," Měi says, "from now on. So I can keep an eye on you."

"So I can keep an eye on *you*," Henry echoes.

A figurine of Mrs. Claus has come to life and is seated at a small desk in the foyer. She sets down her romance novel. "Welcome!"

"Thanks." Henry whips his wallet out. "We'd like a room for the night, if you've got one."

"Just one?" She eyes him over half-rim reading glasses.

"We're engaged," he says, shuffling his feet.

"No. I mean, just the one night?"

He bites his lip. "Yes, ma'am."

"Well, you're in luck. We had a cancellation. The sun porch suite is separate from the main house. It's got its very own entry and two spacious bedrooms with private baths. One has a walk-in shower. You two can fight with this young lady for it!" She winks at Anna, who blinks. Fishing around in a drawer, she produces a blank form and ballpoint pen.

Henry hands his credit card and license over as Měi and Anna linger nearby, drumming their fingers in offbeat harmony on a round, ornamental side table.

Mrs. Claus disappears into another room. Returns holding a menu. "We'll bring breakfast straight to your furnished porch."

"What time?"

"Up to you." She straightens her glasses on her nose. "Just ring down anytime after six A.M. with your order. And there's coffee right here in the lobby, at all hours." She's wearing a ruffled gingham blouse, a corduroy skirt—just as Santa's wife would, Měi thinks, in the summertime—and the "lobby" is simply the home's wide foyer, all hardwood floors, crystal sconces, and ornate mirrors. Hands down, the East Coast beats the West Coast for quaint charm. "Would you like me to walk you to your suite?"

Henry lays the pen on top of his completed form. "Thanks. No. We'll manage."

Her twinkle is undiminished. She returns his license and credit card, along with the menu and two long metal keys. "In case you haven't made dinner plans yet, there are more menus in the room. The best pizza in town is about a mile away, and they deliver till ten."

"Thank you," Měi says. She takes a large metal key from Henry and guides Anna back outside.

Crossing the grounds to the sun porch suite, they pass a firepit. Heavy ceramic planters overflow with bronze cannas, yellow tickseed, and lavender. Sunlight gilds the grass. Henry squints into the sky. "Did the sun creep closer or something?" he says. "I feel like it's sitting on our heads."

"We're at a higher elevation."

Anna drops into an Adirondack chair, peering at the firepit. "S'mores," she says. Of course, she knows this word. All children must know this word. Měi thinks of how Daddy once made her s'mores right there in the living room, with chopsticks for marshmallow spears and a candle for a roaring fire. Daddy would've loved this place.

"What?" Henry says. "Higher than the Bay Area? That doesn't sound right."

"Well, it is." Měi moves on ahead of them.

"Wait up," he calls out, but she's nearly at the door. She lets herself in, shuts it behind her. Inside, motes of dust lift and drop on some soft current that circulates from nowhere—gleaming in bright rays that pass through sheer curtains. She closes her eyes. Presses cool fingertips to her eyelids. Sees Daddy, charring a s'more in the candle flame.

Once, just once, she visited a free grief support group that met in the basement of an Oakland church.

She'd gotten the address from a café flyer and arrived to find there was no licensed counselor. The session was led by a late-night A.M. radio host. Nor was there anonymity. They welcomed her into their circle of metal chairs, trading surnames that were forgettably similar, as though pieced together with limited parts on a factory assembly line: Yoder, Schroeder, Kreuger, Croyle, Doyle. There was even an exact match for her name—another Brown.

She feels, suddenly, as numb as she felt in that basement.

"I'm having trouble," she'd said to the radio host and the circle of nodding heads, "with trusting happiness. Like, anytime things go well, I get scared."

"Happiness is untrustworthy," someone said.

"Your father didn't leave you," someone else cooed. "He just left the pain."

She drops her overnight bag in the suite's living room, on a floral-patterned chair with rolled crescent arms. Goes to the window. Parts the sheers. On the lawn, Henry and Anna are playing cornhole, the girl tossing the beanbags wildly, missing by a mile. Cornbags, not beanbags, she corrects herself, remembering the day she'd learned that the little red and blue bags Lǎoyé handed out at the go-kart track were actually filled with kernels.

He'd taken a long break to play the game with her, as though they were customers.

"They still need better name for the game, though," he'd chortled. "'Cornhole' sound like you talking about your pìgu." Covering her mouth, she'd cracked up, too, with a glance back at the yellowing island of grass where a family waited their turn. You didn't need to be fluent in Mandarin to understand what Lǎoyé meant.

Nearby in the wilted grass, the pimply attendant had shaken his head. "You're not supposed to smoke out here," he bellowed halfheartedly, "or bring your grandkid to work." By now, he considered Lǎoyé a lost cause.

Outside, white sun drizzles the radiant treetops. She watches Henry laugh, mouth wide, his shine desaturating everything else till he's the only thing that stands out. As he moves behind the girl, guiding her form, careful not to crowd her, Měi fights an urge to join them. She thinks of her own mother watching her through the window as she ran out back to knock on Lǎoyé's door.

Though Mama hated the converted garage, sometimes she'd accompany them to the go-kart track, sitting on a shaded bench underneath an awning. Yet she never joined in. "Lái lái lái," Lǎoyé would beckon, and Mama would shake her head.

Wrangling her phone from her pocket, she dials, strolling into a bedroom. The line rings for a long time. So long, she lifts her finger to hang up. Then Mama answers. "Wéi?"

"Mama," she says, "it's me."

"Ah, Xiǎo Bǎo, nǐ zěnmeyàng?"

"I'm fine." She looks around as though this proper room will offer up something to say, but the damask wallpaper and mahogany rolltop desk remain silent.

"You sure? Don't need me to pick you up? No cops poop in your car?"

"I'm really fine. I'm at a bed-and-breakfast."

"What? You sleeping with that Henry your lǎoyé tell me about?"

Irritation grips her, and that unique brand of indignation one can only muster for a parent. "Of course not!"

"Good. Your grandpa think you are."

She waits for her annoyance to subside. "Remember," she says, strolling into one of the bedrooms, "when Lǎoyé took us to the go-kart track?"

"Which time? Time you run car into big stack of tires?"

"That was my first time driving."

"Yah. That time?"

"No. Any other time. I'm just wondering—why didn't you ever race us? Or at least play some cornhole?"

A pause. Mama inhaling, exhaling. "Stupid game."

"Jenga's a stupid game, and you love it."

"Okay, Měi. I tell you." She sighs, the telling clearly a taxing chore. "Because impossible to drive holding my breath."

"Holding your breath? What do you mean?" She lays a hand on the antique bed's carved finial.

"I hold my breath whole time. Too scary. Your kart go so fast around those sharp turn." And now, the metal scrape of the key: Henry and Anna. She ducks into the en suite, shuts the door behind her. Locks it. "I only make one of you," Mama says. "Don't got a spare."

"Okay." She breathes into the phone. This is not what she'd expected. She has never known her mother to express fear.

"Okay?" Mama echoes.

"Okay," she says again. "Hǎo de—"

She hangs up. Oddly self-conscious about the call, she flushes the toilet and runs the sink before emerging.

In the orderly parlor, Anna's pulling the sheers wide, letting the day in. Měi grabs her bag from the floral chair, plopping down with it on a pink settee against the far wall. She rubs her finger over a threadbare spot on the settee's rolled arm. "Who won?"

"She did," Henry says, emerging from the other bedroom. "She crushed it." He wrinkles his nose.

She fiddles with the overnight bag's zipper as, moving to the settee, he sits next to her. When she doesn't speak, he grabs her wrist. His fingers rub at the soft skin there, as though checking for a pulse. "Something wrong? Why didn't you join us?"

"Nothing's wrong." She doesn't slide her fingers through his, but she doesn't pull her wrist away, either. "I just can't throw," she says, "holding my breath." He gives her a quizzical look.

In the evening, they select a menu and pass it between them, circling the items they want.

"Yìdàlì miàn," the girl tells Henry, who circles spaghetti. "No"—she pauses—"meatball? Not halal." He nods. "Coca-Cola!" His eyes catch Měi's, unsure, and she shrugs. With a crooked smile, he circles that, too. Now the girl is practically levitating with satisfaction. She points at the

TV. "Wǒmen kěyǐ kàn diànshì ma?" Henry nods, switching the screen on with the remote before relinquishing it to Anna's extended hand. For a moment, she stares at the buttons. Then she channel-surfs like a pro, settling on *Catfish*.

"Hey." The lower notes of his voice are like a warm, firm touch. His head dips toward Měi's. "Can we talk?" She nods. "In there?" He points to the bedroom he's claimed.

"No," she says, pointing to the other room. "In there."

"Got it. Home turf."

"No," she lies. "I just want to check out the rolltop desk."

"After you." Rising a little too quickly, they walk together toward the bedroom, eyes on the girl, who never moves her gaze from the screen. He closes the door softly behind them, then seems suddenly at a loss. He inspects the heavy bed while she fiddles with the desk, opening and closing its drawers. When he checks out the chiffonier—turning away and bending to examine its paneled door, its tiny key—she takes in the way his worn gray T-shirt clings to the muscles of his back. "Sorry again," he says, not looking at her, tracing an index finger along the foliage decorating the chiffonier's upstand, "for leaving." She waits for him to turn toward her, but he doesn't. The broad span of his shoulders is a curved and untouchable horizon.

"What?" she says.

He turns sharply, the corners of his mouth tugged down, rising to his full height. "I said I'm sorry. I kinda freaked out. Wha'd you guys do after I left?"

"We packed up," she says, "and got back on the road."

A grin. "Well, I kinda figured that much." He moves to sit on the imposing bed. "Scared the bejeezus out of me. And I—missed you guys."

She purses her lips. Averts her eyes. "Did you know older beds were built to stand higher, to separate the sleeper from cold, drafty floors?"

His face crumples a bit, before he smooths it back into a smile. "Hey," he says, his voice slightly too high, "I'm not the bad guy here. And. Uh, I heard from my gān mā."

With slow steps, she traverses the geometric blooms of a faded yet opulent rug. The bed is tall, but not very wide.

Gān mā is a term she knows, because she has one, too: Gān Mā Lily, her godmother, still lives in Texas, attends the same YMCA swim glass she'd once convinced Mama to sign up for.

"Mā is mother, of course," Mama had explained. "Gān mean dry. We call your godmother gān mā because she just my friend. Didn't push you out from all that fluid!"

Měi's nose wrinkles.

"They took my mom," Henry is saying, "but only for a day, to interrogate her. Mom wasn't, like"—a strange, high laugh—"working in a cotton field." Their eyes lock. "You've heard of that, right?" She shakes her head. Sits beside him on the bed. "It's like all the evil regimes go by the same oppression playbook. *Take their books. Change their names. Make them pick cotton.* They've got forced laborers out in Xinjiang's fields. And in the factory, more detainees to spin the cotton into exports." He points at her high-tops.

She raises her hands in the air. Bends forward and unlaces her shoes, kicking them off. "So did they ask your mom about Anna?"

"Yup." He stands slowly, giving her the bed. "But that's not unusual. They're talking to everyone Jimmy's friends with on social media. And Mom's good at playing dumb." Měi nods. Henry is looking at her as though he might bend toward her, lift her into an embrace. Instead, he runs a hand through his hair. They trade a smile that unknots something inside her. "Look, I'ma let you settle in. Get your rest before we're back on the road." He backs toward the door and she stops herself from stopping him. "Sorry again," he says.

10

SYRACUSE TO CUYAHOGA VALLEY

Farmstead Acres is nothing like what she'd imagined: no dairy barn, no grapevines. Instead, a suburban development just outside downtown Syracuse where she must slow to five miles per hour.

"That's tape," Henry says.

"What?"

"The speed limit sign we just passed: someone altered the numbers with tape." He twists in the passenger seat, squinting back at the sign. "Must not want folks speeding through here, plowing down their kids."

"Help me look," she says, navigating rows of near-identical houses that make her think of Monopoly. On either side of the fresh black asphalt, sprinklers water plush green lawns—and in one driveway, a man in golf shorts is hosing off his motorboat. Looking up, he raises a hand. Měi waves back. "Can you imagine," she hisses, "wasting all that water?"

"Hey, maybe he's trying to grow that dinghy into a yacht. But I hear you. I grew up in Cali, too. I still take combat showers. Even when there's no drought."

"When is there no drought? My shower game is on point: two minutes and I'm out." She holds out a fist for some dap, but Henry's distracted, pointing.

"Follow those stroller moms."

She turns right on Loganberry Lane. Up ahead, a brigade of

skateboards and bikes, Rollerblades and sneakers and sandals moves en masse toward a parked food truck. "Is that it?"

"I mean, it's blue," Henry says.

"I can't read the side of the truck." She slows the sedan to a crawl. "Where do we park?"

"Anywhere, I think? Don't ask me! I live in a high-rise condo."

She pulls over between a mailbox and a suburban streetlight designed to resemble an antique gas lamp. "You own a condo on the street I picked you up from? That luxury building in the Mission?" He shrugs. "It's like *Crazy Rich Asians* up in here."

The engine is still running when Anna hops out. "Wait," they call, but she scampers across a driveway. Beelines for the blue truck.

Henry unbuckles his seat belt. "So much for our breakfast discussion of sticking together."

Měi's lost sight of Anna's white shirt in the crowd. "Fuck," she says, slamming the car door behind her, taking off after the girl.

"We shoulda put her in chartreuse, right?" Henry sprints to catch up.

She doesn't reply—there's too much noise. Beyond the idyllic row of houses, a bulldozer breaks ground on an empty lot, and down the block are more construction sounds: trucks beeping, backing up. The clank of metal. Shouts of workers. And all these mundane conversations.

Měi pushes her way past two teens in *Thrasher* gear. Snorts involuntarily. Do they even know how to ollie? With a pang, she recalls her father reading at the skate park under the bridge, on a bench just inside the chain-link fence. It was ridiculous that he insisted on watching, yet she saved her best tricks for when he glanced up from his newspaper. And once, when her middle school friend Laura fell, Daddy ran to them. Lifting Laura's eleven-year-old body like an infant's, he carried her to the bench where he rocked her gently—a modern pietà—smoothing her sweat-tangled hair till she stopped crying. Though Měi herself never took a bad spill in front of him, his heroism had swelled her chest.

She scans the crowd for Jimmy Xīn. Wonders again what will happen if he doesn't show. Up ahead, Anna weaves through the clustered families, earning curious stares—and Měi notes that the entire throng is white.

This is the truth in the model minority myth: the mathematics every Asian American excels at. The risk-assessment practice of counting other people of color in a crowd. She's flung back to the playground, Chris Pringle's spit in her face, *Chink! Chink! Chink!* Funny, she thinks, how many lessons her elementary education taught her. Truths never fully imparted to Mindy, to Maanika, to Una, to Gabriel, who still haven't quite grasped what kind of country it is that they live in. While they understand that it is wrong to put your fingers at the corners of your eyes and pull, shouting "Chink! Chink! Chink!" they've developed no recognition of racism's subtler, narrowed gaze. It is possible that they never will.

"There!" Henry's close behind her now.

"I see her," Měi says. "Up ahead."

"No. Look!" From behind, he grabs her shoulder; spins her gently. "Across the street."

Prying her eyes off the girl, she looks. In a parked SUV, a man in glasses and a snapback is staring straight at them. It takes her a moment to place him as the person in those tiny author photos: Anna's father, Jimmy Xīn.

Henry takes off toward the vehicle.

"Anna," she calls out to the black hair, the white shirt, pivoting left and right in the crowd. "Anna! Nǐ bàba láile!"

In moments, the girl is by her side.

"Zài nǎlǐ?"

Měi takes her hand.

It's strange to be the passenger for once. As they exit Farmstead Acres, Jimmy Xīn driving quickly, familiar with these roads, she alternates between studying Henry's features from the back seat and watching the scenery. She sees what he meant about the region overflowing with water: swamps and bogs, rivers and ponds. The greenery's so vibrant she can almost catch it growing, flowers stretching sunward, vines reclaiming dilapidated wooden structures—dragging the husks of sheds and barns back down into the soil.

Mandarin words fly around her, her consciousness seizing at comprehension now and again: Dr. Xīn misses Anna's mother too? Or does he . . . smell her? He wants to know if the girl's reached four foot two? Or eaten four birthday cakes? "Tā wèn wǒ . . ." Henry says, and Měi's unsure of whether he's describing a kiss or a question.

She gives up. Leans her head against the coolness of the window. Thinks of the petite woman handcuffed to a bed frame, in the video on Henry's phone.

Jimmy Xīn shares his daughter's silken skin and soulful eyes, but Anna's diminutive form is inherited directly from her mother. Jimmy's chubby, broad-shouldered. She guesses he is medium height. But he did not emerge from the vehicle, even to hug his daughter, so she can't say for certain. She wonders if the hugs will come later as he turns his head to ask Anna something, the girl leaning forward from the back seat— tussling with the seat belt to be closer to him as they speak.

Surely Jimmy Xīn has the video on his phone, too. Does he watch it every night? Every morning? Does it give him hope? Or make him cry?

The SUV is slowing now, cruising through downtown Syracuse. She'd expected some isolated safehouse with peeling paint and boarded windows, but they park in front of a bar with outdoor seating and a logo on its sign that reminds her of the Olympic rings. Let history continue to record our contradictions, she thinks, stepping out onto the high curb: that the U.S. joined a diplomatic boycott of the Beijing Winter Olympics in acknowledgment of the Uyghur genocide, even while we sent athletes to compete in the games, TV crews to record them, money to sponsor them. That we banned imports from Xinjiang, yet China remains our number one trade partner.

She blinks as Dr. Xīn slams the driver's door. "Welcome to my humble abode," he says, an arm around Anna as he leads them through an entryway next to the bar. They pass into a narrow vestibule with a cluster of tenants' mailboxes, the door gusting shut behind them, and Jimmy scoops Anna into his arms, kissing her cheeks again and again. This is the sort of father, Měi thinks, a child absolutely cannot lose. Not without internal combustion. But then, in some sense, aren't they all—even the worst of them? They head up a flight of stairs.

Inside the loft, she stares up at a vast cathedral ceiling—white paint between dark, distant beams. Though the long, ratty brown couch and stale air remind her of Lǎoyé's converted garage, the interior here is all wood floors and pricey, exposed brick. Heavy curtains drape a wall of windows. She holds out a hand to the glossy black cat that slinks toward her. Scritches its head as it purrs, sticking a paw out to knead the air. Immediately, Anna slides into place to take over petting the cat's soft fur.

The adults move to the granite counter.

"Pour you something?" In the refrigerator is a curated selection of local craft beers.

"Sure," Henry says, peering in. "What you got?"

"This is a friend's place. He's out of town, and I don't drink, so I'm really not sure. Help yourselves." His smile, like the apartment, is comfortable. Warm. He stretches to pull a glass from a high cabinet, pours tap water from the faucet as Henry bends into the fridge.

She goes to his side. "Peanut butter porter," she says, and he raises an eyebrow. "What? I like my beer thick. I wanna chew it."

Jimmy Xīn sets a bowl of fruit before Anna, silently taking in her sunken cheeks, then rummages in a disorganized drawer, locating a bottle opener. He cracks Měi's porter and Henry's nondescript lager, and they move back to the counter to sit on barstools.

"Cheers," Jimmy says, lifting a blunt finger to shove his glasses firmly into place on his nose. They clink and sip.

As the men chat in Mandarin and Anna tries to get the cat to eat a grape, Měi stares around. There's a bong half-hidden behind a stack of books. This place must belong to another Syracuse professor, she thinks.

Outside, the city goes on with its business. She remembers reading that Syracuse is New York's fifth-largest metropolitan area and thinks about civil inattention, how much easier it is to hide in an environment where ignoring one another is a form of politeness, of granting privacy in public.

Nearby is Armory Square, Syracuse's nightlife hub, with its restaurants and bars. And the Museum of Science and Technology. And Clinton Square fountain, an enormous water feature honoring the Erie Canal. As they passed by the fountain, she'd caught sight of families wading barefoot in the summer heat despite city officials' printed admonishments. These families would return in the winter, with the city's blessing to ice skate.

Jimmy's loft, she thinks, is just a block or two from the ornate, red and gold Landmark Theatre. Maybe also near Onondaga Creekwalk? *My people invented feng shui, yet I've got a crappy sense of direction.*

Her mind drifts out into the afternoon heat, back to the highway, the suburbs. Corfu, Elyria, Rock Island. Elko, York, Tahoe.

Home. Is Lǎoyé sleeping, now, in his darkened garage—sunlight pushing through the murky window? Or up playing *Grand Larceny MMMCMXCIX: The Burglar's Ballad,* or whatever the final title in the series may be?

Suddenly, the word "final" amid thoughts of her grandfather is terrifying. How is it that her estrangement from Mama has kept her from visiting him in a year? Eighty-six isn't necessarily old, not for a Chinese grandpa, but it isn't young, either. He could have twenty more years, or two. She rises from the stool, shaking her head. Chinese *American* grandpa, she corrects herself, as this country is important to Lǎoyé despite his griping (perhaps, in fact, its importance to him is the very reason he gripes).

"Could you point me toward your . . ."

"Over there." Jimmy points to a curtain near the book stack.

She parts the heavy fabric to find a tiny hallway leading to a bathroom that reeks of ammonia. Shutting the scuffed-up door behind her, she tries to ignore the overflowing litter box, banishing thoughts of bacterial infections, roundworms. Toxoplasmosis. She relieves herself quickly, unsteadily, pushing away a persistent memory of squatting in Tilden Park. Returning to the kitchen, drying her hands on her jeans, she pulls the barstool back out and climbs on.

The men continue to speak rapidly in Mandarin. She examines the polished concrete countertop, half listening for words she recognizes, then drifts back home again, to her childhood, when Lǎolao's smile was an invitation to pull a chair up to the mahjong table. Back then, Lǎolao's friends spoke so quickly that their words were a song's melody, one taking the lead as the others accompanied.

But things changed after the first stroke, which landed her grand-mother in a facility where—with the help of a physician, a neuro-psychologist, a rehab nurse, and a rotating cast of speech-language therapists—she'd struggled to form even one sentence. Then the second stroke had hit, leaving Lǎolao utterly trapped in the confounding disar-ray of her own mind. When they visited, Měi watched, horrified, as the old woman grasped at words just out of reach. "It's lucky you were here and not at home this time, Mrs. Lǎolao," said the kind new attendant who didn't realize this was not her name. "It's very lucky you were right here with us." Beaming affectionately at Lǎolao, he'd patted her leg.

Lǎolao means maternal grandmother, she waited for her father to correct him. But Daddy stayed quiet.

Unexpectedly, Lǎolao died there, on a night when Lǎoyé had returned home to catch a few hours' sleep. "How this happen?" he cried when her parents woke him, Měi pressing her six-year-old body into a shadowed corner of the room.

"Dysphagia," her father said.

"She choke to death," Mama clarified. "On candy you sneak in for her."

Years later, when Měi asked Lǎoyé whether it was guilt that had pushed him out into the garage, he guffawed. "Your lǎolao rather die with sugar in her mouth than live a day without it." He cleared his throat, voice dropping low. "They lie when they say she lucky to be there. She rather be at home with me. Also lie when they say she not talk no more."

"You mean the expressive aphasia?" Měi was proud of having learned this terminology.

"Yah, that. Not talk? Psht." His veined hand swatted the air. "Some-times the stroke put words in her mouth instead. She cuss me out all the time when they leave us alone. Call me a bastard, an idiot, a real

húndàn. You believe it?" He coughed quietly, the muted hack of an experienced smoker. "Your sweet lǎolao never say a mean word before in her
life!" His cataract-clouded gaze left hers, drifting out someplace beyond.
"Worst thing, this condition contagious. I open my mouth to say 'You
don't mean that,' to say 'It okay, don't worry, I love you,' and insults fly
out like startled birds."

So maybe, Mĕi thought, it had been the guilt.

Whatever the case, she'd loved his garage hideaway, where she had
him all to herself.

At the counter, Jimmy Xīn gestures emphatically. But a lifetime of
practice with her family has taught her not to get too curious. If she needs
to know something, it'll get translated. She sips her porter, drawing the
cold and bitter sweetness through her teeth, swirling it on her tongue.
Replays the lively harmonies of Lǎolao's conversations over the mahjong
tiles' clicking percussion. It is the memory of her grandmother's marvel-
ous voice, the voices of Lǎolao's friends, that helps her understand why
regulative worship eschews musical accompaniment—deeming human
vocalization the best instrument of praise.

"I'm sorry," Jimmy says suddenly. "I've been so rude! Henry just let
me know you're not fluent in Mandarin."

Henry's hand, chilled by the bottle of lager, lands lightly on her
wrist. "I guess that makes me the rude one, since he really had no way
of knowing . . ."

"It's fine," she says to them both. "Really."

"Let's do this right." Jimmy sits up straighter on his stool. "It's a pleasure to meet you. My name is Ehmetjan, but Jimmy's fine, and I cannot
thank you enough"—his smile strained with gratitude—"for helping my
daughter find me."

"She figured it out herself," Mĕi says. "I'm just the driver."

"Still, Mr. Lee tells me you didn't exactly sign up for this."

"Really, it's fine." She shakes her head. "He hired me as a driver. So
I drove."

"I'm far from the sketchiest client she's taken on." Henry lifts his beer
in a salute.

"Is that so?" Jimmy smiles.

Měi nods. "Or the smelliest. I once drove a guy with a big box that absolutely reeked"—she thinks of the bathroom litter box—"from Kentucky to LA. The recipient opened it immediately, right outside the car. Turned out to be a sloth." She swivels back and forth on the stool.

"Aw, sweet! Sloths," Henry says, "are freakin' adorable."

"Yeah, well. That's one job I regret. And not just because the odor stank up my car for a month. But sloths really shouldn't live inside. And it was just a baby, so you've got to wonder what they did with its mom." Watching Jimmy's eyes darken, she immediately wishes she could suck the words back into her mouth and swallow them. "I'm sorry," she says quietly.

"It's okay. I got a video from Aynur yesterday. She's surviving," he says. "For now." He nods slowly. "I don't know how she's charging her phone. Who she bribes. Or with what." His voice catches. "The women in the camps say the men use electric sticks to—" He scratches at his salt-and-pepper stubbled jaw, blinking rapidly at Anna, as the cat leaps deftly up on the counter. "This is Li'l Bit," he says, and Měi extends a hand, but before her fingertips reach the cat's lustrous fur, Anna materializes at her side to scoop the animal up and return it to the couch, kissing the top of its purring head. "It's been confounding. Before you found me, I nearly gave in to the threats."

"Threats?" She sips, wiping her lower lip with the side of her hand.

"Nearly every day since I went dark. Someone even sent a photo of me teaching on campus. Shot through the classroom window. But mostly, I receive warnings that my wife, Aynur, will only be released once I return to China and 'cease my activities.'" His air quotes wilt and he wraps his hands around the water glass. "You know, we renamed Anna after Aynur. And the messages are threatening her, too, now, saying I'll never see my daughter again."

"Well, that's clearly wrong." She glances at the girl, who's curled around Li'l Bit, glowing.

"Which means you did well." A gracious smile. "They don't know she's here. We are safe."

Měi wants to ask, but does not, about the paperwork: who got the girl to America, and how. She thinks of her left-behind aunties, then of Ānmíng Āyí and Měilì Āyí in San José.

"He's writing a book," Henry says. "A big book, on the atrocities."

"Well, I was." Jimmy turns the waterglass in his hand, back and forth, back and forth. "I take breaks. It can be intimidating." She thinks of the Nguyen twins, the blank screen, and the secret she kept. "Did you know our own president's son invests in the technology used to surveil my people?"

"Hm." She fidgets with her sweating bottle. Picks at the label's gluey corner.

"The last message threatened to release a red notice against me. Through Interpol." Now he relinquishes the glass. Rubs his hands together as though warming them before a fire. "It's rampant, this kind of thing. And not uniquely Chinese. Did you hear about Iran's foiled plot to kidnap a journalist in Brooklyn?"

Měi frowns. Thinks of Lǎoyé. "Maybe those countries are learning from us. The People's War on Terror sounds a lot like our War on Terror. Also known as Open Season on Muslims?"

"Yes," he agrees, "sure. But at least freedom of religion is still protected by the laws we uphold. Did you know that nearly thirty countries are complicit in helping Beijing intimidate and deport my people? Because they're scared of China's power?" He massages his forehead with a fist. "As a Muslim, I remain grateful to America's Jewish population."

She hides her surprise. "How so?"

"They keep stories of the Holocaust alive. So America cannot justify deporting refugees. Cannot forget the horrors of fascist regimes." Měi blinks slowly. Recalls the IBM Hollerith machines that Henry described. And she's back in the carpeted high school computer lab again, Mr. Murphy prattling on, from his pleather armchair, about how it's not enough to tell the truth once: we must keep on telling it. When she opens her eyes, Jimmy Xīn is smiling grimly. "Besides, it's not Judaism or any religion that creates conflict. It's people. How we interpret religion. Whom we listen to. Even we Muslims tend to forget—the other side is also part of the Ummah."

"Ummah?"

He nods. "A word we think of as meaning 'Muslim' now. But Muhammad used it to refer to all monotheistic people: Christians. Muslims. Jews." His tone is bewildered. "Strange, isn't it? To think Muhammad negotiated the Constitution of Medina to try and forge bonds between all the same groups that are at war today?"

Without thinking, Měi stands. Puts her arm around the shoulder of this kind, frustrated man. "People can screw anything up." Are Muslim men allowed to touch women outside of their families, she wonders too late, and yanks her hand back quickly—but just like that, Jimmy is up on his feet, too.

"Thank you," he says, enfolding her in a hug, his chest heaving, "for bringing my daughter to me."

∽

Jimmy deposits them at Farmstead Acres. The crowd's dispersed with the food truck's departure, Měi's car lonely on the emptied street. Anna, too, looks desolate as she waves furiously at the departing SUV. She scratches at the ragged dent in her hairline. Drops her hands to her lap. Bites her lip. But Jimmy's made it clear that the little loft is only a temporary harbor.

"I applied for an early sabbatical," he explained as he drove them here. "My chair and dean understand the situation. They'll be quick and discreet."

So, Anna will return to California with them—Jimmy on their heels as soon as his request is approved. A happy ending. As the SUV turns off Loganberry Lane, disappearing behind the massive shape of a cookie-cutter Colonial, they walk slowly to the sedan.

Back in the familiar confines of her car, she knows she should be relieved. The return trip always feels faster. And this time it actually will be, Anna buckling herself into the back seat like any kid, the dreadful suitcase stashed in the trunk. This time, they'll skip all those long, secretive stops that had allowed the girl to stretch, eat, relieve herself.

Checking the rearview, Měi envisions her finger hovering above a Rewind button. Once pressed, it'll set her free. Free to return to the Lower Haight, where the congregation of First Baptist rattles her bedroom floor with their praise. Free to hit Chances for a drink or two or three with Mindy, then weave down the block to Second Chances. Free to investigate, gently, Mama's unflappable refusal to grieve. And to devise acerbic answers to the inevitable questions about when Měi will return to Dartmouth. She starts the car. Presses Rewind. Throws their journey into reverse.

In college, she'd taken journalism and somehow secured an off-campus internship—growing increasingly despondent over how poorly prepared she was, how misguided Murphy's disjointed assortment of lectures had been. She'd have been better-equipped had he simply leaned back in the pilfered pleather armchair at the start of every club meeting, letting Mindy and Matt handle the lectures. It turned out journalism was not *Just the Facts* and (Murphy's nostalgia notwithstanding) never had been. Journalism was elusive and problematic. It was numeracy, and a code of ethics. It was understanding the whole world in order to tell a small, specific story—and doing so despite a lack of time, resources, and public trust. A lack, oftentimes, of collaboration.

And this was the most disheartening thing—despite Murphy's ineptitude, her high school journalism club had been more collaborative, by far, than the newsroom in which she'd interned, where she would've been laughed out of the room for asking *Who cares which outlet breaks the story first? If it's important, shouldn't we all shine a light on it?*

Was the decline of journalistic ethics an inevitable result of capitalism? Or of the same apathy that greeted her as she waited for the cavalry to appear and save the Nguyen twins—for someone, anyone, even herself, to do the right thing? She isn't sure. But she's certain of this much: the thought of returning to Dartmouth, to her internship and classes, her twin bed at the vegan house (where Lǎolao's hand-stitched bedspread clashed with Maanika's bohemian tapestries and the colorful, tapered candles Una stuck in emptied beer bottles; where her window overlooked a sprawling quad diced up by footpaths and whizzing Frisbees), fills her with panic.

This is why rewinding the road trip affords no relief. It can be tiring, after all, taking one step forward, one step back. Getting nowhere. She wants to move beyond her self-imposed purgatory, like Jimmy Xīn. But toward what? She has no daughter to protect. No spouse to worry about. In the rearview she meets the girl's smiling eyes, and the smile is like a bracing, cleansing wind.

The direct route she's plotted will take them straight to Elkhart, Indiana, skipping Corfu and Elyria. From there, to Omaha, Nebraska; Rawlins, Wyoming; Elko, Nevada; then on to Oakland. Long, efficient days of driving, stopping only for bio-breaks. She accelerates onto the highway. Shifts in the driver's seat, clutching the wheel too tightly till she notices and relaxes her grip.

The shark-gray pavement drifts before her under low clouds shaped like waves. She waits to feel the rush of being in motion again. Street sign, street sign, street sign. Overpass, overpass, overpass. Hour one passes and her body is still tense. Speed trap, speed trap, speed trap. Hour two. Big rig, big rig, big rig. Three. Four. Five. Passing into Ohio, she feels her hands clenching the steering wheel again, squeezing the braided leather cover Lǎoyé bought her off the internet.

She pulls off at a gas station with a burger joint. Behind the building is a dirt lot. As Henry and Anna head to the restrooms, she makes her way over rutted mounds of bulldozed earth to an enormous yellow excavator waiting to claw the land—the arm of its heavy steel scoop bent at an uncannily human angle. She stretches to touch the machine's sunbaked surface, her hipbone tight against the phone in her pocket, and before she's fully aware of her own actions, she's extricated the device and dialed Mama's number.

"Wéi?" She squints at the glowing screen. "Wéi?"

"It's me, Mama."

"Yah, I know"—her voice eager—"you got a special ringtone."

"What's the ringtone?"

"Who knows? I pick from phone menu."

"Oh," she says, thinking, *That's not so special.*

"How you doing? Client okay? You coming home now?"

"Mama," she says, "do you miss Daddy?"

In the pause that follows, two gray herons drop from the sky to trail each other across the dirt, stopping beside a large puddle.

"Of course I miss him."

"You didn't cry."

"I cry," she says simply.

"I've never seen you cry."

"Well, I do."

She considers this. "Once, when I came home from school, you and I were talking about immigration. At the kitchen table—remember? You said my aunties had been blackmailed for fake citizenship papers. Do you remember that?"

"All that happen a long time ago. No point to discuss."

"But then—" She watches smaller, brown birds zoom past the herons' sleek bodies. On foot, they behave like roadrunners, cutting each other off comedically. "Then you said you sacrificed, too. By marrying Daddy." She can feel the corners of her mouth turning down. She has her father's smile, but her frown is just like Mama's. Suddenly, she wishes she were inside the little restaurant, eating french fries with Henry and Anna. But she presses on. "What did you mean by that?"

"Xiǎo Bǎo, nǐ hái hǎo ma? Why you asking all this stuff?"

"Just answer the question, Mama."

Her mother sighs. "You remember Àiguó?"

This is not the direct answer she's looking for. "Of course," she snaps as the smaller birds take flight, the herons remaining still by the puddle, faces upturned to the sun, wings drooping open as though to tan their undersides. She waits with impatience till she realizes her mother is waiting, too. "He was your older brother," she says.

"Yah. Only brother. Die of encephalitis." There is the clatter of pans: Mama putting kitchen things away. "This back in China, before Lǎolao get gray hair and we finally go to America to be with Lǎoyé. I only three or four when we watch him seize and go limp on the floor. Lǎolao strong then. Not like when you knew her. And meaner, too: your grandma"—a deep sigh—"not the same woman as my mother. She change over the years." Feeling herself nod as though she and Mama were sitting across the table and not thousands of miles apart, Měi bites the tip of her tongue lightly, then runs it back and forth between her incisors. *Teeth*, she thinks, *are the body's most useful bling*. "She carry him outside. Bury him near a scrappy tree, tell us never speak his name again. In the night, though, I sneak outside. I talk to Àiguó's ghost. I love him so much." The herons fly off now, alighting briefly on the excavator's hulking form before ascending into the bright Ohio sky. "He the only person in the world," Mama says, "who nice to me. Until your daddy."

Mama's voice suddenly sounds farther away than the distance that separates them. Měi shuts her eyes, imagining her mother staring out through the kitchen window at the fence, the overpass.

"See," Mama continues, "my own lǎoyé, my grandpa, he a KMT military man. By the time I born he missing four fingers, but that never bother him. He tell me once he never experience that—what you call? Phantom limb. But he still haunted. Back in 1937, before I born, he collaborate with the Communists. Both sides agree suspend Chinese Civil War, and he give command to flood entire valley."

Staring down at her high-tops, she kicks at a pinkish rock. "Like, to hold off the encroaching Japanese?"

"Yah. But evacuation order never go through, and soon the valley stink like death. Japanese soldiers row in laughing, poking bloated Chinese corpses with their oars. After that, my grandpa haunted. He hit Lǎolao. Hit me and your aunties, even once we grown, till we all run away to America. Mostly he drunk, say a bunch of nothing. But one day he tell me something true. He say ghosts come back in form of birds, poisonous spiders, and snakes. But also sometimes take human form. He say Àiguó's ghost will haunt me if I don't let it go. Ghost of sickness. Early death. But I can't let go. He my big brother. So I grow the bad luck by talking to ghost."

Pans clank, water runs. She can picture her mother perfectly, bent over the sink in the little Oakland craftsman, the kitchen window cracked and freeway sounds sliding in. "My lǎoyé, he was one mean bastard," Mama says. Then there's a long pause, in which Měi considers climbing up into the seat of the excavator. She paces instead, stopping briefly to glance down at her reflection in the large, muddy puddle. "But he right. I marry a man just like my older brother. Good man, very kind, your daddy. But you know how he get. Stand up from desk and stalk around, back and forth, back and forth, like something inside him trying to burst out. Pretty soon I realize, Àiguó spirit inside him. And I know it gonna end bad. I know long, long time before he leave us. But I don't care. I keep my promise to love him. Sickness and health."

Leaning over the murky water, Měi watches her own face change as long-held anger pours out into the puddle, cold earth below absorbing it. "Oh," she says, confused.

"Yah. Oh." Her mother's voice is no longer far away, but present again. Unperturbed.

"That's not—what I expected you to say." She kicks a pebble into the water; turns back toward the rest stop. "Not how I thought you sacrificed."

"What?" Mama says. "You think your daddy want do weird sex stuff?"

"Jesus! No."

"Butt stuff?"

"Mama! Stop!"

In the back seat, Henry is sleeping again while Anna reads one of the Chinese graphic novels her father had produced from a closet, along with other small gifts: a necklace, a *Star Wars* shirt. She walks straight past the sedan before the girl can look up—into the gas station's bathroom. After relieving herself, she washes her hands, forearms, neck, face. Pats a little water onto her hair.

Street signs blur into one another again, her fingers digging into the leather steering wheel cover.

When the Cuyahoga Valley National Park sign appears, she blinks hard. Takes the exit.

11

BRANDYWINE MANOR (AN INTERLUDE)

"Where are we?" Henry rubs at his face.

She opens the little partition. "Brandywine Manor."

"Sounds delicious."

"Out of the car, wino."

"Are we in Elkhart?"

"Still four hours out." His eyes darken with confusion. He's rubbed an eyelash out and it rests on his smooth cheekbone, so long it's worth more than one wish. "C'mere." She wiggles a finger, beckoning him to the partition. When she plucks the lash gently from his skin, he winces. "Blow," she says, amused, "and make a wish."

"This is a stupid superstition," he says, blowing anyway. "You know that, right? Plus, I was supposed to toss it over my shoulder."

"That's spilled salt," she says. "You toss salt over your shoulder to hit the devil in the eye."

"Eyelashes, too." He grins drowsily. "If it sticks to your shirt, your wish is shot. I'm a writer—remember? I know everything." She smirks as Anna yanks on the door handle, stepping gingerly out to gawk at their surroundings: the sloping green hills, the 1840s Greek Revival bed-and-breakfast with its cornices, its pedimented gables. "We consider other cultures superstitious," Henry yawns, baring perfect teeth, "but think of all the things Americans wish on: clocks that say 11:11, shooting stars, ladybugs. Wishbones, of course, and wishing wells. Birthday candles, eyelashes, dandelions. I could go on."

"Please don't."

"Well, we do a lot of wishing."

She smiles at him. "Birthday candles, eyelashes, and dandelions? We also do a lot of blowing." She shuts the partition on his reply. Exits the car.

Anna's pointing at the sheep behind the carriage barn. "Kàn! Yáng!" She takes off toward the wooden fence.

"Xiǎoxīn," Měi calls out, following a few steps after her, and when she turns around Henry is staring.

"Did you book a room here?" He walks around the front of the car.

"You're the client," she says. "That's your job."

"No informational handout?"

"Not for an unplanned stop." She gestures with an arm toward the front path. He doesn't move but regards her, his lips tugging into a wry, wavering smile. "There's a waterfall," she says, waving vaguely to the east, as though this explains things. Grabbing her overnight bag from the trunk, she tosses him the car keys, strides quickly toward the main building's generous porch, calling back: "Lock it when you've got what you need."

In an empty foyer stocked with pamphlets and menus, she rings a metal call bell until a peculiarly familiar man emerges from the adjacent room.

"Be right with y'all," he says in a deep drawl, disappearing again as the door shuts behind Henry.

"Is it just me," Henry whispers, leaning into her side, nudging her, "or could he be Samuel L. Jackson's twin?"

"Yas! I was trying to place him. *Deep Blue Sea* Samuel?" Through the window, Měi watches Anna wander away from the animals, toward a little grove of pines—bending to sniff the wildflowers but not picking them.

"*The Long Kiss Goodnight* Samuel. But Southern and older, with gray hair."

"*The Hateful Eight.*"

He nods vigorously. The host is back, equipped with a tablet and stylus. "I'm Clark. What can I do for you fine folks today?"

Henry straightens to match Clark's erect posture. "We'd like a room for one night, sir, if you've got one."

"Certainly." He taps around on the stylus. "Is it just the two of y'all? And have you visited the park or the manor before?"

"An eleven-year-old as well. And no."

"You don't say—eleven." He turns to Měi, who points out the window, Anna strolling toward them now, veering through the grass, eschewing the path like an indolent barnyard cat. "Well, you must've had her when you were nine, young lady. You don't look a day over twenty."

"Thank you," Měi says. "But I'm twenty-four, and she's not mine."

"Ah." A chastened smile. "Where did you good folks park?"

Henry clears his throat. "Just out front," he says. Remembering the keys in his hand, he turns them back over to Měi.

"I'll be happy to move the car into our garage."

"Is it fine to leave it where it is?"

"Absolutely." Clark scrolls on the tablet. "For tonight, I recommend the granary suite. Normally it'd run you around four hundred dollars, but right now you can have it for three." He watches her eyes widen. "Worth every penny, I assure you. It's out in yonder in that carriage barn the little one's so enamored by. Got a large main floor and sleeping loft. It looks right out into the hemlock grove, and there's a double-size Jacuzzi tub to ease any stiff muscles from driving. It'll stay warm tonight, I suppose, but on the off chance it cools down, there's also a wood-burning stove." He pulls glasses from a shirt pocket, perching them on the bridge of his nose. "Y'all don't have pets, now, do you?"

"No, sir."

"Good. No pet fee, then. Might you furnish a credit card and ID?" With a quick, bemused glance at Měi, Henry opens his wallet. Clark squints at the license through wire-rimmed spectacles. Swipes the credit card, passing the tablet and stylus to Henry. "We'll bring a candlelight breakfast round about eight A.M. Just need your John Hancock here."

Měi wanders outside to find Anna testing the porch swing. Smiling at the girl, she leans on the white balustrade.

"Looks like Sam Jackson, talks like Sam Elliott." Henry joins them, stuffing his wallet back in his jeans.

"Right? What a character. Sorta walks like a cowboy, too."

"I'm not even gonna comment on that one." The swing creaks as he eases in beside Anna. "Nǐ xiǎng chī wǎnfàn ma?" The girl shakes her head.

"Bú è."

"Waterfall?" he says to Měi.

"Sure. Just let me hit the ladies'." Reentering the manor, she passes quickly through the foyer to find a powder room made trendy with brass fixtures and an ink-drawn wallpaper pattern of ancient Greek architecture. Even the toilet is artful, its stately base and crisp lines mirroring the room's crown molding. But she does not need to go. Only to check in with Lǎoyé. She closes the pocket door, sits on the toilet, and pulls out her phone.

"Wéi?" His voice is tinny. She hears others in the background. "That you, kiddo?"

"Who else? That you, old man?"

"You looking for a old guy, you got the wrong number."

"I guess I'll talk to you anyhow."

In the brief silence that follows, she feels him smiling with her.

"What's up? You on you way home?"

"Yes. Cuyahoga River."

"Oh my god! You drown!"

"Very funny. Cuyahoga River *Valley*, Lǎoyé."

"Still no good: that place stolen. Government promise a thousand dollar per year to every displaced native nation, plus Indigenous hunting rights. How much of that you think they make good on?"

"Well, I can see why they stole it. It's gorgeous here."

"Yah. But why you take the I-90? I-80 quicker."

"Little detour." She hears the phone scrape across Lǎoyé's stubble as he transfers it from ear to ear. "Where are you?"

"Out and about. Perlie take me to Costco. Good air-conditioning, and we like sample the food." Shifting forward on the white porcelain, she hears the busy warehouse's announcements echoing through the phone—envisions Lǎoyé and his friend pushing an enormous grocery cart under blinding fluorescent lights. "You got more questions or something?"

"No," she says. "I just—had a conversation with Mama earlier and wanted to hear your voice."

"Weird."

"I know. It used to be so easy to talk with her. Now we barely talk at all."

"No, I mean weird you wanna hear my voice. Usually you just talk over it."

"Aiya."

"Don't you aiya me. I teach you that word!" A pause. "But you right to talk to your ma. She not always a open book. Need you to reach out first." She hears a woman's voice and his hand muffling the phone as he replies. "Hey," he says clearly, removing it, "you not in no trouble with Mr. Lee, huh?"

It takes her a moment to remember that Henry is Mr. Lee. "No," she says. "You were right. He's very nice. I'll let you get back to your shopping."

"Okay. Perlie say hi."

"Uh, hi. And bye."

"Bye-bye. You be good."

She hangs up, not quite ready to rejoin Henry and Anna. What is she even doing with them, playing family in this bucolic place when she has her own family to sort out?

She pulls up her social media. A message from someone she doesn't know. She stares at the sender's avatar: a skinny, nonthreatening Asian man in enormous black-framed glasses, his handle China510. "Click here," the message says, "to read about the Uyghurs." She is poised to open the link before it occurs to her that Jimmy Xīn, the only Uyghur activist she knows, would not contact her this way; that the link may be malicious.

Instead, she clicks on the avatar to visit China510's page. There is nothing, no content at all, just a background photo of Tàishān, the easternmost of China's five sacred mountains. The earliest traces of human presence there date back to the Paleolithic period—though the mountain's ancient trees, Mama's told her, now bear digital ID cards that calculate their health and record fluctuations. She thinks of Physicals for All, the government program that stores Uyghurs' biometric data.

The account was created today.

Unsettled, she deletes the message.

A trail follows the edge of the gorge all the way to Brandywine Falls. The air cool on her skin, the water's noise intensifies as they approach a sixty-foot torrent cascading in a pattern the pamphlet describes as "bridal-veil" (to appeal, perhaps, to the manor's newlywed guests).

This place, she thinks, does possess a distinctly honeymoon vibe—the charming accommodations, the picturesque falls, and even this well-kept path, which ends in a boardwalk with steep wooden steps descending to a round viewing platform. She had thought of telling Henry about the odd message from China510, but what good would it do? Thinking of Jimmy Xīn and the threats he receives daily from China, she pulls pure oxygen into her lungs. Glances up at the evergreens, oaks, and hickories that shade smaller blue beech and sassafras.

"Nǐmen kàn! Pùbù zhēn de hěn dà!" Anna runs, coltish, toward the steps.

"Slow your roll," she hollers, but the girl has the language barrier as an excuse and doesn't slow. Shaking her head, she recalls the way she'd made her father chase her as a girl: across fields, down sidewalks, through department stores. And suddenly it strikes her that Daddy, six foot two and ever in military shape, could certainly have caught her if he'd wanted to. Instead, he let her claim her own space.

"So, you're twenty-four," Henry says. "A veritable baby." She feels his warm fingertips clasp hers. "Want to hold my hand on the steps?"

She yanks her hand away. Jabs him in the ribs. "Shut up! How old are you? Twenty-six?"

"Cold."

"Twenty-five?"

"Ice cold."

"Twenty-eight?"

"Ooh, now you're heating up." Glancing at her sideways, he narrows his eyes, fishes his ID from his wallet and forks it over. "Be warned, my hair looks like a bad toupee."

"No," she says, studying the photo, which is of course perfect. She hands the license back, blushing inexplicably. "You ain't bad. For a geezer." Henry is twenty-nine. "Did you, like, go to school for writing?"

"I went to school for cute girls and frat parties. But somewhere along the way, I lost sight of those noble goals."

"How'd you break into ghostwriting?"

"I dunno. The usual. How does anyone break in?"

"So you applied for a job and got it?"

"No, I went to a friend's bachelor party and met a famous musician who happened to be his uncle. We got to talking, got food poisoning from the oysters, and at the end of our daylong pukefest, he signed me to write his memoir."

"Ah. Yes. 'The usual.'"

Anna skips down the steps to the platform, shaded by conifers. When the first cold drop strikes Měi's shoulder, she peers up through the trees. This time, when he takes her hand, she doesn't pull back. A low rumble's starting in the sky: divine surround sound reverberating as the day darkens like a theater.

"Hey now, it's the 3D theater experience," he says as though reading her mind. The rain abruptly pummels them and he squints at her, heavy lashes sticking to wet skin. Below, on the round platform, the girl's body trembles and Měi feels herself jerked forward, hunting for the right words to call out. Come here words, comforting words, words Mama wielded like magic whenever a thunderstorm woke the household in the night. But as Anna turns to face them, Měi sees that her trembling is laughter, ecstatic and wild. She throws her skinny arms up, embracing the downpour, and spins in a slow circle as thunder cracks and rolls to compete with the waterfall's roar.

"Look." Henry points past the girl, at the fall's massive vertical drop. "You can see the different layers of rock and earth the water's worn away. That yellowy stuff is sandstone and the red part's shale."

"I read the pamphlet, too, Oracle." She sneers and then his lips are on hers, crushing the smugness out of her with their softness. Lost for a moment, she presses into his warmth, legs buckling, fingernails dug into his shoulders. When she recalls the girl and jerks backward, she slips and comes down hard, and now it's Henry's turn to surge forward, ready to comfort, and her turn to laugh.

Like lightning Anna's beside them, pointing and giggling, one hand cupped over her mouth, as Henry hauls Měi to her feet. And for an odd moment, enfolded in his arms, she feels like a little girl, too. Head spinning, she sees her father. Daddy grinning. Daddy asking, "You all right?" in Henry's voice. Nodding vehemently, she blinks him back to himself. She does not need a protector anymore. Cold rain slicks her face in the waterfall's booming noise.

The granary suite is a cozy counterpoint to nature's sudden assault: sloped roof, area rugs, exposed beams. On the main level, potted plants thrive around a rough-hewn table in a sunroom that the storm pounds, sheets of rain flowing down the glass walls to mimic the waterfall. There is a wide living room couch, a small bedroom—perfect for Anna—and upstairs, where Měi will sleep, a second bed tucked into what was once a hayloft.

Dry and changed into new jeans, a flannel shirt over his gray tee, Henry hangs the clothes they've peeled off before the woodstove. "Way better than an industrial dryer."

"Won't it get too warm?" she asks.

"If it does, we'll just crank the air-conditioning. We paid Samuel L. enough to justify it." He opens the cast-iron door, lights the scrunched newspaper and kindling. Pokes at the fire. "You know the *L* stands for Leroy?"

"I did not know that."

"Yeah. And L. Ron Hubbard's *L* stands for Lafayette."

"You're a fount of vital information."

They crowd onto the small sofa near the stove, Anna wrapping herself in a patchwork quilt pulled from her bed, the TV remote already in her hand. Měi glances at Henry as the girl curls into his side and he wraps a protective arm around her narrow shoulders. Together, the two navigate the menu of kids' films. Is this strange for him, too? Or was he one of those kids who grew up surrounded by family, caring for younger siblings and cousins—practicing for parenthood from birth?

Before Mindy bore her two sons, before her gender reveal parties and attempt to talk Měi into motherhood, she'd forced her oldest friends into glittering silver bridesmaid dresses that had itched going on and off. The wedding was lovely, an indoor-outdoor affair at an inn much like this. But what Měi remembers more clearly than the lights strung through weeping willows, the awkward tango Mindy and her stiff husband, Chip, had rehearsed for weeks in advance, is the way the unmarried couples acted—trading brief, secretive looks that grew bolder throughout the ceremony and reception, as if to say *This could be us.* By morning, those feelings had faded. She recalls McCarthy's stony face at the breakfast table; the way the pierced beauty ignored the bridegroom they'd all seen her make out with. She steals another quick glance at Henry, and through dark lashes, he glances back.

Anna picks out a young adult romance rated PG-13. "What do you think?" Henry asks over the girl's head.

"I'm cool with whatever." Měi keeps her eyes on the screen.

"Do you think her parents would be?"

"What are you asking me for? I'm a godless heathen." Still, she considers the question. It must be hard, she thinks, for Muslim parents in America to find films that send the right message. "Probably not?"

They go back to the drawing board, settling eventually on a Disney classic.

She's seen it before, more than once, so she lets her mind drift back to the ratty couch where she and Lǎoyé would cozy up in blankets to watch movies. Lǎoyé was crazy about movies. One summer, home from school, she'd even managed to drag him out to Grand Lake Theatre for a Spike Lee marathon. "Spike Lee's your favorite director," she'd wheedled.

"Jim Jarmusch my favorite."

"But you also love Spike Lee."

"I love him more from my couch."

"I'll buy popcorn."

"Yah, thirty-dollar small size. Blow all your limo bucks."

"C'mon. Just this once. For me?"

His milky cataracts had glowed in the darkness of the converted garage.

"Oh, fine," he pouted, "but I get M&M's, too."

Parking downtown was awful, of course, but her mood lifted as the entire city of Oakland crammed into line with them, buying tickets and refreshments, laughing bigheartedly as everyone filed into the cinema and spread out, vibrating in anticipation as the lights dimmed. The historic movie palace had been renovated multiple times, but its main auditorium was still equipped with a Mighty Wurlitzer hidden beneath the floor. Soon, the organ rose for a brief pre-film concert and, settling deeper into his seat, Lǎoyé pulled the hood of his sweatshirt on, cinching it tightly around his face.

"Lǎoyé"—she stuck her hand into their popcorn tub—"nǐ lěng ma?" Crunching on the snack, she was proud she'd remembered how to ask if he was cold.

"Nah," he said. "Just don't wanna get lice from these cloth seats."

"You're kidding, right? You look like E.T."

He scowled at this. Kept the hood on throughout the marathon.

The last movie was *Bamboozled*, which ended with a montage of historical film and television clips featuring Caucasian characters in blackface, Black characters in stereotypical roles, and racist cartoon shorts. It was hard to look at, so she turned to study Lǎoyé and found him quietly crying. In the white light from the screen, Měi watched the tears glazing his cheeks, soaking into his cinched hood. Then, behind them, the laughing began. It was hesitant at first, but welled up, louder and stronger, as the cartoon montage continued. Twisting around in her seat, away from

Lǎoyé toward the back of the theater, she saw rows of stunned Black faces among the giggling white ones.

Facing away, she did not see Lǎoyé stand. Then his words spilled out, over her head: "WHITE PEOPLE, that's not how we do things here." Some of the laughter died; the rest became uncertain. "I SAID THAT'S NOT HOW WE DO THINGS HERE," he exploded. In his ridiculous sweatshirt, her stooped grandfather was a strange sight, the theater stunned into a silence that he savored only a moment before he took her hand, pulled her up and toward the exit.

As they left, she heard a man murmur: "Right on, Grandpa."

The walk back to her car had been silent.

"I hire them to prove my point about going outside," he joked grimly as she backed out of the parking space.

Her cheek tingles under Henry's stare.

Above the girl's head, he raises an inquisitive eyebrow. She smiles wanly, shaking her head.

Suddenly remembering China510, she pulls her phone from her pocket.

"Oh, no," Henry says. "Nope. No phones allowed on movie night." Reaching across Anna, he snatches at it.

"Just checking my messages," she says, dodging his grasping hand. "And I wanted to show you—"

"Put it away." He pouts. "If you need something to do, order dinner. Maybe Chinese tonight?"

And so she does. They pause the movie, Henry disappearing into the bathroom as she and Anna explore the menus, then the coffee station, where they make hot cocoa and tea. Měi waits for Henry to return before placing the order. Then she reads him the tea flavors: "Mint? Cinnamon? Echinacea?"

He grimaces. "Ew."

"Echinacea boosts immunity—"

"No, 'ew' to tea in general."

"Are you serious?" He shrugs. "You're gonna get your Asian card revoked."

"Says the woman who won't speak Mandarin with me." He runs a hand through his hair. "Tea's just warm, flavored water. Can you order me a beer?"

"They don't deliver beer."

"Then I guess I'm headed out to the store."

"It's still raining."

"I'll be fine: I'm not the Wicked Witch of the West." He grabs her keys off the counter. "Want anything?"

"Wine, I guess?"

"Red or white?"

"I don't care——"

"Pink, then. And make sure she takes two of the gummy vitamins I left in the bathroom." Then he's gone, locking the door behind him so that she feels devastated, then foolish for missing him so quickly. Is this normal? She hasn't had a crush in years, since before her father left them. Did that fucker give her abandonment issues? Fury surges up from her belly, like bile, and she squeezes the TV remote. This is the first time she's been angry with Daddy, not Mama, for what he did.

Quickly, she diverts her rage to herself. Her stupid, stunted self.

The girl is staring at her.

Anna gestures toward the screen, and she nods. Presses Play.

After dinner, buzzed from the rosé, she heads upstairs to the loft—pausing on the landing to watch Henry tuck Anna in below. Their soft Mandarin tones remind her of childhood, when her parents stayed up talking once they'd put her to bed. It was almost better that she couldn't understand. It turned their voices into lulling white noise.

She brushes her teeth, strips to her bra and panties, and slides between the sheets.

"Hey." Henry's voice in the doorway is low. "Can I get a pillow?"

She pats the bedspread in response.

Hesitant, he moves toward her as she envisions him biting slowly at her lower lip, her neck. "You sure?"

She nods and he removes his flannel shirt, sliding under the covers gingerly in T-shirt and jeans. Pulls her cheek to his hammering chest.

They listen to the rain dwindling away.

Around midnight, she wakes to frightened sounds. Henry is breathing deeply, one arm thrown over his eyes. Pulling on his discarded flannel, she grabs her phone, taps its flashlight on, and tiptoes, barefoot, downstairs, where the air is cool, the wood stove quiet now. Gently, she shakes the girl awake.

Small hands snake around her neck, pulling her in close till her face rests awkwardly on the pillow, too. *This yearning answers itself completely,* she thinks, stretching out beside the girl atop the covers, the memory of Mindy's exuberant face shimmering in the unlit room. It seems, after all, her friend is right: having a child is not like having a lover, which demands so much give-and-take. A child is all take, no give. But the taking itself is a gift.

Anna fidgets, kicking at the sheets, scratching ferociously at the irregularity in her hairline, and Měi waits on the bed till the girl's still again, breaths slowing, evening out. Then, unlacing the small arms from her neck, she rests the girl's hands on the quilt—fingers half-curled in sleep—and, rising silently, sneaks off to the bathroom.

Flipping the light on, locking the door, she blinks at the phone in the sudden brightness before pulling up her social media to find another message from China510.

"We don't know how much time we have. Or how much loved ones have," the message reads. "Our days are numbered. Should return home quickly."

∽

She does not wake Henry to show him the vague threat, but shimmies out of his shirt and slides into bed beside him. Googling "Uyghur surveillance in United States" brings up an article about a Uyghur man in Montana whose grandmother called from Nanjing, requesting photos of his ID, debit card, and license plate in a strained voice. When he asked whether she'd been instructed to help the government track him overseas, the old woman abruptly changed subjects. "The fruit trees in the backyard are flourishing," she said. And when he inquired after his grandfather, she asked which: his lǎoyé, or "Grandfather Xí Jìnpíng."

Gently, she sets the device face down on the floor. She needs sleep, but her thoughts bounce around between China510, the Hollerith machines, and her own phone: a door to the whole world that swings both ways. She thinks of Una in the vegan house, passing a bowl around to collect devices before dinner. "Unplug from your cancer-causing spyware."

Her monkey mind leaps from threat to threat, memory to memory, exhausting itself until there is only the sensation of deceleration, then nothing, then sunlight through the loft's quaintly curtained window.

The morning's hush broken only by Henry's breath, she peeks out at the hemlocks; sees a cardinal lift into the sky. Her parents were not nature-lovers, and Lǎoyé was fond of saying the only branches he liked belonged to banks and libraries, so it wasn't until she left home and began exploring the woods around Dartmouth, alone, that she'd discovered real darkness, real quiet. Now it's something she treasures.

Slipping out of bed, into a soft pair of joggers and a T-shirt, she snatches her high-tops and tiptoes downstairs, where she sits by the woodstove, lacing up. *Clients*, she reminds herself, pulling out her phone to study the route home: *These are my clients. We can power on past Elkhart to Omaha. Make it to Oakland with just three stops. But first, I'll change my phone number. Delete my social media.*

Instead, she calls the Elkhart Inn to cajole the manager into waiving last night's cancellation fee and moving the reservation to tonight. Phoning each remaining destination, she uses Henry's name and the confirmation numbers he's given her to push each stay back, accommodating this brief respite. Then, as he showers and Anna sleeps deeply in the first-floor bedroom, she sits by the woodstove to wait for Samuel L. Jackson.

When she opens the door to his knock, he greets her with a verbal "Knock, knock" as well and she almost responds, *Who's there?*

"Good morning," she says instead.

"Well, morning to you, too. Hope y'all got a good night's rest?" Stooped slightly—a tall man's posture—he pushes the breakfast cart in. "Where would you like to eat?" He smiles. "Some folks favor the Jacuzzi."

"The table, I guess?" He nods, making his way past her to the sunroom as Henry emerges from the loft's en suite and skips down the stairs, toweling wet hair.

"Jimmy texted." He hangs the towel on a chairback. "His department approved the sabbatical. He's got a spot in Cali set up for the two of them already. Took off a few hours after us."

"A spot in Oakland?"

"Alhambra. He knows people there: a dutar-player, a former student, a couple that owns a Uyghur restaurant." He grins. "Good morning, Carl."

"Morning, sir." They watch the older man light a few votives, vanilla infusing the air. "You all enjoy your breakfast, now." And he's out the door.

"Do you think"—Henry locks the door after him, a city habit—"I should've tipped Carl?"

"Nah. We can leave a tip on the table." Moving to the sunroom, she sits on the rustic bench. Stabs a cantaloupe cube with her fork. "But you probably shouldn't have called him Carl because his name is Clark."

"Shit!"

"Language," she chides as Anna's door swings open. The girl appears in pajamas, her hair a fuzzy mess. "Ānnuó, zǎo."

"Good morning," Anna chirps, looking satisfied. "English," she adds for good measure.

"Shuō de zhēn hǎo." Henry crosses to the sunroom, pulling a chair out for the girl before seating himself beside Měi on the bench. "At least I didn't call him Samuel L." He slides close, his thigh pressed against hers. "Kinda weird to light candles in the morning."

"Guessing it's probably better in the winter? On those dark, frigid days?"

"Probably."

"Hey, about last night, that rosé hit me pretty hard, and this place sort of lends itself to, like, cuddling—"

She feels the pressure of his thigh disappear. "Say no more. It was a onetime thing." He leans forward, purses his lips, and blows the votives out.

After breakfast, she packs quickly. "See you out there," she says from the doorway, in answer to Henry's quizzical smile. "Gotta make a call."

Puddles glint along the path back to the main house, and despite the summer heat, mist drapes the trees. Wiping smudges from the phone's screen with her shirt, she dials her mother.

"Wéi?"

"Hey," she says—startled, as she always seems to be these days, by Mama's voice.

"Xiǎo Bǎo! Nǐ zěnmeyàng?"

"I'm fine." A goldfinch shoots up from the grass, a brilliant shooting star, its yellow form flashing and disappearing in the mist. "Can we talk a little more about Daddy?"

In the silence that follows, she steps over a puddle. Remembers skipping to school in the rain, Lǎolao holding her hand lightly and skipping a little bit, too. Her grandmother's electric smile had been wired directly to Měi's heart.

"What, you wanna ask about the butt stuff again?"

"I never—ugh—" she stammers, thinking about every parent's uncanny ability to evoke embarrassment. Embarrassment for them and for you.

"I just yank your chain." Her mother's voice drops to seriousness. "You want me say I miss him again?"

"No," she says. "I'm just wondering why you think he did it."

"Did what?" Měi refuses to answer. "With the gun?" Mama finally asks.

"Yeah."

Now two finches swoop above, the male lemon yellow, the female a muted brown. They are the opposite of her parents, she thinks: Mama the brighter light, outshining Daddy. Since her mother's admission that she cries, that she mourns, Měi's wondered how much of Mama's grief is guilt. Who else but Mama could've broken her father, this coolheaded, composed academic who'd spent years as an international spy? Who else could've put him in his grave?

"The Alzheimer," Mama says.

"Excuse me?"

"He have the Alzheimer. Before he die."

"No, he didn't."

"What—you think I confuse your daddy with my other husband?"

"Mama, be serious." The night's rain has enlivened the landscape. Everything is a too-bright green.

"I am serious. He don't want you be sad."

"Alzheimer's disease is dementia. I don't think you understand—"

"Tsk!" Mama's tongue is quick. "Don't patronize me like the white boss. I understand perfect. Your daddy have the Alzheimer disease. He develop it after you go back to school for junior year." In the driveway now, Měi stops. Stands stock-still. Holds the phone far from her ear, then presses it tightly into the flesh of her lobe. "At first, we not say nothing, figure no reason ruin your spring term. Figure he still have many year. But this sickness work a little different for everyone. Doctor call what happen to Daddy 'unusual presentation.' Like a magic show with monkeys and fire. I get mad at doctor. He always say everything wrong. But the Alzheimer not his fault. Even though he talk stupid." Her mother's words have shed their skin of politeness. Without its drag, they flow faster and faster. "Daddy say don't tell you, I mad at your daddy. I want tell you. You have the right to know. But he argue, and finally we agree: I not say nothing unless you figure it out. He make me promise not let you worry. He want enjoy summer with you."

"You're—lying."

"No. I not lie. I tell him, 'I don't say nothing unless she ask.' But I don't lie neither."

"Mama, Alzheimer's is long-term dementia. Daddy was only—"

"What you know? You spend all summer drive stupid car, go out with friend. Barely talk to us, just your marijuana addict lǎoyé. It not hard hide nothing from you." Dimly, it registers that her mother knows what the old man does in his musty garage. Of course she knows exactly what he does, what the ripe sweet scent of his clothing is from, why he never invites her in. Perhaps she even knows where the gold-gilded saucer from her wedding set has gone. "Xiǎo Bǎo," she says, slower now, lower, almost gentle, "I cover for him"—Měi has reached the car, unlocks the door—"till it reach the point we cannot hide no more."

She tosses the phone on the driver's seat and slams the door shut. Keeps walking. Up the narrow drive leading to the country road. Along the weedy shoulder, rocks crunching, mud squishing beneath her high-tops. She will walk all the way to a new place where nobody leaves and nobody lies. Where nobody bothers her at all. A car speeds by, nearly clipping her left elbow, her balled-up fist. Tears sting her, but she blinks them back.

12

CUYAHOGA VALLEY TO ELKHART

It is the thought of Henry opening the unlocked car and Anna clambering in, expecting her, that turns Měi back to Brandywine Manor: the thought of the girl in the back seat, kicking her feet, doodling in her notepad, waiting for another adult who has left her. The thought of China510 finding her instead.

But when she arrives, huffing under a sheen of sweat, they're on the inn's columned front porch, chatting with Clark. She opens the sedan's unlocked door, grabs the phone off the seat, and gets in. Buckles her seat belt, beset by a buzzing numbness.

Closing her eyes, she recalls the buzz of wasps amid fragrant eucalyptus—wasps nested under the eaves of a Tilden Park maintenance shed. How cautiously she'd approached the nest, thrilled by the forest's waking, thinking this was the most pressing danger that existed till she heard the Nguyen twin's wail.

Surely, Mama is lying.

She would've known if her father was on some steep decline, struggling, losing himself. She's seen on-screen portrayals of Alzheimer's: the white hair, the vacant stare, the dribbled soup. But maybe these versions are incorrect. Or rather, incomplete. General. Not applicable to Daddy's unusual presentation.

A magic show with monkeys and fire.

For her fourth birthday, at Měi's request, Daddy performed a sock-puppet play. Puppets were something she'd begun coveting at a store on Grand Avenue, but he'd dismissed the idea of buying a toy so easy to make at home—so they'd sat below the picture window, in a bright square the sun had painted on the living room's refinished hardwood floor, and created Herbert. Despite several failed attempts, Daddy had let her produce Herbert's signature yarn mustache. He'd even let her thread the needle he used to sew on the puppet's button eyes. Then, he'd performed for her and Mama—announcing Měi as the character's creator when it was his voice, his hand that brought the rough cotton to life.

Now Anna skips down the porch steps, Clark snapping off a crisp salute.

Měi checks her eyes in the mirror: a little red, a little puffy. Nothing noticeable, so long as she smiles. The girl approaches, unfolding an *I fell for the Falls behind Brandywine Manor* T-shirt as she walks. Shaking it out for Měi to see.

Yanking the back door open, she scrambles in. "Clark gěile wǒ yī jiàn chènshān!" Her smile becomes pensive. "Tài dàle, dàn wǒ huì zhǎng dà de." She pulls out the little notebook, uncaps the mini-pen, and sketches a small girl in an enormous shirt. Then she crosses it out and draws a bigger girl in a perfectly fitted shirt. Points to her own chest.

Měi nods. "You'll grow into it. Nǐ zhīdào Samuel L. Jackson?"

"Ohhhhh. Clark zhǎng de xiàng tā . . ." The girl laughs, teeth slightly too large for her face, her wide smile something else to grow into.

Sliding into the back seat with Anna, Henry pulls the door shut. "Ladies!"

"Gentleman," Měi says. It will be strange, she thinks, to ride alone with him in the sedan's front seat once they drop the girl off in Alhambra.

"So," he says, as though listening in on her thoughts, "Looks like we're homeward bound. Got another text from Jimmy. He'll pick Anna up in the Town."

Oakland. Their final stop.

She flashes him a too-bright smile. Starts the car.

At the Elkhart Inn, their suite overlooks the park with its small goose pond. Henry stretches out on the living room couch where he will sleep tonight while the girl unpacks, placing neatly folded clothes in shallow drawers. In the other bedroom, Měi's own clothes are neither neat nor folded: she rolls them, stuffs them in her overnight pack, and never uses hotel dressers.

Parting the sheers, she stares down the street at the Amish creamery and, across from its canary yellow facade, the balcony where Hog and Jake—once bearded and menacing—had clinked pints of beer.

Below, families stroll in the park or perch on sun-warmed benches. Cement steps lead down to a small colonnade, a footbridge to a gazebo on the water where teen girls in matching sequined gowns snap selfies. Closer, in the grass, a bone-skinny woman yanks at her white Chihuahua's leash as the dog inexplicably falls on its side, stands up again, falls on its side, stands up again.

Glancing at the cement steps' handrail, Měi closes her eyes and can almost hear the grind of her skateboard on Lake Merritt's rails, curbs, concrete benches. Back in middle school, when she and Laura were learning their first tricks, her father had always been the one to drive them to the lake. To the skate park under the bridge, or even to Yerba Buena Gardens, where he'd give them their space. Sit at a distance, reading the paper.

"We can BART, or take the bus," she'd say, but he'd shake his head. "I'm almost twelve," she'd say.

"Your daddy a wise man," Lǎoyé replied when she complained. "Last time I take bus, man sit next to me playing with plastic bag of urine. All the way to Sacramento."

"How d'you know it was pee, not lemonade?"

"Oh. When he first sit down, bag empty."

It took a moment for that to sink in.

Now, thinking of Anna, she realizes it wasn't just the buses Daddy had feared, but the myriad other dangers of releasing two girls into the wild with nothing but skateboards and cell phones.

She pulls her phone out. Checks her social media, and, finding nothing new, scrolls to the message from China510. Opens it and stares.

"We don't know how much time we have. Or how much loved ones have. Our days are numbered. Should return home quickly."

Surely there is no way to track her car, unless—she squints at her phone.

Should she show Henry? Ask him to notify Jimmy? Or maybe, now that someone's apparently aware of their connection, simply message Jimmy herself? How many mysterious threats has he received at this point—tugging him toward home? She regrets deleting the message before this one: "Click here to read about the Uyghurs." Perhaps she should've saved it as—evidence?

The girl's bony elbow brushes Měi's. "Kàn! Nà tiáo gǒu tài dòule."

Mei clicks the phone off; slides it in her pocket. She recognizes "gǒu," which means "dog."

"I'm not sure what it's doing," she says. "Hěn qíguài." They stare at the Chihuahua, which falls and stands and falls.

"What what's doing?" Henry joins them at the window.

"That dog." She points.

"Rolling in goose poop," Henry answers, as though this is obvious. She squints at him and he laughs. "My dog, Cindy, does it every chance he gets."

"You've got a dog named Cindy?"

"Cindy Brady. Yes."

"Wait—where's Cindy Brady now?"

"Revealing more dark secrets about the other members of the cast."

"I'm serious, Henry. Where's your dog while you're away?"

"At home. I'm paying a neighbor to take care of him."

"Her."

"Him."

"Cindy Brady is male?"

"I haven't heard that one from the paparazzi yet, but I wouldn't be shocked. Cindy was full of surprises. Did you know she made out with Bobby in Tiger's doghouse while Marcia did bumps of coke?" She produces a flat stare. "Okay, okay. He's a yellow Lab, okay? Something about his ears reminds me of Cindy Brady's pigtails. But he was never in porn."

Měi scowls. "For a bigtime writer, you can't talk in a straight line." She glances at Anna, who's still watching the dog. "And thank god she doesn't speak English. Speaking of which"—she moves to the couch, pulling Henry by a belt loop—"I got a message for her dad." They sit on the edge of the sofa, knees touching.

"A message from Jimmy?"

"No, *for* Jimmy." She hands over her phone. Watches him read what China510 sent.

"510. They've been tracking us since Oakland?" He gnaws at a thumbnail, pensive. "We can't tell him," he says.

"That's what I thought, too, initially."

"But?"

"But he should know they've connected us to him."

He frowns. "You. They've connected *you* to him."

"If they know about me, they for damn sure know about you."

His dark lashes drop to half-mast. "Let's not assume. And I mean"—there's an odd friction to his voice, thoughts and emotions rubbing, dragging, on one another—"this is just an intimidation tactic, right? So long as the CCP wants Jimmy to keep his mouth shut, they've got to protect Aynur. She's their only leverage." He taps a foot on the broadloom carpet. "We've gotta keep him here. Where he and Anna are safe. I mean, if he gives in to the threats . . . if they even travel outside the U.S."—the foot taps faster—"if they visit Mecca to perform the hajj, say . . . Saudi Arabia, Dubai, Morocco, Egypt, Thailand: they're all extraditing Uyghurs based on Chinese terrorism warrants."

"I mean, maybe those people are terrorists, though."

"Some, sure." He studies her, nodding. "But all of them? Even the teenagers with blogs? You can't tell me a million-plus, maybe two million, Chinese detainees are terrorists. No, the worst thing would be to go home now. And for what? Once people disappear, it's impossible to track them from the outside." His jaw works back and forth, the foot tapping, tapping, till she rests a hand on his knee.

"I just think," she says, "he should be aware that they know about us."

The girl turns from the window. "Bù hǎo yì si, wǒmen qù kàn é ba?"

"Of course," Henry says, standing. Měi tilts her head. "She wants to see the geese."

"Go on without me, you two."

"You sure?" He rubs his palms on his jeans.

"Yup. I've got a call to make."

After Daddy's funeral, she'd stood quietly at the picture window wishing it would snow in July as it sometimes did up in Tahoe, soft drifts whiting out nature's ugly mistakes: fire-charred land, dirty puddles, rotting carcasses. But Oakland barely saw snow once per decade. In Oakland, merchants spray-painted fake flakes in their windows during the holiday season.

There would be no whiting out.

The funeral was brief, the reception reminiscent of her sweet sixteen party. The few high school friends who could make it had clustered around, trading stories of college, as her parents' friends chattered in Mandarin and ate thousand-year-old eggs.

The night before, when Měi opened the wrapped dish a friend had dropped off, her mother had slapped her hand away. "No meat."

Měi had gaped. "I thought vegetarianism was 'stupid'?"

"The gods don't eat meat. And how you gonna eat so good tonight when your daddy can't eat nothing at all?"

The reception was another story. "Eat, eat," Mama said to Měi, to everyone, shoving candy into guests' hands as they left.

"Are you trying to give them diabetes?" Měi asked through her teeth.

"To purify them after they see death," Mama answered, once again proving that the baffling gulf between them was too wide to cross.

But perhaps now? Měi stares out at the little footbridge to the gazebo on the pond. Perhaps we can hammer something together now. Some span to help us meet in the middle. She closes the sheers. Moves into the bedroom, shutting the door in case Henry and Anna return.

"Wéi?"

"Mama"—sitting on the queen bed, throat suddenly dry—"how are you?"

"Ah, Xiǎo Bǎo. Wǒ hái hǎo. Nǐ ne?"

"I'm good. I wanted to apologize."

"Yah! You hang up on me. After all my effort, too."

Effort? When has her mother reached out to her? When has she ever held out an olive branch? Měi takes a deep breath. Another. Another. "I was just—surprised, Mama. By what you said." Her mother is silent. "Mama?"

"Go on. Apologize."

"I mean, that's kinda what I just tried to do . . ."

"Apologize more."

"I'm sorry. It was disrespectful to hang up. You've been a wonderful mother, the best mom anyone could ask for, and you were only trying to respect Daddy's—"

"Too much."

"What?"

"Too much apology. We family. No need stand on ceremony. You eat yet?"

"I mean, breakfast, yes."

"It almost two o'clock."

"I'm not hungry."

"You need eat some chicken or something."

She sighs. "Mama." Recalling her mother's dry, blank, grief-molded face as they laid her father to rest, she tries to think of something kind to say. What comes out is, "Daddy was always very nice to you, wasn't he?"

She can almost see her mother's appraising expression; braces herself for an extended silence. She stands. Moves to the window and opens it, letting in a tickling breeze. In the park, Anna's stalking a large goose that pivots suddenly, sending her running back to the bench where Henry laughs with her. The sequined girls are still taking selfies, endless selfies, but the Chihuahua and its owner have moved on.

"Yes," Mama says abruptly. "Daddy good to me. Maybe I don't agree with his decision, but I promise keep his secret because I know if it is me, he do the same." Then, as though weighing her own equivalency and finding it lacking, she adds hastily, "Also he only want protect you. And no matter you believe me or not, I want the same." Now Měi hears something that might be her mother's dry, tiny hand smoothing salt-and-pepper hair back behind an ear—something she does compulsively when she's nervous. Her mother is making an effort, she knows, not to pull the newly formed scab off Měi's trust. "Xiǎo Bǎo," Mama coos, "I marry your father"—she pauses and Měi pictures her turning her gaze to the little kitchen window, her distant eyes so black that more than one Indigenous American has approached them, asking what tribe Mama belongs to—"because he remind me of somebody I lose too soon. Someone I bury long ago. I know you suffer, wondering why he leave us, but you will learn we all gonna suffer. It's unavoidable in this life." A quick exhalation. "Let's not talk about him anymore," she says, leaving Měi uncertain of whether she is still talking about Daddy, or about the ghost of her older brother Àiguó, buried someplace in China near a scrappy tree. "We just leave him buried this time."

Hanging up, Měi cannot tell whether she feels better or worse.

Less alone or more alone.

She goes to the window and looks out. Anna's chasing the goose around again, Henry watching, chatting on the phone.

Because it's in her hand, and because it's a habit, she looks at her phone, too.

Stares at the ominous words of China510.

Flicks the message off the screen.

By the time they return, she's put on a brave face. Anna heads straight for the remote control, while Henry pulls her into the bedroom. Shuts the door, his skin radiating warmth. She moves into his arms, but his embrace is stiff. "I spoke with Jimmy," he says tonelessly. "Told him about the message."

"And?"

"I think we really fucked things up, Měi." He steps backward, releasing her entirely. "Everything. Everything we did. We fucked it up." He exhales sharply through his nose, rubbing at his chin. "He's scared for

Aynur's life now. Now that they know Anna's location. That we stole her from the orphan school. He's certain they'll start playing hardball. Leverage Aynur to silence him. Torture her. Says it's gotten worse over there, says"—trailing off, he shakes his head—"I don't know how much of it's paranoia, but he's backed against a wall. He's going home."

"What?" She steps backward. Steps into a near-perfect vacuum—like space with its space dust, devoid of air and atmosphere—where she struggles to breathe. To understand that "home" means China.

What Mama's always told her about the Chinese government: the officials are like parents. They act in the people's best interests.

"But your own family fled to America!" she rebuked, shortly after learning of her two bonus aunties.

"No," Mama said evenly. "We just come for better life."

"What about Tibet? Hong Kong?"

"What about them?"

"The people there hate Beijing."

"Who tell you this?"

"Lǎoyé."

Her mother swatted the air between them as though blocking Měi's best shot before it reached the rim. "Lǎoyé got funny American ideas. Once I get here, I seen how the white people treat him. How bitter he get, every time. Then try win their approval again, till he run out of energy. I know why he turn into a hermit. Only talk to one little girl. That's why I do different. Make all Chinese friends."

"But you married Daddy!"

"A husband is not a friend."

She'd rolled her eyes. "Mama," she said, steering the conversation back to its intended destination, "you've seen the bumper stickers in Berkeley. Surely you know about Tibet. And Hong Kong, where civil rights have diminished sharply."

"What you mean?"

"Like, the rights to expression, association, and peaceful assembly?"

"What, like music festival?" Her mother had wrinkled her nose. "Who cares? Young people don't understand that China protect the people. Protect the national security."

"They arbitrarily impose rules suppressing people who speak out for democracy or independence!"

"Psht," Mama spat. "Those people troublemaker."

"You can't even be queer in China!"

"Weirdos everywhere."

"I don't mean weird. I mean 'queer' like gay or trans—"

"Trans?"

"Transgender!"

"What you think the imperial servants were? They eunuchs."

"That's not the same. In China, you're stuck with the gender some stranger assigned you at birth. And gay people can't even get married."

"What, you gay now?"

"No."

"You a man?"

"No, but—"

"First vegetarian, now gay man."

"No!"

It was all too confounding.

∞

"We can't give her up," she says.

"You mean we can't give up?"

"I mean we can't give Anna up to Jimmy. They fly back, they disappear."

"I mean, I agree. It sucks. After all this." He sits on the bed, glaring at the carpet. "But we don't have much of a choice."

"We have a choice." She sits beside him.

He looks at her. "He's her father."

"Exactly. And you told me yourself, they separate Uyghur kids from detained parents. She'll go back to orphan camp. You see how skinny she is already. How quiet. You see the bald spot at her temple, like someone tore out a clump"—he rubs at his stubbled jaw—"do you want her to lose both parents?" She clutches at his knee, but he says nothing, glancing at the closed door.

"No."

Standing, she paces between the bed and the window; scratches at her shin with the heel of a high-top. "No. So we aren't going to Oakland. We can't give her up." Her overnight bag is on the bed. She opens it and pulls the clothing out, placing rolled items one by one in the top drawer of a dresser.

Then, grabbing the bag, she moves to the bathroom and empties its remaining contents on the counter—toothpaste, toothbrush, floss, hairbrush, lip gloss, expensive lotion from Brandywine Manor. When he follows, leaning in the doorframe, she's arranging everything neatly. "What," he says, "we're going to live here forever now?"

"I don't know what we'll do," she says quietly, meeting his eyes in the wide mirror, "but Anna isn't going back."

"She'll go where her parents want her to."

"Her parents hired us to hide her."

"Well, now one wants to take her home."

"And the other?" Turning sharply, she faces him. "I bet Mrs. Xīn wouldn't want that."

"But Jimmy is—"

"Her father. I know. He's the man. What, are we back in the fucking fifties?"

"No, Jimmy's—"

"Our friend? Fuck that! We had one beer with the man. And he was drinking water! You tryna tell me Anna's mother is less deserving of our respect?"

"Měi." He steps into the small room, shutting the door; hovers near the toilet. "Jimmy's paying me now. A lot."

Her jaw drops. "Are you for real right now?"

"I'm very for real. Back in Syracuse, we struck a deal."

"Oh, so the man with the Third Street luxury condo wants stacks on stacks?"

"Everyone wants more money. It's just a fact. But the point is, Jimmy's Anna's father. And he's my boss." His index finger stabs the air. "And, frankly, I'm yours. We do what he says."

A coldness sinks in her chest like a stone falling slowly through water.

She turns back to the mirror, preferring his reflection to his beautiful face.

Bending, she slams the faucet on. Splashes its bracing flow across her brow. Grabs one of the hand towels hanging on the wall and pats her forehead, her cheeks, dry. Her hair is delicate, ink-black brushstrokes across the pale canvas of her skin.

When he leaves, she feels absolutely nothing.

The girl's hand in hers is warm. As they move from the muggy outdoors into the boutique's air-conditioned comfort, Měi feels the numbness lifting. Time alone with Anna is time spent in another atmosphere. One that absorbs fear and anger and carries them off, in clouds, to rain down another day.

The boutique is larger than it looks from the outside. It extends back and back and back, every object in its preordained place. Necklaces shine on driftwood jewelry hangers. Bright clothes are folded in neat stacks or hung along the wall. She lifts a heavy glass paperweight in her hand, unsure of whether the jellyfish inside is real. "You like that?" The saleswoman moves closer. "It's a paperweight. Great gift. Let me show you something." She extends a palm, and Měi sets the paperweight there.

They follow the woman to the back of the store, where curved rods draped with champagne curtains form elegant fitting rooms. "C'mon in," the woman urges, and they crowd into one together. As she pulls the curtains closed, the jellyfish lights up in her palm, a frozen, phosphorescent glow in the dim space.

"Wah, duōme jīngzhì," the girl breathes.

The saleswoman laughs: "You two aren't from Indiana, are you? What did she say?"

"She said it's really cool," Měi says, "I think."

Anna meets her eyes, nodding, and Měi has the odd sensation that the girl understands every word. The saleswoman throws the curtains open again, sunlight beaming in through the store's facade of windows. "You like?" She places the paperweight in Anna's hands.

Měi follows them out of the fitting room. "Is it real?"

"The jellyfish?" The saleswoman offers a lipsticked peach smile. "No. Entirely handblown glass. But it looks real, doesn't it?" She moves behind the register. "Enjoy looking around and let me know if you have more questions."

The boutique's buyer, Měi thinks, has a good eye and a fair mind— the merchandise trendy yet timeless, and not too exorbitant. When the girl flips the paperweight over, showing her the price, it's nothing like what she'd expected, and she nods.

They approach the register, passing a wooden rack of socks, and Měi's eye is drawn to a pair that says FUCK OFF: I'M READING. She's tempted to buy them for Anna, when another idea occurs.

"Do you have plain white socks?" she asks the saleswoman.

"You mean, like, tennis socks?"

"No." She points to the rack. "Just like those, only white."

"We do," the woman replies, surprising her. "Susan, the owner, prints the black-and-white paisley pairs herself. They're her own design. Very bespoke."

"How much for a large pair?"

"Of white socks? They're one-size-fits-most." The woman wraps the paperweight and stashes it in a small bag, then runs Měi's credit card. Glancing at Anna, she says, "I think we can spare a pair for free."

"Hǎo jí le!" Anna beams, accepting the bag as the woman excuses herself. Disappearing into a curtained doorway behind the register, she reappears with the socks.

Henry is still gone when they return to the inn, so they sit on a sheet spread over the broadloom carpet, in a patch of sunlight, scattering materials from the local craft store between them. Anna's pulled up a digital art folder created during her first visit to America. Scrolling through thumbnails on Měi's phone, she pauses once in a while, clicking. The images she opens are a mishmash of sketches and photos that she seems proud to share.

Some, Měi realizes, she must've drawn on Henry's tablet recently, and uploaded herself. A spot-on image of Mickey Mouse climbing into a suitcase. Lightning McQueen parked in front of a sign that reads ROCK ISLAND CASINO AND HOTEL. She squints at a photo of Anna and her father in China—Xinjiang, she imagines, though she can't read the red street sign—marveling over how a tween who can't read English has managed to access this folder again.

The girl clicks another thumbnail and her mother appears: Aynur Xīn, napping on a colorful sofa, midday sun streaming through an open window to light her hair. Měi admires the woman's vibrant clothing, her glowing skin.

"Māmā xǐhuān tiàowǔ," Anna says in a faraway voice.

"Tiàowǔ?" Does this mean nap? Her mother likes to nap?

The girl rises to her feet. With a smile she twirls, her stick-skinny arms suddenly flowing, graceful, expressive, her fingers held elegantly in place. "Sanam," she says when she stops. "Sàinǎimǔ?"

Měi shakes her head.

The girl pulls the little notebook from her pocket. Draws a map. "Xinjiang," she says, pointing. "We. Dance. Sanam," she says. "Teacher happy." Now her movements quicken. Still gripping the notebook, she skips from one foot to the other—then stops and points at the little hand-drawn map again, her finger moving south. "Samaa," she says. "Here. They dance Samaa. Make Chinese teacher smile."

Měi cannot find the right Mandarin words, but when she asks, "Your dances tell what region you're from?" the girl nods.

Circling the entire map, she grins. "Hip hop," she says. "Everywhere."

"Nǐ bàba yě xǐhuān tiàowǔ ma?"

Anna shakes her head furiously—no, her father does not dance. "Bùshì měiyígè Wéiwú'ěr rén dōu huì tiàowǔ. Bàba yóuqíyǒnglái jiù xiàng yíkuài dà shítou; tiàoqǐwǔláine, jiù xiàng yìzhī hēzuìle de dà xióng!"

"Swims like a rock?" The girl nods. "'Hēzuìle de dà xióng'? What's that?"

"Bear. He good writing. Bad swimming. Very bad dancing. Like dizzy bear." She flails her arms.

Mei laughs.

Dropping to sit cross-legged on the sheet, grabbing Měi's phone, Anna traces a finger across the image of her mother. "Māmā zhēn de hěn xǐhuān tiàowǔ," she says softly.

If only one could crop memories like photos, she thinks, *Anna might frame those moments with her mother. Keep the dancing. Leave out the worry, the disappearance.*

Měi's own mother would always be smiling, she thinks, frying yóutiáo in the kitchen. Lǎoyé always cackling laughter, blowing smoke rings into the joists. And of course, she would crop out Daddy's death. Lǎolao's, too. Goose bumps raise on the back of her neck as she feels her lǎolao's trembling hand run a hairbrush through her hair.

There is a shop owner in San Francisco who looks like her grandmother, has Lǎolao's dimples, Lǎolao's hairstyle. One summer, after glimpsing her photo in a news article, Měi had visited the store just to see her.

The article had made it to the top of her newsfeed because *if it bleeds, it leads*: another hate crime against an Asian shopkeeper. The criminal enraged when she refused to sell him cigarettes for a dollar. A dollar, he shouted, was all he had to his name. Then he pummeled through the plexiglass barrier, sending shards into one of the woman's eyes, and ran away. No cigarettes.

When Měi arrived at the store, she'd expected Lǎolao's ghost. But the woman was nothing like her grandma: spoke fluent English, was third-generation. "Thanks," she said when Měi approached the counter shyly to commend her for standing her ground, "but I really had no choice. I've got four grandchildren in college, and one trying to make it as a comedian. He's also a substitute teacher. To pay the bills, you know? On payday, the administration lines up to throw peanuts at him." She shook her head. "I should've given up the damn cigarettes," she said.

"The hospital bill, repairs, and lost revenue from closing set us back twenty-five Gs."

There are no ghosts, Měi thinks bitterly. *Only the people alive right now.*

She wants to shout this at her mother: *Ghosts don't fucking exist.* It's not Àiguó—ghost of sickness, of early death—who pulled that trigger. And if Mama hadn't hidden Daddy's sickness from her, she might've spent her summer differently. Been attentive, been nicer. Been there.

Anger flushes her face as she sets her phone aside; rips open packages from the craft store. Then the girl makes a silly, excited grin, sticking just the tip of her tongue out and biting it with her white teeth as she pulls open a bag of googly eyes, and the feeling fades—all that red rage bleached away by the sun that is Anna.

She fingers the cotton sock in her hand.

Because she can't remember exactly how she made Herbert's full brown yarn mustache, she's purchased black pipe cleaners to twist into the correct shape, creating a stylized version. She pulls a needle and thread from the Rock Island Casino and Hotel sewing kit in her overnight bag.

The girl is confident with a needle, and soon each sock is a puppet with sewn-on googly eyes. Anna introduces the two to one another.

"Wǒ shì Xí Jìnpíng Zhǔxí," the boy puppet on her right hand says. "Wǒ yǐjīng zhǎngle húzi." Then, pulling the girl puppet onto her left hand, she solemnly intones, "Wǒ shì Billie Eilish." The Chinese president bows to the pop star.

Even after Měi orders pizza (which the girl has drawn on her little notepad) and Caesar salads (to balance out the junk), the puppets' banter continues. "Nǐ xiǎng chī shénme?" Anna asks, her right hand manipulating the President Xí puppet: What would you like to eat?

Měi pulls Billie Eilish on. "Wǒ xiǎng chī *nǐ*!" She opens the puppet's mouth wide and devours President Xí as Anna giggles.

At night, she dreams of the gazebo on the pond. Henry's arm is snug in hers as they cross the footbridge, he in a tuxedo, she in a white tulle gown.

Around them, cameras flash: Hog and Jake and the generous saleswoman from the boutique. Mama and Daddy and Mindy Johnson and the smiling Nguyen twins, along with Lǎoyé, Lǎolao, and all of her relatives. Even two sun-browned women in loose tunics and straw sandals—the left-behind aunties—are in attendance.

The bouquet of lilies in her hand delights her until, looking into the water, she's distracted by a shimmering light. It nears, and she makes out the shape of a florid pink jellyfish. The animal is exquisite, otherworldly, pulsing softly with light, its long tendrils reaching back into the darkness of the pond. But it is shrinking as it rises. Smaller and smaller it gets, till it nears the surface and she sees delicate fingers stretched around its pink bell.

Blinking, she steps back from the gazebo's edge—aware she is dreaming, wanting to change the dream. But it's too late. She must glance back at the water.

At the two white faces floating there with black button eyes. At Anna's fingers clutching the heavy paperweight to her heart, her slim form wrapped in her mother's arms. Tendrils hang, limp, from Aynur. And then Měi understands that they are not tendrils but glittering chains. The woman is handcuffed to the floor of the lake.

She scrambles out of the tulle dress, prepared to dive in. But Henry turns her around to face him, his lips closing over hers hungrily, tongue seeking, and the cameras flash, their old-fashioned bulbs crackling as she wakes into darkness.

Her arm flies out to the empty pillow beside her.

She hears the TV, low, in the living room. Strains to hear Henry's breath under its tinny sound, but of course she cannot.

13

ELKHART TO OAKLAND

Cities fly by, her leg cramping as they reach Omaha, Nebraska, the "Gateway to the West" and birthplace of the honorable Knights of Aksarben (or *Nebraska*, backward) as well as the Aksarben Knights, a hockey team.

Omaha has been celebrated, at various points, as a national transportation hub, a meatpacking industry leader, and home to an assortment of gambling houses, saloons, and honky-tonks. In fact, the goal of the original Knights of Aksarben was to develop the city beyond these dens of iniquity so it could continue to house the Nebraska State Fair, whose organizers had laid down an ultimatum.

"Did the Knights succeed?" Unpacking together in the Grand Deco Hotel's upscale suite, he sets the printout atop the dresser.

"Sadly, no." She tucks tomorrow's bra quickly in a drawer, wishing she'd brought the lace rather than the cotton. She is keenly aware that unpacking again is senseless, that she could leave everything rolled in her overnight bag as usual. "The fair moved on to Lincoln." She unrolls, folds, and puts away tomorrow's T-back tank, a clothing item even less deserving of folding than the bra. "But the Knights are still around, doing good deeds. They've even got their own rodeo."

"Do the cowboys wear armor or ten-gallon hats?"

She shakes her head. "You'll have to ask around while we're in town."

"But we're leaving right after breakfast, yeah?"

"Yeah. The way we planned in Syracuse."

"Then I guess I'd better ask somebody real quick . . ."

In the adjacent bedroom, Anna reads one of her new graphic novels—a compromise between sleep and TV—and Měi feels a slight, irreconcilable relief, even as she misses the girl's presence. How do parents ever manage to do adult things, talk adult talk, with their kids around? She's been trying to discuss yesterday with Henry since they set out from Elkhart: starting conversations in her mind and aborting them; biting her tongue during meals and bathroom breaks, trying to shake the nagging feeling that Anna understands more English than she lets on. "You promised not to leave again," she says now, quietly.

He frowns. "And I haven't." He stacks boxer shorts in the drawer next to her tank top.

"You left yesterday."

He turns to her. "In Elkhart? But I came back. I'm right here." Putting a finger under her chin, he tips her face up, so near his breath warms her lips.

"But you didn't get back to the inn till after bedtime." His face is a still pond. She sees herself reflected: needy, uncertain, injured. "I just—wasn't sure you were coming back." *Neutral face*, she thinks, *cards close to your vest*. She steps backward. Picks up her empty overnight bag.

A half grin. "Thanks for not taking off in the middle of the night again, I guess?"

"I almost did."

"You did not!" He shoves her arm.

"No. I didn't." Tossing the bag in the closet, she spins to face him again. "But where'd you go?"

"Just wandered around. Drank a pint or two."

"Or three?"

"Maybe four," he says, sheepish. "But I was never more than a mile from you and Anna." Shutting the dresser drawer softly, he grabs a pillow from the bed and follows her into the suite's generous living room, where he settles into the umber couch as she paces between the wet bar and an abstract brass coffee table that reminds her of a puzzle piece. "This is some heavy shit," he mutters.

She nods. "Did you know," she says, "China is basically leading the solar power movement with forced Uyghur labor? It was in one of Jimmy's articles. And they've auctioned off like eighty-five million dollars in detainees' property since 2019. They're stacking loot."

"Well, countries are built on the backs of the powerless. Even ours." She pictures Lǎoyé's leaning bookcase. Nods again. "But I thought about what you said, and you're right," he adds. "We can't let them go back. Not after the threats, the intimidation. Not with China wielding Interpol to capture activists. Blocking diplomatic visits to Xinjiang."

She bites her lower lip. Sits next to him. "Okay, boss. So what're my new orders?"

He slaps his forehead. "I can't believe I said I'm your boss. I'm such an asshole."

"You really are."

"Your boss?"

"No. An asshole."

"Thanks." He lunges at her, tickling, and she squirms away, standing.

"Seriously." She stares down at him. "What do we do now?"

"I dunno," he says, stretching on the sleek couch. "Go back to Oakland as planned, I guess? Try to talk sense into Jimmy? Keep the Xīns alive?"

Rawlins, Wyoming, was once a lawless place. Here, one can visit Carbon County Museum to bone up on the state's notorious outlaws, such as Big Nose George Parrot—or swing by Wyoming Frontier Prison Museum to browse in the Old Pen Gift Shop and follow the walking path up to the cemetery where unclaimed inmates were laid to rest. Though the prison shut down in the early 1980s, it was once equipped with a dungeon and a "punishment pole" where inmates were whipped in the Wild West days. The old penitentiary had churned out goods meeting the demands of four major industries—though the workers in its broom factory were apparently dissatisfied, as they burned the building down during a riot.

She cringes and rethinks this information sheet, envisioning Aynur cuffed in her cell. Eons have elapsed since Měi and her roommate, Shayla, stumbled in from some East Oakland warehouse party, hugging before she shut the bedroom door and sat down to print her handouts. They were waiting in the printer tray when she woke six hours later. She snatched them up. Threw her duffel in the car. Pulled up to the curb where Henry Lee waited in his tie, his Bulgari, beside an enormous black suitcase. She leaves the handout in the car as they check into their suite.

It's late (the drive clocking in around eleven hours, stops included) and everyone's tired. Their suite is simple: all business, with one king bed. No wet bar, no brass table, no thoughtful touches. Anna's shut the door to the bedroom, leaving them a pullout sofa—but, despite her weariness, Měi isn't ready to lie down beside Henry or negotiate who'll take the floor. "I'll be back," she says, and he raises his eyebrows over the magazine he's reading. She shuts the door softly behind her.

In the tidy retro lobby, she claims a butterfly chair near the stone hearth of a fireplace that appears to be hibernating for summer (a decorative wooden horse in its mouth) and dials Lǎoyé. When he answers, there's background noise. She remembers the time difference.

"Where are you?" she asks, and he laughs.

"Perlie and her friends take me to Joshua Tree."

"The park?"

"No. Califusion restaurant in the city. Got a dance floor."

"Oh," she says. "Is it good?"

"The dancing? Not so much. Mostly whites and Asians."

"The food, Lǎoyé! The food."

He lowers his voice. "Děng yīxià." She hears him excusing himself from the table; walking through a bustling space. "Kinda gross."

"What do you mean by 'gross'?"

"I mean, why I need lemongrass in my burger?"

"Ew. That is gross."

Now he's outside, where it's quieter. She hears the flick of his lighter. "So. What's crackalackin', kiddo?"

"We'll be back the day after tomorrow."

"Client and you? Mr. Lee?"

"Yes. Him and—another person." He inhales, and she envisions him on some trendy restaurant patio. Even if it's a cigarette, she knows, he's holding it like a joint. Winking at the other stoners. It's funny how easily we recognize members of our own identity group. "We're in a sticky situation."

He exhales. "What?"

"I can't tell you."

"Why you bring it up, then?"

She sighs dramatically. "Just to torture you, Lǎoyé."

"Perlie already got that covered. She gonna make me dance again."

"I'd argue that it's you who'll torture her, then."

"Fair."

They enjoy a comfortable silence, Lǎoyé smoking, Měi picking at a small hole in the chair's upholstery. "Anyway, I just wanted to thank you. For urging me to talk to Mama."

"Well, one of us got to, and it ain't me," he says, but she can hear his affection for her mother in his voice.

"Okay," she says.

"Okay."

"I'll let you get back."

"Yah." Another inhale, followed by a rush of exhaled words. "I don't get back in there, Perlie gonna order me a avocado eggroll."

The drive through Wyoming's big spaces is breathtaking if you pay attention. But her back is sore after the pullout bed, which they shared judiciously, more than a foot of space between them.

In the night, she woke to find him staring at her. It wasn't that she could see him, exactly, in the dark, but she sensed his wakeful gaze. Or perhaps this was only a projection. Regardless, between Henry and the mattress, she slept poorly, and now her mind wanders.

There's a spot near here on the I-80, Měi knows, where the road appears to lead up into the sky. But each time she's crossed the state, searching for the optical illusion, she's missed it. And now she wonders whether perhaps the spot is actually nicknamed the Highway to Heaven because this stretch of the road is so mesmerizingly straight, it lures people to sleep, causing accidents.

In Utah, climate change is drying up the drinking water—yet the landscape looks almost too perfect, sun haloing the silvery ground till it's indistinguishable from the sky.

Anna raps on the partition and Měi opens it. "Qǐng tíngchē." The girl points down the interstate at a small rest stop.

"Yes, ma'am," she says, pulling over.

Immediately, Anna's stick-thin legs are out of the car, carrying her away. "Zhèlǐ xià xuěle!" she calls back over her shoulder.

In the back seat, Henry yawns. "She thinks it's snow," he says.

They follow the girl across the asphalt, along the edge of a sprawling salt flat. "Zhè bùshì xuě," Henry explains when they reach her. "Shì yán."

Her eyes widen. "Zhēn de ma? Shì yán ma?"

He nods. "Shì de. Dàn bùnéng chī."

Laughing, she points at the phone in Henry's hand. They crowd in for a selfie.

Bending into the shot, Měi's cheek brushes the girl's, and her heart thuds. There is something about a child's soft skin that's almost tragic, perfection inviting ruination.

She is exhausted by the time they reach Elko, Nevada, home to the National Cowboy Poetry Gathering, Jarbidge Canyon, and the man-eating giant *Tsawhawbitts*. But these facts are no longer what Měi will recall about this place. She will remember, with equal clarity, both the beautiful hotel they're checking into now and the first place they stayed in Elko, with its warped, moldy carpet. Its mealy apples. And the bright, tiled bathroom where she first acknowledged her attraction to Henry. Yes, she'll remember it all, she's sure—but in what context? Does his promise not to leave again extend beyond their contract?

"Last night in a hotel together," she can't help noting over the sandwiches they've ordered from room service. And the girl gives her such a long look that she is certain Anna understands.

"Sad," Henry says. "Hotel beds are so comfortable."

"Not last night's," she says.

"Not last night's." He shoots her a grin.

After dinner, they hide out in her bedroom, strategizing. How to approach Jimmy? What to do if he's stubborn? She recalls, suddenly, how Anna had darted from the car after the white van cut them off. How she'd wrapped herself around the girl like a turtle's protective shell. But in the end, maybe she cannot protect anyone.

Either way, Anna can't be present for whatever argument may transpire. "We'll drop her off for a bit," she whispers to Henry, "with my lǎoyé."

He heads off to the couch, and in the morning, charged with an electricity that jolts her, she slams the trunk on their overnight bags, on water bottles and scattered items. On the ugly suitcase. She is still buzzing as she navigates back through Tahoe, sugar pines towering above— casting shade on the dusty shoulder where she stood a lifetime ago. Her pulse sparks as they reach Oakland's city limit and cross into the world that she thinks of as hers.

She steers the sedan past the cinema, the lake. Past her favorite Thai joint.

Past the street signs and houses and lawns she'd walked by with Lǎo-lao on the way to school. Here is where she fell, taking her skateboard out for its maiden voyage, and wound up with the scar under her chin— faded now, but still visible, a pale crescent moon. Here is the house that gave out the best Halloween candy. The tree shading the sidewalk square where Mama caught her and Laura writing their names in freshly poured concrete and screamed words Měi had never heard.

"You sure she'll be okay with your grandpa?" Henry had asked back in Elko, before they checked out. "No offense. I really like the guy, but—I mean—"

"Yes." She'd nodded fervently. "The safest I ever felt as a kid was with my Lǎolao and Lǎoyé." His lips had twisted into a slow smile. "Besides," she added, reaching for his discarded gray T-shirt, which she intended to annex, "nobody will find her there."

She pulls the sedan into the crumbly driveway.

Getting out, she leads them to the backyard, the girl gawking up at the freeway on-ramp, the tops of whizzing cars. They walk past Mama's kitchen window, open just a crack. And here are the familiar sights, sounds, and scents. Morning glories spilling through the fence. Her mother's music playing somewhere in the house. The traffic accelerating, a dog barking nearby as car exhaust mingles with the fragrance of honeysuckle.

She unlatches the gate. Leads them to the converted garage.

Her hand is poised to knock when the door opens from the inside.

And there, behind Lǎoyé—in the clutter and shadows of her grand-father's little refuge—is Jimmy Xīn.

14

LǍOYÉ'S GARAGE

Involuntarily, she steps in front of the girl. But Anna's seen. She runs around Měi, launching herself into her father's arms. Eyes wide, Henry follows her inside.

"Hey, kiddo," Lǎoyé says.

"Hey, old man—" Her feet do not move. She stands outside in the brown weeds that poke up between the pavers. "How'd he find us?" She gestures at Jimmy.

"He not find you." Lǎoyé chuckles, poking a finger at her chest. "You find him."

She peers into his rheumy brown eyes. "You know him?"

A curt nod. "I know the Xīns. Just like I know the Lees. How you think I get you client? Freeway billboard?"

"You knew—what was in the suitcase?"

"Yah."

"But it's illegal!"

"Drive karura illegal, too. Smoke weed illegal in lots of places, too." Her eyes widen as she notes the absence of a live joint between his lips, and he seems to read her mind. "I not smoke or cuss around the Muslims," he whispers. "Disrespectful."

"Why didn't you tell me?"

"Then you prolly not gonna take the job."

"Goddamn right I—"

"Disrespectful . . ."

"—goshdarn right I wouldn't have taken the job!" She attempts to manage her volume, talking through her teeth. But Anna and Jimmy turn and stare.

Like a sputtering radiator, she forces out warmth—smiling so the girl isn't scared. She takes Lǎoyé by his sleeve (noting that the robe, too, is missing: he's wearing a button-down shirt and slacks) and pulls him out into the yard. With a little wave at the three inside, she pulls the door shut.

"You okay, kiddo?"

She looks him up and down. "Who the fuck even are you?"

"You hit your head or something? I your lǎoyé."

"My lǎoyé cares about my well-being!"

"Listen," he says, "all my life I teach you history. So you can be on the right side of it. But a good life about more than knowing. A good life about doing, too. Your ancestors not gonna build a railroad across America sitting in some Ivory League classroom, bitching about capitalism." A little coughing laugh. "Now you more than my hero. You a real hero." He pauses, letting his words settle. "Besides, I always know you gonna like Henry Lee." He elbows her. "You two an item?"

"That's not important," she shouts. "What's important is—"

The door opens, Henry poking his head out.

"You okay?"

She scowls. "Why does everyone keep asking me that? I'm not the one in fucking danger. Did you know about this? That he'd be here?"

"No." He puts his hands up as if she's got a gun. "I swear—"

"Only Jimmy and I know," Lǎoyé interjects. "Better that way."

"Better my muthafuckin' ass."

Henry and Lǎoyé trade a look. "She like cuss when she scared," Lǎoyé says.

"Don't I know it." Henry grins.

⌒⌒

With Anna nestled into the ratty couch, Lǎoyé's battered and duct-taped TV remote in hand, they pull chairs up to a tempered-glass patio table that her grandfather has moved inside. "Perlie and I like your ma's patio table"—he whispers, whisking away the ash-smeared saucer stolen from Mama's wedding set—"but we not like her prying eyes." He pours lemonade from his mini-fridge. Hands the first glass to Anna.

"I'm sorry again," Jimmy says, unsmiling, "for involving you in all this. We hoped you'd make it to Syracuse and back unaware of—the situation. At which point we planned to come clean." He adjusts his glasses on his nose.

"The situation," she says, "is something I"—a glance at Henry—"something we want to talk to you about."

He raises a hand in the air between them. "There's nothing to discuss."

"Hear me out," she presses in a rough whisper. "Please. Because you did involve me in this. So I've got at least some small say." Lips a pale line, he nods. "I know you've received threats. We have, too. I know you're worried about your wife."

Jimmy lifts his glasses to his forehead, pinching and rubbing the bridge of his nose, then drops them back in place. "You get threat, too?" Lǎoyé asks Měi. She pulls up the message from China510. Hands the phone to Lǎoyé, whose eyebrows rise.

The air is very still. She glances at Anna, their eyes meeting for a moment before the girl's gaze returns to the TV.

"Listen," she presses Jimmy, "it's too dangerous to go back now. Clearly these people mean business. They found me, didn't they? If you give them what they want, you give up your power. You disappear. Then Aynur becomes dispensable, too. And Anna."

"She's right." Henry shrugs. Lǎoyé is nodding vigorously, knuckles crammed against his lips. He passes Měi's phone back without a word.

"I understand that"—Jimmy taps at his head—"up here." Four lemonade glasses sweat on the table, untouched. "Not here, though." He thumps his chest. "I can't let Aynur rot in there, alone. Do you know what they're doing to female—" He glances at his daughter.

"Maybe she get sent home," Lǎoyé ventures.

"Maybe not."

"But who's to say you'll be reunited if you go back? Most detainees are separated." Měi thinks of Mr. Murphy, of her abandoned internship, and grasps at straws. "I know journalists. Writers. They'll spotlight your case!"

"I *am* a writer." He shoves his glasses into the bridge of his nose again. "Trust me. That won't work."

This man is a wall. "I have a friend," she says, not quite knowing where this is going, "that once told me parenthood is a different kind of love. A love more selfish than the lover. I know you must miss your wife terribly, but"—subtly, without raising her hand from the table, she points at the couch—"think of her."

The corners of his mouth droop.

And in that moment, she knows she's blown her chance. Jimmy Xīn is a parent. She is not. "I'm thinking of her all the time," he says simply. "She needs to feel her mother's touch. Even if it's a supervised visit."

Měi opens her mouth, then closes it, as Daddy's face flashes before her. What would she give to touch his hand, his shoulder, to eat ice cream with him just once more?

"That's not how it goes, Jimmy," Henry says. "You know this. Family on the outside may have occasional access to the orphan camps. But not parents who are locked up."

"I—" Jimmy falls silent as Anna sidles up between Měi and Henry.

"Zěnmela?" Henry asks, tousling the girl's hair, but Anna's fingers are already digging into Měi's pocket.

"Wǒ kěyǐ jiè nǐ de diànhuà ma?" She beams. "Wǒ gěi nǐ fā duǎnxìn."
Měi looks to Henry. "'Fā duǎnxìn?'"

"She wants to send you a text from your phone. Probably a new animal."

Handing the girl her phone, she grins at Jimmy, who looks on with raised eyebrows. "She's quite the text artist."

"Ah." He smiles. "Ānnuó," he says gently, "nǐ kěyǐ qù wàimiàn wán." Bouncing on her feet, the girl nods, then runs to the door and yanks it open, disappearing into its rectangle of light. The door slams shut and Jimmy's face falls serious. "I'm sorry," he says. "But it's clear they know what we've done now. Where we are. The 510. So these are no longer empty threats, and risking detainment is better than risking my wife's life. Death is a disappearance nobody returns from." He holds his palms up. "I have no choice."

⁓

Her own father had so many choices.

He could've moved into a long-term facility where professional care might've extended his lucidity, his life.

He could've joined an adult day center offering professional caregiving, social interaction, and staffed activities, cutting Mama a break—helping her balance his needs with her own.

He could've stayed right where he was. With the house paid off, Mama, Lǎoyé, and Měi might've managed his care together. Kept him home with them, where he'd have access to his study, to all of his books and possessions.

There is respite care and hospice care.

And.

And he could've moved to the city with Měi. She knows this option is farcical but can't help imagining Daddy in her little Lower Haight apartment, Mama and Lǎoyé visiting him there, Shayla and Tim doting on him—showing him all the kindness they'd heaped on her in the wake of his death, treating her like instant family though she'd found their rental ad online.

She sighs, forcing her mind to follow the Disney film Anna chose upon her return from the backyard. Thrusting Měi's phone back at her, she'd tapped her nose, "Boop," with a sprig of honeysuckle, the bottom leaves crushed.

Jimmy's at the tempered glass table with Henry, browsing flights to Xinjiang.

She glances at him: certain in his decision, glasses lit by his laptop's reflection as he taps away at its keys. "Stops in Seattle, Taiwan, Beijing," he murmurs. "Then, home."

Henry avoids her eyes.

When it's done, the flight booked, he closes the laptop. Scrolls idly on his phone as Anna giggles at the animated antics.

Lǎoyé shifts on the couch beside them. "I know you like spend last night with Anna," he whispers, "but you got plenty time. Takeout not even arrive yet." He pinches her wrist. "Go see your ma. She gonna get mad she know you out here with me, not say hi."

"I will," she lies.

"Tsk."

He assumes she hasn't forgiven Mama. But she has.

In fact, she's come to the realization that there's nothing to forgive.

The issue is that she's not ready to forgive herself. For dropping out of school so rashly, when Mama never attended college at all. For dropping out of the family, too. This is what happens, she thinks, when you don't pay enough attention to the people who love you. When you're embarrassed of your own. When you give all your time away to the pierced high school girls and savage high school boys who once watched a bully spit in your face. To your college friends. Your clients. Anyone but the parents who paid so much more than money to clothe, house, and feed you. The parents who paid in time, emotion, exhaustion.

Perhaps the real reason Mama kept Měi's two youngest aunties a secret was that Měi had never asked. She scours her brain for even one instance when she sat down with Mama and asked about her life.

"Hey," Lǎoyé whispers. She turns to him. "You know who China510 is?" Her forehead wrinkles.

"No. Do you?"

"World's worst driver."

"What?" she whispers back.

"Yah. I think you get everyone worried for nothing. That not Chinese spy. That your mama's new social media."

She stares at him. Says, in her quietest voice, "What are you talking about?"

"She try reach out. Connect like you young people do. Make a big effort. I help her. You know I got almost fifty follower! I tell her you helping the Xīns, she say, 'I change my mind about Uyghur situation.' We talk about how Chinese constitution guarantee minorities can speak their own language. She disappointed Beijing deny its people this right." His gnarled hand swats at her knee. "First she send you article about genocide. Then urgent message, say she miss you. But she say you never respond. Then hang up on her."

"China510? Is *Mama*? But the avatar is a man!"

"Crowd Lu."

"Excuse me?"

"Vitas Lu?"

She stares blankly.

He rolls his eyes as though this combination of words should mean something to her. "Taiwanese singing sensation! He her favorite now. Replace the Uyghur Bieber."

Měi puts her hand to her pocket, fingering the hard edge of the phone as she tries to recall China510's exact wording.

"Aghk." Jimmy stands from the table, hands at his throat.

At first she thinks he's choking, but there's nothing for him to choke on: as Lǎoyé's pointed out, they're still waiting on dinner. She stands, too. Goes to him, placing a hand on his back.

With a movement that's almost languid, almost relaxed, he gestures to the door. "Could I"—he directs his gaze from her to the two other men—"could we adults step outside?"

Anna looks up, curious but unalarmed.

"Wǒmen mǎshàng huílái," Jimmy says, and the girl smiles, eyes back on the TV.

Though it's 7:00 P.M., the sky is still bright with that movie-worthy California filter applied by God. Jimmy pulls the door shut behind the three of them. They wait for him to speak, but he doesn't. Only hands his phone over to Henry and sits down on the dry brown lawn.

Henry peers at the screen. "Oh, shit," he breathes, barely audible, handing the phone to Lǎoyé.

She watches her grandfather squint, then draw back with a sharp inhale.

"What?" she says. He hands her the phone.

Jimmy has his social media open. "James Ehmetjan Xin," the message on-screen reads, "I am sorry to announce your wife has died in state custody. She was cremated at our regional Burial Management Center and her remains will be returned to your family. Please contact us if you will claim them. Your daughter's whereabouts remain unknown. —Xinjiang Vocational Education & Training"

She looks at the sender's handle: XinjiangVocEd. The avatar is the Chinese flag.

"This isn't real," she says immediately.

Jimmy looks up from the dry, crumbling dirt, the parched grass. "Open the attachment."

She opens it. Looks at the photograph. Drops the phone.

15

OAKLAND TO SAN FRANCISCO

When Měi was little, workers began construction on the Bay Bridge. She doesn't recall what it was like to ride over the old, crumbling eastern span, but Lǎoyé told her stories.

Now, approaching the bridge from the Oakland side one week after parting ways with the Xīns, she thinks back to something the old man said a few days after she withdrew from Dartmouth. "You know where stereotype of bad Asian driving come from?"

They'd stood in front of Mama's house. "Where?"

Navy blue, pin-striped satin pajamas peeked out beneath Lǎoyé's pink robe to pool on the dusty sidewalk. She was shocked that he'd ventured outside to meet her. "Same place woman driver stereotype from," he said.

"Where's that?"

"Your ma."

"Lǎoyé!"

"One hundred percent true. Not just a *yo mama* joke. One time, I with her on the 880 at night, she miss her exit. You know what she do?" Měi shook her head. "Throw car in reverse."

"You're shitting me."

"I shit you not! I wrench around in my seat, look behind. Big black eighteen-wheeler bearing down on us. Get so close before he swerve, I see driver clutch the wheel. Probably soil his pants, too."

"Dang—"

"Yah, dang, that's what I say. But your ma don't think she done nothing wrong. She back up, take the exit, never say a word." He sucked his teeth. "Another time, we driving on the Bay Bridge when her old junker stall out. Your daddy beg her get a new car, but she proud of that busted-up scraper with a skateboard spare." A scowl. "So you know what she do?"

"Call for help?"

"She put the blinkers on, hop out."

"Into traffic?"

With a tight smile, Lǎoyé nodded.

"What lane were you in?"

"Slow lane. But who cares? This a highway, not a sidewalk."

"So, what did you do?"

"I do what she tell me! Got no choice! She hollering at me get out, get out and push, so I run around car to the back, she stand in open driver's door, and we push." His wrinkled lips were pursed. "Come to think of it, your ma and me probably also why white folks run around car like idiot shouting 'Chinese Fire Drill!' Good thing we on a decline. And her hooptie itty-bitty, like a smart car but dumb. And muffler fall right off the day before, make it even lighter. So once we get it going your ma hop back in, pop the clutch, I run around, hop in, too, slam passenger door, and she drive." In the shifting shade of an oak's rustling leaves, he shook his head. "All this time, people honk at us. You blame them? I almost have a heart attack." He grinned at Měi. "So, I buy you a little something." With his veiny, arthritic hand he waved toward the curb, where he'd parked the sedan. "Almost new. Automatic. More importantly, now you never got to ride with your ma."

He handed her the keys.

She'd stood dumbly for a moment while it registered. Her father had blown his brains out, she'd dropped out of an Ivy League school, and her mother hated her. But Lǎoyé had bought her a car. She broke into tears.

She recalls how Lǎoyé patted the roof of the sedan and watched her dry her tears. Then, digging in the pocket of his robe, he'd produced a folded slip of paper. She took it. Unfolded it. Read Ling Ling's name and phone number. "Quit the limo gig," her grandfather said. "I hook you up with client from now on. No more cop poop in console."

∽

Now, cruising over the dark bay into the city's lights, she envisions the demolished span; the potholed highway where her tiny mother once pushed a car back to life.

After Jimmy's phone fell from her hand, she did not knock on Mama's door.

But the next day, she phoned. Asked to come over. And in the week since, she's spent her days in Oakland, with her mother.

Navigating toward the Lower Haight, she is plagued by images: the sickly hue of the corpse's skin, once a smooth, warm tone. The drab walls of Aynur's cell. Did she die there, handcuffed to the bed? Or in a packed and sterile clinic? A black room without surveillance?

The rape, torture, and forced sterilization that former detainees report are impossible to verify, but their claims are disturbingly similar, their timelines corroborated by journalists, their hand-drawn maps aligned with satellite imagery of the camps. And then there is the latest whistleblower: another former police officer who now struggles to sleep, recalling the innocent people he arrested and abused. Perhaps no one will ever know exactly what happened to Aynur Xīn.

At least, she reminds herself, Anna and Jimmy will remain in America now, the university allowing him to teach online—safeguarding his location. She thinks of the freedoms he's guaranteed here and is impressed and heartbroken that it took Aynur's death, the death of hope, for him to choose those freedoms.

She recalls one of Jimmy's articles, featuring a Uyghur journalist. This man disappeared years ago, reappearing recently in a Chinese news video where he claimed he was trying hard to "earn the leniency of the Party and the many readers I have wronged." In the video, he apologized for the "bad citizen" he'd been. "One needn't be a linguist familiar with Beijing's propaganda," Jimmy's article had observed, "to recognize that these were not his words. He had no choice but to read the script Beijing handed him. His son and wife have disappeared now, too."

A linguist . . .

She thinks of Daddy explaining the word "tramp," years before Mama slung it at her. He'd been reading at his desk when she crept down the hall after kindergarten, turning the Victorian crystal doorknob to his study. "Daddy, what's a tramp?"

He'd looked up. Set his book down on the gleaming mahogany desk. "In what linguistic context?" She'd tilted her head. She must've been five or six. "How'd you hear it used?"

"Liv said Evie is a tramp because she wore her mama's lipstick to school."

Because Mama was not a native speaker, it had fallen upon her father to cough up the definitions of every word she asked about. (In another year Daddy would tell her, after the playground incident, what "Chink" meant.) He nodded his head. "In that context, 'tramp' refers to a person who kisses lots of people on the mouth"—she'd grimaced—"and may even charge them money for the kisses." His voice was calm; he'd understood what she could and could not absorb. "It's illegal to charge money, and often dangerous. A tramp is also referred to as a prostitute." He rubbed his chin slowly, ever the diligent linguist. "Or a harlot. A hooker, a strumpet, a whore." He drummed his fingers on the cover of his book. "A courtesan, hussy, jezebel, concubine, or painted woman. Though a tramp need not be a woman."

"What color," she'd asked, causing his studious face to dissolve into a grin, "are the painted women painted?"

If only her father had retained the ability to understand her limits. If only he'd warned her of his plans, it might not've taken driving karura or tending to another family's wounds to start her own family's healing.

Before she left Lǎoyé's the night they learned of Aynur's death, she'd watched Henry say his goodbyes—wrapping Anna in his arms for a long hug, tousling her hair. "Zàijiàn," he'd said, which is commonly translated as "goodbye" but actually means "see you again." And then it was Měi's turn. She gave Jimmy a clumsy hug, patting his back. Then she and

Anna moved together, the girl filling her empty spaces. *A yearning that answers itself.* Měi hadn't understood these words, standing amid the blue crepe streamers in Mindy Johnson's decorated kitchen, noticing a grape that had rolled under the table. But now, she thought, maybe she did.

The blue neon cross of First Baptist Church is a steady beacon that draws her out of her thoughts. She circles the block a few times before a spot opens up. Unlocks the downstairs entry. Trudges past dented metal mailboxes, up the stairs to her apartment, calling out to Shayla and Tim as she opens the door. Nobody else is home yet, so she goes straight to her room. Shuts the door without turning the light on. Walks to the desk.

In parting, the girl had grabbed her hands and pressed something into them: the notebook and mini-pen, obsolete now. Anna could speak Mandarin or Uyghur with Jimmy—and the dutar-player, the Uyghur restaurant owners, and any children they had. And in the fall, when she returned to school and to English, it would be on her own terms, in some bustling Alhambra school with athletic fields instead of perimeter alarms. Freed by her mother's death.

It's been a week since Měi touched the little notebook. Beneath the bedroom's high ceiling—her unilluminated glass chandelier a lambent jellyfish swimming in darkness, lit externally by the neon blue—she opens a desk drawer. Pulls the book out, the mini-pen detaching, dangling from its string. Switching the desk lamp on, she flips through the pages, astounded anew by the girl's artistic skill. Certainly, Anna will succeed as an animator if that is what she decides to do.

Dà xiàng, elephant.

Yú, fish.

Māo, cat.

Dàngāo, cake. Nánrén, man. Hǎilí, beaver. Màozi, hat. Mótiān dàlóu, skyscraper.

Flipping slowly through the sketches, she reaches the last of them.

On the opposing page, something is written in tiny letters. She squints. Makes out a URL. Anna's digital art folder? She inhales deeply and opens her laptop.

Painstakingly copying the URL in, she clicks on neatly laid-out thumbnails, one by one. Anna's added a new sketch, dated yesterday, of a fantastical, bird-sized butterfly beneath a purple honeysuckle sprig. She looks closer; sees it's a photograph, the colors and proportions modified.

There are more photographs than she'd thought the girl could take in a week. Alhambra, nestled in the San Gabriel Valley. Anna's empty bed-room—or perhaps a friend's—a unicorn carved into the headboard. An old woman in enormous sunglasses with a tilting coiffure, lounging poolside. Strangers watching Anna blow out twelve birthday candles, likely captured by her father, a boy with bruised knees on a tricycle, a dog sitting oddly erect on a stone wall, each image artfully tweaked: shadows lengthened eerily, Anna's candle flames licking the ceiling, trees' bark smoothed away.

This is the stylized sort of art that Anna will hone. Enter in middle school competitions. Bring to life with animation, and work hard to per-fect; to turn into a career. Yet she stares longest at the older, unmodified pictures: the one of Jimmy and Anna on a Chinese street; of Aynur nap-ping on the couch. The region surrounding the girl and her father is no tourist-ready Chinatown but a shifting, conflicted landscape of demolition and construction; police checkpoints and mazars dotting the Taklamakan Desert. A land where alcohol battles abstention, pork is politicized, and grapes are grown in fertile Turpan soil watered by an ancient system of gravity-powered underground irrigation canals built by Anna's ancestors. Where the boots of police officers meet innocent citizens' skulls.

She studies Aynur Xīn's features. The peaceful smile on the sleeping woman's face puts a hard lump in her throat as Mama's words play again in her head. "Of course there will be war. Men going to fight over who got more like little boys battle on the playground with sticks." The grainy video on Henry's phone and this bittersweet photograph, taken by a child, are all she knows of Anna's mother. Yet something about the composi-tion, the angle of the head, is familiar. Měi's forehead creases.

Then it strikes her. How the vivid clothes and couch were white-washed, the texture and opacity altered to create death's sickening pallor. Yes, the original looks different. Yet she is one hundred percent certain this is the same photo she saw last week, before she dropped Jimmy's phone in the grass.

16

HOME

The sun is a stifling blanket on her back. She shifts in the café's metal patio chair, inhaling crisp morning air—last night's much-needed rain having rinsed away the smoke of an ever-earlier, ever-scarier wildfire season.

Curious about the little creek that once ran behind this row of buildings, she rises to peer over the patio's splintery wooden fence, through the trees, down the embankment. She's unsurprised to find the creek bed dry. California is drying up, flaring up, drying up—a vicious cycle. Grabbing the menus and napkin-wrapped silverware, she attempts relocation to a shaded spot, but as she nears, the host cuts her off to seat a party of three. She slinks back to her own infernal table. Recalls a time when there were plenty of tables to choose from at 10:00 A.M. on Tuesday in an Oakland hole-in-the-wall.

When Henry emerges from the shadowed interior, squinting into sunlight, she's struck by his appearance. Usually she goes for scrappy sorts: the bipolar, tatted-up drummer in an all-girl band, the limping bartender who'd insisted she cut his hair with his vintage Flowbee. But Henry's contoured exterior is like a luxury vehicle for his soul, stamped from a sheet of soft gold in God's manufacturing plant. He is precise and streamlined, even in fraying jeans and a worn green T-shirt (*Does he buy the clothes this way, or just keep them too long,* she wonders). Not the kind of look she seeks out.

"Hey!" She waves him over.

He grins, crossing the room quickly, then hovers uncertainly before scraping a chair back to join her at the table. "Hey," he says. "What's good?"

"I always get the salmon scramble," she says, "but I haven't been here in a while. The menu's changed."

His grin collapses into irritation. "I meant, what's good with you? It's been a week. Did you break your fingers or something? Couldn't answer my texts till now?"

"I'm sorry—" She blinks uncomfortably, simmering in white sun, willing her legs to stand so they can hug.

He holds a hand up. "It's cool. I'm sure you had a lot to catch up on with friends."

"Actually," she says, "I've been spending time with family."

A hint of a smile. "Did your lǎoyé finally shell out for *Grand Larceny X: Aggravated Assault*?"

"Nah. He's got a bunch of new hobbies." His eyebrows rise, but he remains silent. "Dancing with his girlfriend, Perlie. Exploring new restaurants with his girlfriend, Perlie. Shopping for groceries, planting fruit trees, doing tai chi at Lake Merritt with his girlfriend, Perlie. You get the point. You'd barely recognize the man. He puts on daytime clothes during the day."

Returning from the cross-country trip, she'd expected the same old Lǎoyé: still grieving Lǎolao's death in his ratty robe, looking almost like a skeleton himself. Instead, her grandfather brims with life. "Gotta dress like the hot young thing I am," he quipped when she asked about his sharp new clothes. "Perlie say good Black don't crack. But neither do good China!" He'd pointed at his own face, then at Mama's gold-edged wedding saucer, and cackled.

"He still smokes weed, right?" Henry asks.

She laughs. "That, you can always rely on." She tries to twist her mouth out of its smile, but she's ridiculously happy to see him. Jesus, those eyelashes. Those lips. "So, I've actually been spending more time with my mother than Lǎoyé. Kinda getting to know her as a person—not just as my mom." His focused gaze makes her light-headed. She turns the spotlight away: "And you?"

"Me?" A wry snort. "Locked inside with my laptop, racing against a deadline."

"Aw, poor Henry. Stuck in his air-conditioned luxury condo, figuring out how to tell Timothée Chalamet's story authentically? My heart bleeds for you."

"It's not *all* sitting around in comfort, you know. Sometimes the doorbell rings and I have to get up and retrieve whatever gourmet meal I've ordered."

"Wow. Rough."

"Yeah. And this morning, my maid messed up. Forgot to iron my ten-year-old T-shirt."

"You have a live-in maid?"

"No! Of course I don't. But I do iron my T-shirts . . ." She stares at him, trying to determine whether this is true, before peering into the café. She still knows a few of the waitstaff here; loves how professional they are, how attentive. She's read someplace that women are the best tippers— that servers ought to dote on them, rather than the men—and this is one place where the staff has always seemed clued in. Today, though, they're no place to be found. "So. I heard from Jimmy."

She refocuses. "You did?"

"They're settled in. Anna loves Alhambra."

"Yeah?"

"Her dad bought her a cell phone. And their apartment complex has a pool."

"Oh, yeah. She's all about the pool." Uncrossing and recrossing her legs under the table, she kicks one of its wrought-iron legs with a thunk. "Ow," she says, though it doesn't hurt. Then, "I, uh, knew about the phone. And the pool. We've been texting. And she found me through social media."

"Yeah?"

"She knows more English than you'd think."

"Don't they always? Has she sent more little doodles?"

"A few. And she's teaching me Mandarin. Slowly." The heat draws droplets of sweat down her spine. She isn't sure what to say next. Momentarily, she panics. What if they only get along when transporting refugees across the country?

"Listen," he says, face going serious, "I've got a theory I want to run by you."

"Does it have to do with making Jay-Z more relatable?"

"I told you, dream hampton writes with Jay-Z. And she's amazing in her own right, by the way. It's like having Tony Hawk as your skateboard instructor."

"Ugh." Her nose wrinkles. "Clearly you don't skate."

"Tony Hawk is a bona fide badass!"

"Yeah. Also, the only skater people like you are familiar with."

"Actually," he says slowly, "I skate a bit. Since I was, like, nine." He bites his lower lip. "Want me to prove it later?" Hesitantly, she nods. "You're on, then." A half smile as he lifts his menu. His lashes drop, hiding his eyes, but she can tell he's still looking at her.

"Listen," she says, "wanna cut out? I'm starving, and this is taking forever. We could, like, grab bananas at the corner store. Hike the urban trails."

"You mean the sidewalk?" He grins at her. "Sure."

Lake Merritt is not really a lake at all. Alternately favored by Oakland's well-to-do and its impoverished until an uneasy coexistence was achieved, the tidal lagoon has also welcomed leopard sharks, sea lions, rays, jellyfish, otters, and eels that glide from the Pacific into the bay, then the Lake Merritt Channel, winding up in its briny depths. Also, bicycles wobbling from nearby pubs. Mannequin heads tossed in by playful anarchists. Old-fashioned typewriters, an assortment of clothes and cars and, once, an upright piano. Beyond this, the lagoon's home to an assortment of New England wildlife imported by settlers who, in 1870, made it our nation's oldest nature sanctuary by packing transcontinental railroad cars full of live Atlantic oysters, striped bass, and gaggles of geese.

For a moment, she envisions her ancestors at the train station, hardened railway men smiling with satisfaction as the cars roll in—geese flapping their wings in tight enclosures as the cargo is unloaded. Chinese workers, Lǎoyé once told her, also built railroads in Canada, the Caribbean, and elsewhere, which is why there are so many Chinese Jamaicans. She blinks this history away.

Měi has never written a fact sheet on Oakland, but if she did, she'd stuff it into a glass bottle and set it afloat here. "This is my favorite place," she says softly.

"Lake Merritt? Despite the homeless hidden in the trees?" Henry nods toward a sleeping bag tangled in the weeds of an embankment— empty on first appearance but, on second look, containing an emaciated form whose bony hand protrudes as an indictment of how this city fails.

"Yeah. Well." She kicks a pebble down the shoreline's tidy, three-mile path. Thinks of Cherry, who called for a ride last week. Not to a client's hotel, but to a Temescal real estate office, to drop a down payment on a two-bedroom. "Nothing's perfect. But at least Oakland never stops trying."

They pass a teenage couple snogging on a blanket at the base of a sturdy oak, and Henry points to a wooden bench. Near the bench, the trees are smaller, their gnarled trunks twisted like heavy rope under hundreds of delicate white flowers. She snaps an oval leaf from one. Crushes it between her fingers, producing the scent of tea tree oil. These trees, like so much of the lake's wildlife, so many of its devotees, were imported: shipped from southern Australia's coastal dunes to stabilize the sand. She hands the broken leaf to Henry, who lifts it and sniffs.

"So. My theory?" He flicks the leaf toward the water. They sit on the splintered bench. "It's about Anna's mom."

"Yeah?"

"I'm suspicious of her death."

"How it happened?"

He shakes his head. "No," he whispers.

Měi gestures pointedly around at the dog walkers. The students on summer break and strolling retirees. "Why are you whispering?"

"Because despite what Hollywood would have us think, spies don't try to run people off the road in vans." She jabs him in the arm, and he whispers slightly louder. "They get at you through your devices. Your cost-efficient Chinese cell phone."

"This thing," she says, pulling her phone out and slamming it on the bench between them, "is far from cost-efficient. It's the most American phone ever, no matter where it's manufactured, and according to the proverb, using it once a day keeps the doctors away. So it's all gravy." They watch a pelican cruise in as though to make a water landing. But the bird plunges, scooping something up in its beak, and soars off again. She leans toward him. Presses her shoulder briefly into his. "So? What's suspicious about Mrs. Xīn's passing?"

He frowns. *"Xinjiang Vocational Education & Training."*

"What about them?"

"Do you really think they'd notify people of a death in the family that way? The language seemed cribbed from, like, a veterinarian's office or something."

"I mean, no. Obviously they wouldn't. Not officially." She grimaces. "But maybe someone on the inside—"

"What, like the guard Aynur got her phone back from?" She nods, but he's shaking his head. "Way too risky. I think the sender is a catfish." He draws slightly away, peering down at her through his eyelashes. "From here in the U.S. Because the timing was suspicious, too."

"Okay—"

"The very same day Jimmy buys airplane tickets, he gets that photo?"

She says nothing.

"He's neck-deep in research about deaths, disappearances. This is probably just what he expected. It didn't have to be convincing. And that photograph, it's solid evidence, right?"

She closes her eyes, tilting her face to the sun, and envisions Aynur Xīn napping in her cell, dancing hip hop with Anna in her dreams. Will the girl admit to what she's done? That she's sacrificed her father's heart, temporarily, for his freedom? And for her own?

Someday soon, Měi will join the troops. Bombard the Chinese embassy with arguments for detainees' release. She'll resume her internship at the newspaper or find another. Go back to school. Become a journalist, no matter the annoyances, the obstacles. She'll write. Boycott companies that use forced Uyghur labor. Contact Bay Area nonprofits and faith-based organizations to ask what they're doing for refugees, and whether she can help. But for now, she'll keep these plans to herself. Deny any personal connection to a living detainee. Because only the girl knows her father well enough to determine when to disclose that the picture he saw was a fake. XinjiangVocEd, just a clever preteen catfish . . .

She opens her eyes to the bright sky.

Down the shoreline path, in the dappled light falling between branches that extend over the water, an elderly Chinese man casts a line into the lagoon. "See that guy?" She nudges Henry. "He's going to pull up a fucking bull shark." She thinks back to the mealy apple she choked down on their first overnight stop. The dreary Elko, Nevada, inn. "Told you we can't pass up free food."

"Unless it's fake," he says.

"Like junk food?"

"No"—an exasperated snort—"the photo of Aynur. It could be fake."

She cocks her head. "You're really not letting this go, huh? Remember when you called me paranoid? When I freaked out about the guys in the van?" His full lips press into a line. "And now you're suggesting someone obtained a photograph of Mrs. Xīn? Doctored it and sent it to Jimmy with that cold, gruesome message? Who'd do that?"

His eyebrows leap. "Who indeed, Měi Love Brown?" She shrugs. "Someone prepared to decimate the only reason he'd return to China?" Now it's her lips that press tightly together. He stares, his dark eyes making her think of the smooth black rocks hidden below the lake's shining water. "Someone who wants to keep that kid safe?" She looks away. "Someone buying time? For Jimmy to clear his head and see that, no matter how scary or lonesome it may get, he's got a better chance of freeing his wife if he toughs it out here in the States?"

"And you think—"

"Someone who wants Anna here, too, cared for and thriving, until he unravels the truth? Because he *will* learn the truth. But maybe this someone figures by then, he'll have come to his senses. And avoid putting his daughter at risk."

"And you think that someone is me."

"I mean—"

"You think *that's* why I've been dodging your texts?" A shrug. "Well, you're dead wrong. That's not why."

"No?"

"No."

"Then enlighten me. Please." His eyes shine with pride. In his mind, he's got it all figured out, and this gives her pause.

Perhaps she will let him be right.

Perhaps this is how to protect the girl's secret.

All her life, she's hated secrets. She thinks of the Nguyen twins— how furious she was with their refusal to come forward and speak truth to power. She still wishes they'd spoken up. But it turns out power is a tricky thing, like driving on the freeway. Not everyone can throw the car into reverse when all the traffic's flowing one way. Not without getting crushed. Who are we to demand still more from the wronged?

A summer breeze riffles her thoughts, Mama's face flashing before her. "I not lie," her sharp voice had asserted over the phone. "I tell him, 'I don't say nothing unless she ask.' But I don't lie neither." It was, she thinks now— shifting on the slats of the bench—Mama's final gift of privacy to Daddy.

The lake's brackish, still surface reflects skyscrapers.

She's aware of Henry's closeness, and aware, too, of a shift that's occurred in her universe: untethered briefly from Mama's orbit, running amok, going karura, she's become her own center of gravity. She feels her own mass, her heft, her weight on the peeling bench. She does not deny sending the photo.

"The truth is," she says instead, "you and Anna and I—we—felt like family, you know?" He nods. "But I've got a real family to deal with. To love." His face falls and he fixes it just as quickly, as two muscular men in spandex pass by speaking Spanish, holding hands. They smile hello and Měi smiles back. "After Daddy died, we kind of fell apart." She peers into

Henry's pained eyes. "You know that Chinese saying, 'While drinking water, remember the one who built the well'?"

"I do," he says slowly, "but I'm surprised you do, Banana."

She socks him in the arm. "Yellow on the outside, white on the inside? No more than you, Prep School. No more than most Asian Americans. Even if Beijing regards us all as overseas Chinese who may still come home one day." Far overhead, an airplane glints like a daytime star. "You know, I used to hate being a half-breed. But it grants two perspectives. And I don't ever want to forget that again. So I've been, you know, cooking with my mom. Talking with her. And getting to know the dapper new Lǎoyé—"

"Pimpin' Lǎoyé."

"Pimpin' Lǎoyé. Covered in octogenarian drip." She chuckles. Meets his eyes. "I wanted to text back before now. I did. I kept tapping half your name into my phone, but—"

"You tapped half my name into your phone? Multiple times?" He squints, a half smile forming. "Really?"

She nods. "But every day there was more scary news: a Uyghur activist's niece dead in state custody. A dissident's fiancée abducted in Dubai and tossed into some Chinese black site there. No rights. No recourse. No cavalry coming." She tilts her head, staring up into his face. "It's not just Jimmy and Anna who are lucky to have each other, you know? To be in a safe place? So I just had to make things right with my family before"—the breeze lifts a few strands of her hair. She pats them back down, exhaling—"before I gave my time to anyone else."

Wasn't it Rainer Maria Rilke who claimed the lover's highest task is to protect the beloved's solitude?

In the week since her return, she's learned more about her family than in all the years before. From the outside, her parents appeared to be opposites: he, tall, blond, erudite—she, short, dark, practical. Daddy always the last to speak unprompted. Mama so straightforward. But ultimately, they were both private people.

All of Daddy's reminiscences (about the time he hit his brother in the head with a hammer, waiting gleefully for a halo of cartoon stars to appear; the time he selfishly blew out the candles on his best friend's cake to claim the birthday wish; even the time he jumped off the railroad bridge as the train shook the tracks, the trusses) had served a purpose. They were not about him but about Měi. Parables leading to a lesson. A lesson meant to shape, protect, or soothe.

She recalls being five years old, eating ice cream with him at 3:00 A.M. after he'd discovered her over the open freezer. Had he intuited that she'd had a nightmare? If so, he hadn't let on. He'd let the cold, sweet treat speak for him.

And Mama? Měi had only a handful of stories about her mother—not because she'd assumed Mama would always be around to talk to, but because she'd mistaken her for a one-dimensional character. Only this past week, through an intentional line of questioning, was she beginning to map out more. More depth, more breadth, than she'd imagined. (It reminded her of third grade, when she and Mama had bumped into her school principal on Telegraph. He was wearing a Tupac shirt, chewing on a corn dog, and she'd suddenly realized he didn't simply sleep in his suit, folded into an office supply cabinet.)

"You ask so many questions," Mama remarked yesterday, chatting on the couch. "Before, nobody interested. Nobody but Àiguó and Daddy." The thought filled Měi with sadness and shame.

But better late than never, she told herself. They could still earn each other's trust.

Then Mama had stood up briskly. "Oh!" she'd exclaimed. "I forget!"

"Forget what?"

"Have something for you."

She'd disappeared down the hall into her bedroom, then reemerged to stand, hands behind her back, in a square of sun that shone like a spotlight. She was so solemn, a bolt of fear struck Měi until, loudly, Mama sang out: "Ta-daaaaa, here he come!" And from behind her back, she produced Herbert, the sock puppet from Měi's fourth birthday.

Despite decades of hard time in a cardboard box that had moved from Měi's closet to who-knows-where, he looked exactly the same, his yarn mustache glorious beneath his shiny button eyes. And suddenly, in contrast, Měi became aware of how much her mother had aged—more salt than pepper in her hair now. Lines in her face etched deeply, where they'd once been lightly drawn.

As Mama opened and closed the puppet's mouth, belting out some Chinese pop song, she'd burst into tears.

Henry emerges from the bathroom just as her roommates enter the apartment. He's wrapped in a blue towel, and from down the hall, Shayla catches her eye, her expression definitely not one of disapproval. Grinning, leaning out the bedroom door, Měi gives them a little wave. Grabs Henry, pulling him back in.

What she hasn't shared, won't share, is that she's dreamed of him almost nightly since they said goodbye—Henry kissing her softly, tentatively, then harder.

Her dreams still end poorly, souring to nightmares. But here he is, real, safe and solid in her bedroom, with freshly shampooed hair. *Better to wake from horror into loveliness than the other way around*, she thinks. Later, when he's gone home, she will give thanks for her life on her knees.

She shuts the door, and he leans his back against it. "Why do you have all that hotel shit?" he says.

"You went through my things?"

"I thought you might have a hair dryer in the cabinet. And you *did*. Plus, like, forty miniature toiletry bottles and a stack of hotel robes."

"I paid good money for those things, okay?"

He points to the blue towel's stitched logo. "Is this from a hotel, too?"

She snatches the towel off his body. "Feel free not to use it."

"Give that back!" He lunges onto the bed after her as she tosses the towel in a corner. "Fine. I'll hide under here." She dives beneath the colorful bedspread after him, and in the lamplight filtering through the fabric, they grin at one another. "It's like we're in a church," he whispers, "and the sun's pouring through stained glass windows." As though on cue, strains of gospel reach their ears, then fade, from the church below.

"My lǎolao built this church." They stare at the hand-stitched squares.

"Amen," he says, his lips a soft prayer on hers. When her phone dings on the nightstand, they both scramble out, reaching. She gets to it first. "Blasphemer," he pouts. "No checking that thing during the service."

"It's from Anna."

He props himself on an elbow. "What's it say?" She chews her bottom lip. "Isn't it a bit late for her to be up?"

"It's not even nine. We let her stay up past that, on the road."

"But we're crappy caretakers."

"True."

"Can I see?"

She stares at him. She's deleted anything that might incriminate the girl. "Sure," she says.

He snatches the device. "Wǎn'ān," he reads. A sharp glance. "You know what that means?"

"Of course! 'Goodnight.'"

The phone dings again and she grabs for it, but he holds it just beyond her reach. "Aww."

"What?"

"Wǒ ài nǐ. You must know that one."

"I love you," she says, laughing.

"I love you," he repeats slowly. "That's right."

Another ding. "Give me that," she says, uncomfortable. "This is a private conversation."

"It's just a doodle."

"It's a private doodle, then. Gimme the phone."

"Only if you can tell me the Mandarin word." He turns the screen toward her:

```
/\_/\
/>^ ^<
\ _y _/
```

"Māo," she whispers, making another grab as he rolls on top, pinning her arms. "Cat."

The phone dings again.

"Okay, last quiz for the night. I swear." Grinning above her, he shows her the screen:

><(((*>

"Yú," she says. "Fish."

Satisfied, he hands her the phone.

ACKNOWLEDGMENTS

A thousand thanks to Victoria Sanders, my superhero agent, and Shannon Criss, my brilliant, clear-eyed, and patient editor. This book was born from our collaboration and nurtured to maturity with the expertise of literary agent Bernadette Baker-Baughman and editors Micaela Carr, Benee Knauer, Deborah Jayne, and Hannah Campbell. Thanks, too, to Marion Storm, Marinda Valenti, Muriel Jorgensen, Julia Ortiz, Alex Foster, Catryn Silbersack, Arriel Vinson, and Christine Kelder—and to Kirby Kim, who once wisely advised me to infuse stories about solemn issues with humor and light.

Much respect and gratitude to Myra Goldberg, Joan Silber, and Peter Cameron at Sarah Lawrence College; each of you taught me something crucial about writing. And to Arisa White and Quinn Madison, who told me, "You're a writer," and made me believe it.

IOU big-time, always: Jason Rylander, Woo Williams-Zou, Akemi Johnson, Jenn Tanguay, and Bianca Waddell. And xièxiè to my family and the circle of brainy folks who are a part of my literary life, including Jendi Reiter, Adam Cohen, Keenan Norris, Juliet Giglio, Laura Donnelly, Leigh Wilson, Robert O'Connor, Michael Raicht, Donna Steiner, JK Fowler, Miah Jeffra, Tomas Moniz, Alex Dolan, Daniel Handler, Michael Nye, Laura Cogan, Oscar Villalon, James Mattson, Michael Ray, Lisa Bowden, Clem Cairns, Jula Walton, Noley Reid, Josh Aaseng, Matthew Limpede, and Linda Swanson-Davies and Susan Burmeister-Brown (the

miraculous engine that powered *Glimmer Train* all the way to its last stop),
as well as Kelly Edwards for giving me an eye-opening day in LA with
the showrunners and TV writers who lent their time to the HBO Access
Writing Fellowship program. I cannot name everyone in my literary circle, as the names would comprise another book, but I hope this short list
serves as evidence for my students that the world of writing is not as cut-
throat as some make it out to be: you will be welcomed here.

Li Hua-yuan Mowry, thank you for reading every page of this book
closely and helping me smooth the Mandarin portions—oh, yeah, and
for giving me life and whatnot! SUNY Oswego colleagues past and present, including Dean Kristin Croyle, Rodmon King, Courtney Doucette,
and Celinet Duran, thank you for helping me maintain some semblance
of sanity.

I am thankful to you, reader, for picking up this book.

And, finally, please allow me to acknowledge my many fellow writers
who lack the freedom or voice to be heard. Your silence reverberates.

ABOUT THE AUTHOR

Soma Mei Sheng Frazier's work has earned nods and awards from numerous authors and entities. She has been published in *Story, Glimmer Train, Zyzzyva, Mississippi Review,* and *Hyphen,* among others. She relocated from California, where she was a San Francisco Library Laureate, to New York, for a professorship in creative writing and digital storytelling at SUNY Oswego. Frazier has taught at the University of Silicon Valley, the Sarah Lawrence College Summer High School Writers Program, the University of San Francisco, Oakland School for the Arts, Holy Names University, Gavilan College, and Valhalla Women's Correctional Facility—and she worked at KQED, a premier national public media source in the Bay Area.